MURDER BY
NATURAL CAUSES

MURDER BY NATURAL CAUSES

Helen Erichsen

MUSWELL
PRESS

First published by Muswell Press in 2023

Typeset in Bembo by M Rules
Printed and bound by CPI Group (UK) Ltd, CR0 4YY

A CIP catalogue record for this book
is available from the British Library

ISBN: 9781739638276
eISBN: 9781739638283

Muswell Press
London N6 5HQ
www.muswell-press.co.uk

MIX
Paper from
responsible sources
FSC® C171272
FSC
www.fsc.org

For Espen

1

Choices

Somewhere out there in the future is the day of your death. One day it will become an anniversary: the day you died. Almost certainly you don't know when that day will be. It just lurks quietly, patiently, waiting for you to arrive.

Or maybe it doesn't. The future is fluid, it's not written in stone. The date of your death is not pre-set, which sounds comforting until you realise that what this actually means is that you are always standing on the edge of the abyss. At any moment you could fall into its depths. Or be pushed.

These were the thoughts that were running around Maurice Malinowski's head as he lay fully clothed on his bed, stout and sweating. Perhaps not his exact thoughts; he was feeling rather anxious so his own internal dialogue was a little crazier and more disjointed than this. But it all came back to the same thing: whether the date of his death was pre-set or not, he would still do his best to avoid it if he could.

He was currently wrestling with the decision of whether to take a cab or the tube to the airport. The cab was ordered and would arrive at 6 a.m. Yet there was something disconcerting and vulnerable about sitting in the back seat of a car driven by a stranger. In whose employ might that stranger be? Vlad had people everywhere. Perhaps the tube was a safer choice after all.

An hour later he sat in the third carriage of a Piccadilly line train which had slowed to a snail's pace on its approach to Acton Town. He was trying and failing to quell the surge of panic which rose in his throat as the train came to a grinding halt. He closed his eyes in an attempt to bring his fear under control. Tubes often stopped on their approach to Acton Town because it was a busy junction. Vlad might have people everywhere but he was not in charge of the London Underground. The carriage shuddered back to life and moved slowly forward. Maurice opened his eyes.

Without further delay the journey from Acton Town to Heathrow Terminal 2 would take approximately twenty-five minutes; ample time for Maurice to reflect on the choices that had brought him to this point. Playing in the £10 game at the TGR's club had seemed like a reasonable idea at the time; a way to get his foot in the door. He was a competent bridge player. Nothing special, but he knew that his losses were unlikely to extend beyond a couple of hundred for an afternoon's worth of cards. It had seemed like a good investment at the time; to get his foot in that door. Of course he hadn't been interested in the bridge at all. What Maurice was interested in was the backgammon side game. The unofficial high-stakes backgammon side games which carried on into the small hours; the games where large sums of money reputedly changed hands on a single turn of the doubling dice. As far as backgammon was concerned, Maurice was an expert.

But he wasn't known in England; which was a good thing. It gave him an edge.

Initially he concentrated on the bridge. He won a little bit, he lost a little bit. He paid his debts on time. He talked over the hands with the rest of the rubber players; commiserated with them about their bad cards, bad breaks and bad partners. He built trust. Then he started playing some backgammon. Losing strategically when it looked right, making his wins look like luck, affecting a growing addiction to the game. That was all he had to do. He never suggested playing for high stakes, he just waited for someone to suggest it to him.

After four and a half months the day came. Maurice had played cards for several hours, lost eighty-seven pounds, and was collecting his jacket from the cloakroom when Artur, the manager of TGR's, waylaid him.

"Maurice, my friend, where are you off to?" Artur said affably. "There's a party tonight. Maybe some more cards, some backgammon. Young Daniel's coming in. He's heard that you're turning into quite the backgammon player and he'd love a game."

Maurice didn't really know Daniel Crawford. As far as he was concerned, Daniel was just some rich little red-headed schmucko who played high-stakes rubber bridge and fancied himself as a backgammon player. Maurice had seen him at the club a few times but they'd never sat down at the table together. Maurice only played in the low-stakes game and Daniel had not deigned to make his acquaintance. Maurice would enjoy taking his money. He shrugged his shoulders nonchalantly and started taking off his jacket again.

"OK, I'm in," Maurice said.

Now it would have been perfectly acceptable to take Daniel Crawford for fifty thousand. It would have simply created a new story, another small legend to be told and retold at TGR's.

"Hey, do you remember the time that schmucko kid got taken for 50K by some Pole – what was his name? Michal? Milek? I heard the kid had to sell his Porsche to pay the debt."

Even a hundred grand might have been within the limits of propriety. A hundred thousand would have secured a little flat on the outskirts of Gdansk, with enough left over for an annuity. Maurice even knew the apartment building he would have chosen. It was two blocks away from his favourite café. He would have been able to wander down there every day to drink krupnik and play chess. One hundred thousand would have represented a comfortable old age. Now there might be no old age, comfortable or otherwise.

The problem was that Maurice didn't stop at a hundred thousand. The party had been in full swing and there were people watching. The more Maurice won, the bigger the audience became. All those people who had watched him lose at the bridge table and despised him for it were now watching him win. Greed, ego, call it what you will, the feeling was heady and irresistible. He no longer had a choice, he couldn't stop. And Daniel wouldn't stop either. The idiot thought he could win it all back if he just had one more game. Daniel's play became increasingly impulsive and erratic and all the time the losses mounted.

Finally it was Artur who brought matters to a close. As they were setting up the board one more time he put his hand on Daniel's shoulder.

"Message from your father. Time to call it a night."

"I don't want to call it a night," Daniel barked in response. "I want to win my money back."

"He insists."

Daniel flung the counters in his hand onto the table; some

4

of them rolled onto the floor. He stood up. His face had flushed to the same colour as his hair. He pushed through the onlookers and nearly ran out of the room. There was every possibility that he was crying. Daniel Crawford had lost two hundred and thirty-three thousand pounds.

Maurice stood up as well. He beamed at the audience around him. He was expecting people to pump his hand and congratulate him but the room was strangely quiet. No-one would meet his eye except for Artur.

"I don't really know who you are," Artur said gently. He pointed at the empty chair. "But do you know who that is?"

"Daniel. Daniel Crawford," Maurice replied. "What of it?"

"Yes, he has his mother's surname. Do you know who his father is?"

Maurice shrugged nonchalantly for the second and last time that evening.

"His father is Vladimir Haugr. Do you understand what that means?"

Maurice stood there, his mouth opened and closed a couple of times but no words came out.

"I think, if I were you, I would probably leave now," Artur concluded.

There had been no question of collecting on the debt. Maurice had gone back to his bedsit in a state of shock. At four in the morning he decided to pack and leave.

How could he have known that Daniel Crawford, that little ginger twit, was Vladimir Haugr's son? They didn't look remotely alike. The kid had red hair for Christ's sake. On the single occasion that Maurice could recall having seen both of them at TGR's at the same time, they hadn't even spoken. In fact, Daniel Crawford had pushed past Vladimir Haugr in the doorway to the playing area. Maurice had seen it with his own eyes. It was very rude behaviour; an insult.

5

Vladimir Haugr would never let such an insult pass without consequence. Except when the perpetrator was his own son. As the tube rattled into a tunnel Maurice put his head in his hands. He wanted to sob at his own foolishness.

He peered left and right anxiously, aware that his odd behaviour might draw scrutiny. But it was still so early in the morning that there were very few people in the carriage: just an elderly couple, a young woman with a pushchair and two schoolboys dressed for football practice.

There was fifteen minutes left of the journey to Heathrow in which to consider the reputation of Vladimir Haugr. He was the owner of TGR's Bridge Club. He held a major interest in several large London casinos and was rumoured to control several percent of the cocaine trade for the city. He was sometimes known as Haugr the Ogre on account of his volatile temper. But his more common moniker was Vlad the Impaler. This nickname was a nod to his maternal Romanian lineage and his ancestor of the same name who had ruled over Wallachia in the fifteenth century. It also referred to his aggressive style of bidding and play at the bridge table. But there were other more sinister reports associated with the nickname, whispers of individuals who had "fallen" or "jumped" from the upper storeys of various buildings over the years only to find themselves skewered on the iron railings below. The only solace that Maurice could find during that nightmare tube journey was that he was fairly certain there were no iron railings at Heathrow airport.

Once he entered the main terminal building Maurice felt marginally better. He purchased a one-way ticket to Warsaw using the last of his sterling and checked into his flight. He only had hand luggage. There was something soothing about the smell of the terminal. It felt anonymous and safe. The

CCTV cameras strategically located to cover every angle of the interior were comforting to him; designed as they were to prevent terrorist attack, they might just prevent Maurice from being set upon by men with iron railings before he reached the relative safety of an aeroplane.

Before going through security Maurice stopped at a newsagent in order to buy a paper and some cigarettes. He was feeling calmer now, more in control. He selected *The Times*, one of the few things he would miss about England, and stood in the queue to make his purchase. There were two men in front of him and a woman with a buggy behind. Maurice liked babies and he peered into the pushchair to take a closer look. It was a young baby, no more than three months old, probably a boy if the soft blue cap on the infant's head was anything to go by. The child was deeply asleep. Maurice could see his little chest moving rhythmically up and down through the padding of a striped navy romper suit. He was about to say something to the mother, a platitude, a compliment, something of the sort, when a bee stung him on the side of his neck. At least that was what it felt like. The panic came rushing back. He cast about himself wildly looking for the insect but there was nothing there. Maurice put his hand up to his neck only to feel the stinger painful and protruding. He pulled it out with his forefinger and thumb. As Maurice opened his mouth to scream a sudden weight seemed to crush his chest and he found himself unable to draw breath. His legs buckled beneath him and he collapsed to the ground flopping and flapping like a dying fish. The young woman knelt down and leant over him, an expression of consternation in her pale eyes. She took his right hand and held it firmly. Then she looked up.

"Someone get a doctor!" she shouted. "He's having a heart attack."

There were no choices left for Maurice any longer. His last coherent thought was one of surprise. Despite all the commotion, the baby in the pushchair was still fast asleep.

❦

The baby was still sleeping when Cilla unlocked the front door to her flat some time later. She was also thinking about choices, although in a somewhat more detached manner than the late Maurice Malinowski had been. Cilla was contemplating the following remark:

"'Tis not unreasonable for me to prefer the destruction of the whole world to the scratching of my finger."

She liked Hume's observation. It was one of those simple secret truths, hidden in plain view. People failed to see it because their eyes were closed and they couldn't even remember having shut them. Cilla thought about the man on the floor in WHSmiths. She was certain that he was dead even as she began calling for help. She could see it in his eyes. Or rather that they weren't his eyes anymore, just blank blown spaces; the eyes always gave it away.

Once inside the hall she lifted the baby carefully out of his buggy and carried him through into the back bedroom where she laid him gently on the double bed. It was a pleasant bright room overlooking a long narrow garden which extended all the way down to the railway line. The baby's eyes remained closed.

"What a good boy you've been, Tommy," Cilla said. She began to remove his clothes and fold them into a neat pile on the pillow beside him. She was very fond of the navy striped romper suit. It was a French design bought in Paris when she had been doing a job out there. "Maybe next time you can be Tammy instead." Once the little body was naked she rolled it over and flicked the tiny switch halfway down its back from

8

"on" to "off". The baby's chest stopped mid-movement and was still.

The True-to-Life doll had been an excellent purchase. This was the third time that Cilla had used it. The baby was made out of silicone and if you didn't actually touch the skin it was quite impossible to tell it apart from a real baby. Most importantly, its presence, peacefully sleeping in the push-chair, conferred on Cilla the golden halo of motherhood. Motherhood placed her beyond suspicion, which was very useful in her line of work. Although, obviously she never used the young mother persona for a job which might require a swift exit. It was impossible to move at any speed with a buggy in tow.

She left the baby lying on the bed and wandered over to her dressing table. There were five mannequin heads there, four of which were wearing wigs. She looked in the mirror. Her short fair hair was soft and manicured, artfully highlighted with gold and platinum shades. It was a good look for a sub-urban stay-at-home mum. Cilla peeled off the wig, placed it on the naked mannequin head and began to brush out the blonde hair. Her own head was shaved. She had tried grow-ing her hair and wearing a skull cap but it just didn't seem to work. No matter which wig she wore she always overheated and then her forehead and upper lip would begin to perspire. This was unacceptable in so many ways. To begin with it was distracting. There was also the possibility that it might draw attention: a sweaty person looks nervous and guilty. Consider poor Maurice; he had been sweating so much for that entire tube journey, he had actually left two dark round buttock marks on the seat when he stood up. Also, Cilla found that the act of sweating seemed to create a loop in her cortisol and adrenaline production which in turn affected her precision. It was much simpler and easier to shave her head.

She hated these rush jobs. They were always so crude and improvised. It was difficult to match the man to the death under such circumstances. But equally it was impossible to refuse Vlad anything when he was in one of his moods; he wasn't called Haugr the Ogre for nothing. It was just lucky that Maurice Malinowski had been in late middle age and slightly stout, not overweight as such, but harbouring a hard little paunch under his dapper suit which would tend to indicate high cholesterol and some internal fat around the organs. A heart attack would be the obvious cause of death.

She had compounded this diagnosis by announcing the heart attack to onlookers as it happened. By the time the airport doctor arrived Cilla was long absent, but the spectators who remained could be relied on to have breathlessly relayed this information to the attending medic, and this would have simply served to confirm what he was already thinking. No-one would notice the minute wound in the back of Maurice's neck and Cilla had carefully recovered the dart which had caused it.

She looked out of the window into the garden. The sun was shining through the two cherry trees, making dappled shadows on the lawn. There were jobs to be done in the greenhouse. Cilla slipped on her everyday wig: mid-length, light brown, nondescript, an approximation of her original hair as far as she could remember it. Then she opened the drawer of her dressing table, took out some disposable latex gloves from an open box and went outside.

The greenhouse and potting shed were located past the two ornamental cherry trees towards the end of the garden as it approached the railway line. Both had running water and electricity. The only other way in which they really differed from a normal greenhouse and potting shed was that they were both scrupulously clean. The greenhouse doubled as a laboratory and there was a fridge and freezer in the potting shed to provide cold storage where necessary. Cilla always took the precaution of wearing gloves when she was working with her plants and stores. It was probably unnecessary but some of the chemicals were extremely potent and there was certainly no point in putting herself at risk with repeated handling. It was what she had been taught to do. She began by checking several batches of corncockle seedlings, watering and pinching out where necessary. She adjusted her grow lights. Then she moved on to assess her stores. The stores had become a matter of serious concern to Cilla. It was not simply the fact that she was running low on certain key compounds which could not be replaced; she was worried about the efficacy of those remaining. Each of them probably had a shelf life if only she knew what it was. Mixing the perfect toxin was both a science and an art form, but the potency of the final product was only as good as each of its constituent parts. There was no point in giving a man a heart attack only to find that he was sitting up drinking tea in his hospital bed three hours later.

The art of poison was not Cilla's only talent. She spoke five languages. She was a competent forger. She was proficient in the use of a number of small weapon-delivery systems, blowpipes, catapults and miniature crossbows. She was fully trained in the tactics of retreat and evasion. But it was the combination of these skills that created Cilla's real area of expertise. Her speciality was the Dry Job: an assassination disguised as a death by natural causes. The term was a derivative of the more infamous Wet Job. The basic difference between the two was an absence of blood. But the subtle and far more important distinction was that a Dry Job did not involve suspicion. It was the perfect murder.

Vladimir Haugr was her main client. He provided her with

11

an apartment, a reasonable retainer and expenses in return for approximately five jobs a year and some babysitting. He did not object to her taking on freelance projects as long as there was no conflict of interest, i.e. she couldn't bump off any of his major suppliers or customers, unless of course he asked her to.

The problem was that Vlad didn't really understand the level of planning and forethought that went into a proper Dry Job. He wanted someone dead and he wanted it now. What Vlad failed to appreciate, in Cilla's opinion, was the existential principle behind the Dry Job, which was this: everybody dies. Each person's death is out there waiting for them at some unspecified point in the future. Cilla's role was not simply one of executioner; she provided the assessment and execution of probability. By examining a person's life in detail it was possible to predict the likely time and cause of their demise. Then Cilla would seek to tailor her method to this prediction.

Of course if her prediction was that an individual would likely die in their bed at the age of ninety, it didn't help very much. But that was what brake tampering was for.

Cilla usually took on several private projects a year. Her fee was fifty thousand pounds. The process was always the same: three meetings with a client, a large deposit followed by payment upon completion, no further contact, no repeat business.

The first meeting was the introduction. This was often a rather strained and emotional affair. Clients frequently sought to justify their prospective choice of target with long and intense diatribes about how it was just and right that their partner, parent, sibling, etc. should die. Cilla generally listened to these denunciations quietly and when she was certain that the orator was done, she would explain the information

12

that she needed the client to compile and provide her with so that the assignment could be completed.

Then followed a cooling-off period of two weeks before the second meeting took place. At this meeting the information that Cilla had requested was handed over along with a non-refundable deposit of twenty-five thousand pounds. About fifteen percent of people failed to attend the second meeting. Another ten percent changed their minds at some point later on in the process, which was why the deposit was non-refundable. She never informed clients how the target would die, only the time frame within which the death would take place – which was generally three months. Cilla often took this opportunity to remind clients that, should they "forget" to pay the remainder of their fee after the deed was done, they could expect their own demise within a further three months – from natural causes, of course. So far, everyone had paid up.

At the final meeting the remaining twenty-five thousand pounds was handed over. Clients sometimes expressed jubilation at this point, but were equally likely to demonstrate anguish, guilt and regret. Cilla was fascinated by this. It seemed to exemplify the cautionary message from one of Aesop's fables: be careful what you wish for.

As a result of her freelance work Cilla had savings of £350,000. This money was buried in cellophane-wrapped bundles of fifty thousand pounds at seven strategic locations around the garden. Obviously she couldn't put the money in a bank account. But even if she could have done, Cilla didn't actually have a bank account. Nor did she have a passport or a driver's licence or any other form of identification. In fact, officially, she didn't exist at all; which represented a problem, but also an opportunity.

Once Cilla had finished her jobs outside she got ready for an appointment with a client. This would be meeting number two. The client was a stockbroker at Gerrards who wanted to murder his wife. He was convinced that she no longer loved him and was having an affair with her personal trainer. He had found solace in the arms of the Spanish au pair, Matilde. He felt that divorce would be both prohibitively expensive and emotionally damaging to their two small children. Death was preferable. Once his wife had been disposed of he planned to take on the role of grieving husband for several months before proposing marriage to Matilde. From what she knew of him Cilla felt that it was unlikely that the au pair would accept his offer, but so far she had kept this opinion to herself.

Cilla arrived at the rendezvous twenty minutes ahead of schedule. This was her standard practice. She scoped out the meeting point, in this case the flower stall outside Embankment station, and positioned herself in a local café which afforded her a good view of the stall. All that was left to do now was to drink her coffee and wait. If anything did not look right or feel right or smell right about the meeting she could always just slip away.

The stockbroker arrived promptly on the hour and stood outside the station pretending to read his paper. He was every inch the city boy: double-breasted suit, black oxfords, dark coat with a velvet collar. He looked twitchy but that was to be expected. He carried a brown leather briefcase and a large plastic bag. Cilla materialised softly at his elbow.

"Shall we go to the park?" she said in way of greeting.

Her meetings always took place in London parks. She particularly liked the ones with ponds and ducks. Victoria Embankment Gardens did not have a pond but it was next to the river Thames so there were ducks and moorhens in abundance. Cilla rummaged in her satchel for the bag of stale bread she had brought with her.

"What are you doing?" the stockbroker enquired irritably.

14

"I'm going to feed the ducks," Cilla replied evenly. "Do you still want to go ahead?"

"Yes, yes of course I do. I'm here aren't I?"

"Do you have the money?"

"Yes."

"And the rest? All of it, everything I asked for?"

"Yes."

"Well hand it over then."

The stockbroker passed Cilla the plastic bag. In return she handed him some bread. She could see that his hands were shaking.

"What the fuck?" he said, holding the bread with distaste. His voice was high and strained.

"Just feed the ducks," Cilla instructed him. "It'll calm you down."

For a minute or so they stood in silence tearing up the stale slices and throwing them to the birds. Some brazen seagulls appeared, swooping down from the slate-grey sky to intercept pieces in mid-air.

"Now let's walk," Cilla said when all the bread was gone.

"If all goes well, the assignment will be completed within three months," she began. It was a prepared speech that she had repeated a number of times. "When it's done I will make contact and you will pay me the balance. Is that clear?"

"How are you going to do it?" the stockbroker demanded.

"You don't need to know."

"But I want to know."

"It's much better that you don't know how or when," Cilla replied patiently. "That way when it happens you will be as surprised as everyone else. If you're asked any questions you won't need to lie. It's safer that way."

"I want her to suffer," the stockbroker insisted. "The way she's made me suffer. Can you torture her first?"

"Torture leaves marks. Marks raise questions," Cilla said firmly.

"But can't you just make the body disappear? It's my money that's financing this, don't I get some say?" The stockbroker spat his words out. Cilla looked sideways at him. Was he was going to be troublesome? Walking away was still a possibility.

"Not really," she replied. "If there's no body and no explanation for your wife's disappearance then that leads to questions. Even the most obtuse detective will have no choice but to entertain the prospect that she might have been murdered. As the husband you would be the principal suspect. Is that what you want?" Cilla held up the plastic bag towards him. "It's not what I want."

The stockbroker turned away from her but he didn't take the bag.

It wasn't the first time that a client had made this sort of request. Cilla always refused. If truth be told she actively disliked torture. For the most part it was distasteful and unnecessary. The only possible justification for it was to extract intelligence from a reluctant informant and Cilla had drugs that would do a better job of that anyway. She hated the sound of torture. And even worse than the sound was the effluence that always seemed to accompany the noise: blood, sweat, tears, urine, diarrhoea, vomit. In any case, Cilla wasn't a sadist. She took a certain satisfaction in her work, the completion of a job well done, but she had little interest in pain for its own sake.

With some reluctance, the stockbroker capitulated and Cilla brought the meeting to a close. She left him standing by a park bench, his shoulders hunched, his hands thrust into the pockets of his overcoat, staring gloomily at the brass inscription on the wooden seat.

"In memory of my beloved wife Amy and the many happy hours

16

we sat here," he read out. "My wife's name is Amy." The stockbroker gave a short bitter laugh but the irony of this was lost on Cilla. It was one of those subtle emotions that she sometimes failed to understand.

2

Limits

Cilla spent the evening sitting on the floor of her living room examining the contents of the stockbroker's plastic bag and eating a Chinese takeaway. She had ordered a chicken chow mein, some prawn dumplings and a portion of fried seaweed. It was probably just cabbage rather than real seaweed but Cilla loved its sweet taste and the way in which the crisp strands melted on her tongue. Even after all the time that she had spent in England she could not get used to the volume and variety of food that was available. She could still remember the first time she went into a British supermarket and saw the meat counter; how she had stood there in wonder staring at the profusion of pork, lamb, beef, chicken, duck, turkey, even some venison, lying there glistening and inert, available to anyone.

She had taken a long hot bath when she got home and ate the takeaway in her pyjamas; her cropped head was sleek like a seal. The twenty-five thousand pound deposit sat in five fat envelopes. Each freshly minted bale was still enclosed within its bill strap. Even though the money was bank fresh, she counted it carefully. Then she wrapped the whole lot in cling film and placed the lone package on top of the middle kitchen cupboard where it was out of sight but accessible. Once the balance was paid she would consider digging another hole in the garden.

Cilla hoped that the stockbroker had had the sense to withdraw the deposit on five separate occasions as he had been instructed to do. Transactions of a few thousand could be explained away with drugs, call girls and expensive bottles of champagne in grotty nightclubs. But a single withdrawal of twenty-five thousand pounds plus a dead body might arouse the curiosity of even the least imaginative police officer. Of course, the police would need due cause to access his bank account in the first place. If they had due cause then it would mean that Cilla had not done her job properly. Cilla never gave the police due cause. What she gave them instead was The Story.

The Story underpinned the Dry Job. It was the piece of living theatre: the straightforward, predictable, but highly orchestrated account of the end of a person's life. It was Occam's razor in motion based on the principle that, all things being equal, the simplest explanation for something is usually the correct one. The Story provided that simple explanation for the death. If The Story worked then there would be little or no involvement of the police. Instead there would be a funeral, one which preferably involved cremation, and everybody would get on with their lives.

Some stories were easier to write than others. In fact some stories practically wrote themselves.

Take the example of the psychiatrist she had bumped off two years earlier. In this case the client had been an elderly patient who claimed that Dr Khayad was blackmailing her. (It was unclear whether he actually had been blackmailing her or whether this was a paranoid delusion, a feature of the old lady's dementia, but it was a moot point.) Doctors were easy to dispose of because they were generally unhappy, over-worked and had access to lethal medication. Dr Khayad was no exception in this regard. He was on his fourth marriage, estranged from his children, and was a heavy drinker who was given to prescribing himself repeated doses of nonbenzo-diazepines. All that was needed was some ethanol, a Valium chaser and a suicide note. Being a doctor, his handwriting was illegible but Cilla had attempted a faithful representation of his scrawl on the assumption that one of the wives or kids would probably be able to decipher it. She made reference to each of the children by name, told them that he loved them, it wasn't their fault and recommended that they get on with their lives without him, etc. etc. She didn't mention any of the wives. The first three probably hated him and the fourth must be an idiot or a gold digger.

Over the years one thing that Cilla had learned from experience was that an unhappy person was generally a better subject for a Dry Job than a happy one. Unhappy people tended to have bad habits, bad health and often made bad choices. Any or all of these could be exploited and manipulated to create The Story. Unhappy people also made enemies, which was how they ended up as the target for a Dry Job in the first place. In fact when Cilla thought about it, most of her freelance work dealt with unhappy people: unhappy clients and their unhappy victims.

Her work for Vladimir Haugr was different. Vlad might be a brutal narcissistic sadist but he wasn't unhappy. Nor were some of his victims. Over the two years that Cilla had worked for him she had despatched twelve people on his behalf. This included one ex-girlfriend, three employees, three customers, two suppliers and several miscellaneous persons (including Maurice Malinowski) who had offended Vlad deeply in one way or another. She hadn't impaled anyone on a railing. Her methods were usually more subtle than that, even when it wasn't a Dry Job. Ten of the twelve hits were part of her contractual agreement with Vlad but the first couple she had done for free. They had been penance.

In her life Cilla had seen a lot of death. Most people seemed to end without realising it. If they died in their sleep or with a bullet to the back of the head, this was self-evident. There was no warning of the momentous event that was about to occur. But even those individuals who had looked right into her eyes at the moment of their demise did not really seem to understand what was happening to them. They might look pained, frightened, surprised or furious but Cilla could not recall ever having seen a look of comprehension. It must be as Wittgenstein surmised:

"Death is not an event in life: we do not live to experience death . . . Our life has no end in the way in which our visual field has no limits."

But Cilla also knew that she was the exception to this rule. She had been so close to death so many times: death she had caused, death she had witnessed, and her own near death on at least one occasion.

The last time had been six months or so before. Cilla had been doing a job for Vlad. It was a simple enough operation: one of his men, Jacob, was cutting the coke and skimming the profit. Vlad had tolerated this for a while; he had given Jacob a warning, but nothing had changed and then customers started to complain about the product. An example had to be made. If Vlad let one man get away with this sort of thing then all the others would start trying their luck as well.

Cue Cilla. It was not a Dry Job as such. Vlad wanted the man removed discreetly but he didn't care if there was a murder investigation or not. The police wouldn't care much either. Jacob was a known thug and they wouldn't want to allocate resources towards investigating his death.

Cilla decided to adopt a sleep-and-stick approach. She would chloroform Jacob and inject him with one of her remaining vials of Compound 146: the distilled poison from a western taipan sometimes known as the fierce snake. Its most important component was a powerful neurotoxin which led to paralysis and suffocation over a period of about forty-five minutes. Only a very astute pathologist would be able to identify the compound in his system afterwards. In all likelihood they would miss it completely and Jacob's death would be attributed to some nebulous cause.

Everything went off well to begin with. Cilla broke into Jacob's first-floor flat at 3.35 a.m., one hour after she had seen the lights go off. She stood outside his bedroom door for a full minute timing his snores in order to assure herself that he was completely and deeply asleep. Jacob was a large sullen man and she had no desire to encounter him conscious. After the minute had passed she unwrapped the chloroformed rag, held it in one hand and turned the door handle to his bedroom with the other. Once inside she closed the door and paused silently to allow her eyes to achieve partial dark adaptation. Only when she could make out a clear outline of Jacob in the bed and was certain of the position in which he was lying did she proceed. In one nimble movement Cilla darted towards the bed. As Jacob completed his exhalation her hand clamped over his nose and mouth so that his next intake of breath was pure chloroform. He tensed for a moment and slumped. Having completed the tricky part of the procedure, Cilla turned on the bedside light, removed her backpack and took out the rest of her equipment. Once set up she rolled back the brightly patterned seascape duvet and took stock. Jacob lay there naked and hairy; he had good veins. She put a tourniquet on his right arm beneath the elbow, tightened it and prepared the hypodermic.

Once she had administered the dose all that was left to do was wait. The ensuing three-quarters of an hour passed slowly. Cilla still had her gloves on so at least she could examine the contents of Jacob's bedroom with impunity as long as she put things back where she found them. Not that there was much to examine. The space seemed devoid of sentiment or personality. The walls were bare; the bedding looked as if it hadn't been changed in months. On the bedside table was a glass ashtray, a half-empty pack of cigarettes, a lighter, two girlie magazines and a detective novel. She flicked through the magazines but there was nothing to interest her there. She smoked half a cigarette, taking care to put the butt in her back pocket rather than leaving it in the ashtray. When she picked up the detective novel a dog-eared photograph fell out. Perhaps Jacob had been using it as a bookmark. It was a picture of a little boy sitting cross-legged and holding a puppy on his lap. The boy was squinting up at the camera with a big smile on his face. Cilla wondered if it was the child or the dog that was the object of interest for Jacob. The photograph stirred something in Cilla and a memory of her own threatened to surface. She pushed the thought away, placed the photograph back inside the book and rearranged the objects on the bedside table into their original positions. It was time to check on Jacob.

His body was pale and had taken on the yellow waxy sheen of a corpse. Cilla sat on the side of the bed next to him. His skin was cool to the touch. She could not find a pulse and a mirror held to his mouth indicated that he was no longer breathing. Cilla leant over his face and pulled up one of his eyelids to do the final check. The pupil contracted.

Before she could move Jacob's hands were around her neck; pushing, choking, squeezing out the life. Cilla's first instinct was to claw at those hands with her own, but she resisted this impulse. If she did that she would merely waste time and then she would die. As stars exploded in front of her and the inky black edges of darkness began to bleed into her consciousness she forced herself to grope around the bed for the hypodermic she knew she had left there. Her fingers found the syringe and with one final exertion she took hold of it and stabbed Jacob blindly in the face.

Cilla was lucky on two counts. Firstly, when she picked up the syringe it was the right way up so that she stabbed Jacob with the needle rather than the plunger. Secondly, the needle found his eye.

Jacob bellowed in pain. He released her throat and put both hands up towards his face. In the same instant Cilla took hold of the ashtray, smashed it against the bedside table and holding the remaining shard, she turned back towards the groaning man and sliced open the femoral artery on his inner right thigh. Clearly the neurotoxin in Compound 146 was not working properly, but perhaps the hemotoxin was still effective. Apparently it was: Jacob bled to death in less than two minutes.

The whole incident was something of an embarrassment. What was meant to be a discreet Wet Job had turned into a blood bath. Vlad hadn't actually minded very much. The violent nature of Jacob's death served his purpose quite well. It made the other employees anxious and compliant. But Cilla had to wear a scarf for a month until the bruises faded. It also raised other issues.

The first issue was her stores. Unless she had miscalculated

24

the dosage for a large man like Jacob, Compound 146 had become unreliable. It must still have some efficacy. At full strength Jacob would have snapped her neck like a twig. A combination of chloroform and poison had clearly weakened him but it had not killed him. If one compound in her stores was compromised, how reliable were the others?

The second issue was her limits. Wittgenstein was wrong. Cilla's visual field had limits, her life had limits. She had seen them, the dark ragged edges of the abyss. After Jacob's death she knew with complete certainty that if she kept straying beyond those limits her own life would end, just as she had seen all those other lives end. There would be another Jacob and this time she wouldn't be so lucky. Or she would anger Vlad in some absurd way and he would turn on her. In fact the more she thought about it, the more improbable it seemed that she was still alive at all, after everything that had happened. She must be an anomaly, a statistical outlier, she had defied the odds. But the thing about probability was that it always evened up in the end, which meant her luck really couldn't last.

The third issue was herself. During those torturous moments when Jacob's fat meaty fingers were pressing down on her windpipe Cilla experienced something close to an epiphany. The epiphany was this: she liked life. Sometimes she enjoyed life. She wanted to live. This came as something of a revelation. Cilla had always held a deep ambivalence towards life: other peoples' lives, her own. And then on the verge of annihilation she realised that she didn't feel ambivalent towards her own life at all. It was like waking up from a coma; she had been sleepwalking through a monochrome world and all of a sudden it had exploded into colour.

This realisation was somehow fused with an impression of Jacob's blood-soaked duvet. He was a big man, there was a lot of blood. The crimson stain had expanded outwards, engulfing the tessellating blue and green fish below. Cilla held the image delicately in her head, turning it over time and time again in the weeks that followed: the colours, the precision of the pattern on the duvet, the fish swimming in a slow-moving sea of blood. The memory had a reassuring clarity and coherence to it amidst the chaos and confusion that her epiphany had created. Only one other thing was clear to her. In order to preserve and cherish this life that she had so recently discovered she valued, she would have to find another way of living. There was no future in the way she lived now. Her life was nasty and brutish; without change it would be short.

But what could Cilla do instead? How would she live? And what of Vlad? He would never willingly let her go. The only solution was to disappear and reinvent herself, to pupate and emerge as something new. Again.

"The snake which cannot cast its skin has to die."

Friedrich Nietzsche. Not a first-rate theorist in Cilla's opinion, he tended to over-dramatise, but good for the occasional aphorism.

She flicked her mind back to the task in hand and emptied the rest of the contents of the stockbroker's plastic bag onto the living room floor. She couldn't just walk away from her life. Metamorphosis took time, preparation and funds. She had done her sums and estimated the cost at half a million; which meant three more Dry Jobs.

A miscellaneous collection lay before her on the carpet. There were keys to a house, photographs, school reports, letters, copies of bank statements, club memberships and a variety of other documents. The wife's Filofax had also been obtained. All these items represented the foundation on which Cilla would build a picture of Amy Levine's life, and then, in due course, her death.

26

The stockbroker's wife appeared to be a typical example of her type. She was thirty-five, married with two children: Samantha and Michael, a pigeon pair. She had been born and raised in Kent, the Garden of England, had attended a private girls' school where she had distinguished herself on the school tennis team and had risen to the position of deputy head girl. Afterwards she studied Politics, Philosophy and Economics at Bristol university where she met Paul Levine, her future husband. She achieved a creditable but undistinguished 2:1. Paul got a First in Maths. After graduation they came to London; Amy joined the graduate scheme at Saatchi and Saatchi, and Paul started life as a Blue Button, an unauthorised clerk on the stockbroking floor. At some point there had been a separation between them. There were copies of three letters from Paul to Amy from around this time and Cilla read this correspondence with interest. It was difficult to connect the lovelorn author to the bitter twitchy man she had encountered, but the letters seemed to have achieved their desired intention and the two were married soon after. Michael was born a year later. The couple bought a large house in a West London square and Samantha made her appearance in due course. The children were now aged five and eight. Amy no longer worked full time and her CV described her as an independent qualitative research consultant, whatever that might mean. There was little indication that she worked at all. A series of nannies and au pairs had been employed over the years. The current one was called Matilde. There were black-and-white copies of photographs of all the main protagonists: Amy on the tennis court, blonde and lithe; Amy and Paul getting married; school photographs of Michael and Samantha with freshly combed hair and gappy teeth. There was only one slightly blurry image of Matilde sitting at a dining table with the two children. From what Cilla could see Matilde was a dark, plump girl, pretty enough, but an unlikely object of infatuation; an infatuation so obsessive that it would cause a man to murder his wife. Not that Cilla knew much about infatuation. What mattered was that Matilde and Amy looked nothing alike so there could be no possibility of mistaking one for the other at the crucial moment.

Cilla finished the remnants of her chicken chow mein and turned her attention to Amy's Filofax, the small leather-bound personal organiser which would provide the details of Amy's daily life. She was a member of an expensive health club. She saw a personal trainer once a week and played tennis three times a week. She did yoga. She belonged to a book club. They were currently reading *The Beauty Myth* by Naomi Wolf. Amy had several female friends whom she met regularly for coffee, lunch and cultural activities: visits to art galleries and the theatre. She had a private gynaecologist. It was all standard stuff.

The notes at the back of the Filofax were somewhat more revealing. There were shopping lists, book titles, film titles, the odd jotting down of thoughts or intentions. Amy had round childish handwriting which slanted slightly to the left. She did not dot her i's but formed a tiny circle above them and her lower-case l's were widely looped. Cilla traced her fingers over a couple of the words; it was not a complex style and would be simple to forge if necessary. The most interesting page divulged a list of New Year's resolutions. The first of these was: "Win Mixed Doubles", followed by "Lose half a stone" and "Cook vegetarian twice a week". There was also "Do your Kegels!!" and the rather generic: "Be Kind". These all seemed rather banal aspirations for the year but the final two goals were more intriguing. One read "Hold it together" and the other "Keep to the plan".

But there was nothing in the contents of the plastic bag

to indicate how Amy Levine might be persuaded to meet a premature end in an inconspicuous manner. She had no identifiable health problems and no bad habits. There wasn't even any indication that she was having an affair with her personal trainer, whatever her husband might think.

Cilla could only hope that closer observation would dredge up some dirt, divulge some hidden detail of Amy's life, something Cilla could work with.

3

Origins

Cilla's name had not always been Cilla. For the first few years of her life she had had another name, which she did not like to think about.

She had been born and raised in a small dilapidated house on the outskirts of a village whose name she was no longer sure she could remember correctly, and didn't want to, even if she could. A lot of her impressions from this time had a dim, surreal quality to them like half-remembered dreams; a shadowy realm broken up by a few sharp fragments of memory.

One thing she could remember was that things were always broken and that it was her father's job to mend them. There were broken things all over the house and other broken things rusting in the yard: old bicycles, various engine parts, a lawnmower, a chainsaw. He was the village handyman of sorts. Apparently he wasn't a very good handyman because most of the broken things stayed broken.

They owned a few chickens. In the days when Cilla's name

was not Cilla it was her job to feed them. She performed this chore grudgingly and regarded the chickens with derision. They were excessively stupid. Her father had constructed some sort of rough hen house in the corner of the yard with a fence around it. Periodically the hen house was raided by a fox and no matter what her father did he could never seem to prevent the fox from eventually gaining access again. What he did do was to build the chickens a high broad wooden perch which could act as a refuge when the fox launched his attack. Even though the chickens couldn't fly for any distance as such, they could flap their wings sufficiently to become airborne and reach the perch. Cilla knew this because if she put some of the feed on the perch a few of them would always manage to retrieve it. She even attempted to train the chickens to evade the fox by using various lures and deterrents. But it was no use. Every now and again Cilla would go to feed the chickens in the morning only to find that they had all been massacred during the night. One would be missing and the rest would have been decapitated. She wondered why the fox murdered all of them instead of just killing and taking one. The only possible explanation that she could think of was that he enjoyed it.

She was one of five children. Her position was number four. The two eldest siblings had already left home and her next sister was seventeen and more like an adult than a child. Mostly it was just her and Tomas. He was four years younger than Cilla and the only boy of the brood. She often wondered why her parents had had three children in quick succession, waited eight years, and then decided to have two more. It seemed ridiculous. But one day, when she was ferreting around her parents' bedroom, she found a little box under their bed. Inside were all sorts of strange treasures: locks of hair tied with different coloured ribbons, little teeth, a family photo of her parents with three young children and a new baby who couldn't have been her. She was so engrossed in the contents of the box that she didn't hear her mother come into the room. There was shouting and her mother chased her out, slapping the backs of her legs as she fled.

Most of the time life was dull. When Cilla wasn't doing chores at home she attended the local village school. It was divided into two classes: Elementary and Transition. You were supposed to stay in the lower class until you were ten years old and then move up. Cilla quite enjoyed her time in Elementary, but not for the usual reasons. The school work was pitifully simple and the other children were, for the most part, gormless and gullible. What she found pleasure in was telling tall tales. Her peers in Elementary were such idiots that she could tell them practically anything and they would believe it. On one occasion Cilla succeeded in persuading the rest of her classmates that the world was due to end on the night of the next full moon. This was just the sort of intricate fabrication that she loved to construct. As the moon waxed and the fateful day got nearer, many of the children started to experience night terrors. Parents complained.

"But why did you tell them that the full moon would crack like an egg and its yolk would pour down onto the earth, engulfing the planet and causing everyone on it to drown?" her mystified teacher demanded.

But Cilla just stared at her shoes and said nothing.

She only lasted in Elementary for a year before the teacher announced that she had nothing more to teach Cilla and that she was too disruptive to stay with the younger ones. So at eight years old Cilla graduated to Transition and donned the small red pin of a Little Octobrist. The older children did not tolerate Cilla's silly stories or her unruly behaviour and they sat on her hard. She often came home with bumps and bruises. Not that it mattered much. Cilla was mostly impervious; both to pain and to the disapproval of others. She also had a vicious streak. If one of the bigger children bullied her, she always managed to exact some curious revenge of her own devising. On one occasion she even sacrificed her morning meal to get someone back, which was quite something given that there was often not really enough food to go around. At breakfast time, instead of eating her millet porridge, Cilla carefully secreted it into the pocket of her school dress. She carried it around in there all morning, cold and congealing. In the afternoon the class was scheduled to do PE. Most of the children did PE in their everyday shoes but one boy, Gregor, was the proud owner of a pair of plimsolls. He brought them into school every week in a string bag which he hung over the back of his chair. At lunchtime, when all the children were playing outside, Cilla slunk back into the classroom and transferred every last morsel of cold porridge from her pocket into the toes of Gregor's plimsolls. Then she carefully washed her hands and went back outside to join the others. How Gregor howled when he tried to put them on. It served him right for giving her a black eye two weeks earlier.

Cilla found the school work easy. It was mostly rote learning and the digestion and recitation of State-sanctioned moral doctrine. But she had no friends. This was not simply because she was the youngest and often the naughtiest child in the class. Several of the other girls had, at different times, tried to initiate closer bonds with her. The problem was that she could not seem to understand the rules of friendship. However carefully her mother explained it to her, Cilla struggled to grasp the concept of sharing. If she wanted something she attempted to take it, even if that involved hitting someone or being hit herself.

33

But the fact of the matter was that Cilla wasn't really interested in making friends because she had Tomas and Luna. Tomas finished his Kindergarten half an hour earlier than she finished school and every day he would wait breathlessly at the gate for her with Luna barking joyfully beside him. There was no issue of having to share anything with Tomas because, if she wanted something of his, he gave it to her immediately. Whatever game she was inclined to play, Tomas was honoured to play it with her. It was simple really: she was his sun, moon and stars.

Cilla's feelings towards her little brother were less intense. She often found him irritating. At times he could be babyish and he always cried if he fell over and ran to their mother to be comforted. But he never told tales, even when she was cruel to him, and his frank and blatant adoration of her gave Cilla a warm feeling inside. All in all, she preferred Tomas over every other human being in the world.

They had great adventures together in the back yard. One of their favourite games was pirates. Cilla was always the pirate captain Stenka and Tomas was her first mate. They would pretend that the hen house was a neighbouring merchant vessel which they were going to attack and plunder. Cilla would make an elaborate plan and then the two of them would take command of the hen-house ship with great gusto, waving pieces of wood as their swords. The chickens squawked, Luna barked. If their mother or their older sister Martha was home from the farm collective one of them would usually appear at the back door, hands on hips.

"Will you stop terrorising those chickens half to death. They'll stop laying and it will be your fault."

Luna always accompanied them. She was often given some sort of honorary role in their games, such as cabin boy, messenger or go-between, which she was then encouraged to perform with the throwing and retrieving of sticks. She was an exceptional dog and both children adored her. At night Luna was supposed to sleep in the yard but invariably one or other of them would creep downstairs and let her in so that she could come and spend the night in their room. She was such a clever dog that she always knew not to bark.

One day, shortly after her tenth birthday, Cilla arrived at school to find a sleek black car parked outside. It didn't look like any of the cars in the village. Two men sat in the front with the windows rolled down. They were both smoking. When Cilla went inside there were two other smartly dressed strangers talking to her teacher in low voices at the front of the classroom: a man and a woman. The woman seemed to be in charge. Cilla went to her desk and sat down. There was a buzz of anticipation in the room but a glance at the other children told Cilla that they did not know what was going on any more than she did. After a few more minutes of murmured conversation the teacher turned to the class and clapped her hands for silence.

"Good morning students," she said. "Today we are honoured to have visitors from the Ministry of Education. Please show them every courtesy. They are here to conduct a test. The test will take two hours. You have five minutes before it begins. If you need to go to the toilet now is the time to do so. Make sure you have two sharp pencils on your desk."

The test was divided into two parts. The first part was mathematics. It was easy enough to begin with, just lots of simple sums, the sort of thing they did in class. Then gradually it became more complicated. The questions were presented as long wordy problems which needed to be solved:

Q36: Victor, Igor and Dimi are three elderly brothers. The sum of Victor and Dimi's ages is 148. The sum of Dimi and Igor's ages is 157. The sum of Victor and Igor's ages is 139. Which brother is the youngest and how old is he?

Cilla was perplexed. She had never encountered questions like this before. But she didn't find them very hard.

The second part of the test consisted of a page with a series of photographs on it like a large cartoon strip and a comprehension exercise below. But it was unlike any sort of comprehension that Cilla had done before. In the first photograph a man and a woman were sitting at a table eating a fancy meal. They looked happy. In the second picture the woman had pushed her plate away, even though the food was only half eaten, and was saying something to the man. She didn't look happy anymore. In the third photo, both man and woman had stood up and were gesticulating at each other. In the fourth photo the woman had picked up her knife from the table and was brandishing it at the man. In the fifth photo the man was lying on the floor on his front, the woman was still standing up and the knife was nowhere to be seen. Now she looked stricken. There was clearly a box for a sixth photo but the space itself was empty.

There were only six questions to answer in the comprehension. The first five questions asked for a detailed description of what was happening in each of the corresponding photographs. The sixth question read:

6. Please describe the photo that you would expect to see in box six? Provide a comprehensive account of what is happening in the picture.

It all looked fairly obvious to Cilla. The man and the woman were having dinner together. Then the woman had got cross with the man about something. They'd had an argument.

The woman had picked up her knife and she had stabbed the man. He had fallen to the floor, dead. It was strange that there was no blood but maybe it was all underneath him along with the knife. Cilla wrote a thorough explanation for each photo accordingly. She even made the couple man and wife and suggested that the woman was angry with the man because he got drunk too often. She'd heard her own parents row about this issue numerous times so it seemed a suitable topic for an argument between adults.

Cilla pondered over the possibilities for the sixth photo, but she could only come up with one sensible outcome.

"In this photograph the woman would be sitting back down at the table eating the rest of her dinner because she is still hungry," she wrote. "She would have to borrow her husband's knife to cut up the meat." Then, since this explanation of events seemed rather bald, she added a lengthy description of the food and what it tasted like for good measure.

At the end of two hours the visiting guests from the Ministry of Education collected in the tests. The lady said that she was impressed with the class for concentrating so well and gave all the children a chocolate bar and sent them outside for an early break. Cilla was delighted; chocolate was a rare delicacy, but her elation was curtailed when her class teacher sought her out in the playground.

"They want to see you," the teacher said. "You're to go and wait in the corridor until they call you in to the classroom. And behave yourself," she added with spiteful emphasis.

Cilla stood in the corridor listening resentfully to the sound of the other children playing outside. She couldn't believe that she was in trouble yet again. What had she done this time? There was a muted but intense discussion coming from within the classroom so she crept closer to the door.

"Her scores are off the scale," the lady visitor was saying. "We have to have her. In any case we're under-subscribed for girls."

"But she's so small and malnourished," the man replied. "Do you really think she'll be a useful addition to the programme?"

"Her numeracy skills alone would qualify her, but her answers to the Burkov Test – they were conclusive."

"Could she not simply be an autistic savant?"

"No, no. I've explained it to you before. An autistic child would not be able to understand or describe the photographs properly. And they entirely lack the ability to link one photograph to the next so they might say that the man had fallen over, for instance, or that he's gone to sleep. Her answers demonstrate a fully developed understanding of emotional sequencing. But it has no consequence for her. It doesn't mean anything in her world. That is a key trait."

"Shall I send someone to pick her up?" the man asked.

"No, let's take her with us today. I'm not interested in any of the others and there's room in the car."

There was a scraping of chairs and Cilla moved swiftly away from the door. It opened and the man came out.

"Go in," he said.

The lady was sitting at the teacher's desk at the front of the classroom, writing.

"Sit down here." The lady said, pointing towards a chair in front of her. Cilla approached the front of the classroom and sat. The lady continued with her writing and glanced up at Cilla as she spoke.

"Do you like school?" the lady said. Cilla nodded.

"Do you have lots of friends?" Cilla nodded again.

"Are you a good student?" Cilla nodded vehemently for a third time.

Finally the lady put her pen down and looked Cilla directly in the eye.

"That's not what your teacher says," she stated. "She says that you are wilful and disobedient; that the other children avoid you and that you demonstrate many undesirable qualities." The lady hesitated for a moment. "I don't agree." She continued, "I think you are at the wrong school."

This remark caught Cilla's attention.

"How would you like to go to a different school, a boarding school, where there are other clever children, children like you?"

Cilla was silent.

"It is an honour to be chosen to go to this school. I see a great many children and very few of them are selected."

Cilla opened her mouth slightly. There was a question that she wanted to ask, but she was unsure how to phrase it politely.

"Go on," said the lady encouragingly. When she heard Cilla's request a glimmer of a smile appeared at the corner of her mouth.

"I expect that can be arranged," she said.

Cilla's parents were bewildered but resigned. There was no question of them defying a directive from the Ministry of Education. In fact the only person who made a fuss was Tomas. When he realised that Cilla was going away he started to cry and shout. He became so distraught that, in the end, Cilla's older sister Martha had to drag him off for a walk so that he missed saying goodbye to her altogether.

Cilla herself was not particularly upset; if anything she was excited. She was going to get to ride in the big black sleek car and, in response to her request, the lady had promised her another bar of chocolate.

4

Players

When Cilla went to bed that night she left the contents of
the stockbroker's plastic bag scattered across her living room
floor. The mess was made on purpose; seeing all the documentation and photographs strewn over the carpet gave her
an overview. Out of chaos she would create order; out of
order she would write The Story; and The Story's ending
would be death. It was the beginning of a process.

The following day Cilla had an appointment to see Vlad
at TGR's. He conducted much of his business, both legitimate and illegitimate, out of a small office on the bridge club
premises.

The letters TGR stood for The Great Rose, which in turn
referred to the colourful bridge player Irving Rose, who
had been the first manager of the club. It was based on the
Bayswater Road near Marble Arch and inhabited the basement of a huge cream-coloured Georgian mansion in what
would once have been the servants' quarters.

When Cilla arrived play had begun and there were already two tables of players tossing cards. Cilla noticed, with irritation, that Vlad was sitting at one of the tables. That meant he could be hours. There was nothing much to do but wait. She sat down on a stool at the bar hoping that he would become aware of her presence and cut his game short. He took no notice but a player at the other table beckoned her over.

"Hey girlie," he said. "A cappuccino over here please."

Cilla sighed. The only way to explain her repeated presence at the bridge club was to pretend that she was one of the waitresses. She nodded, retreated to the kitchen and turned on the coffee machine. Whilst it was warming up she filled the portafilter with coffee.

Most of the regular staff at TGR's knew Cilla by name but they rarely spoke to her. None of them were quite sure what it was that she did for Vladimir Haugr, but they knew that she wasn't a waitress. Today there was a new girl in the kitchen that Cilla hadn't seen before.

"Hi," the girl said and smiled pleasantly at Cilla.

"You have to turn the coffee machine on as soon as you arrive," Cilla replied blankly. "It takes time to warm up."

"Oh sorry, I didn't know," the girl replied. She smiled again. "I'm new. The agency sent me."

"Go out and see if any of the players want anything," Cilla instructed her.

"OK," the girl said agreeably. She did as she was told but was back in the kitchen moments later.

"It's like they're all in a trance out there," she said. "What are they playing?"

"Bridge," Cilla replied.

"Honestly," the girl continued, "I think I could have taken all my clothes off and done a pirouette. No-one would have noticed."

"That actually happened," Cilla commented. "I think it was for a bet. Someone got a naked woman to sit opposite an expert whilst he played a hand."

"And?" the new girl said. "What happened?"

"Nothing," Cilla replied. "He never realised that she was there."

The girl laughed. Cilla sidestepped her to deliver the cappuccino out to the playing area. She placed it carefully on a small side table next to the player who had ordered it.

"That'll be two pounds," she said. "Cash or account?"

The player handed her two pound coins and a fifty pence piece.

"Keep the change," he advised.

Cilla sighed. At this rate she would only need to serve 24,999 more coffees to equal the payment for one Dry Job.

She sat down on the same bar stool again but Vlad was still engrossed in the cards and showed no indication of quitting.

Cilla went back into the kitchen where the new girl was fiddling with a packet of cigarettes.

"Want one?" she said. Cilla nodded.

The two of them leant out of the kitchen window blowing smoke into the basement courtyard outside.

"I'm Nancy," the girl said.

"Cilla," Cilla replied.

"How long have you worked here?" Nancy enquired.

"Two years," Cilla said.

"That's a long time."

"I'm thinking of quitting."

"To do what?"

"I'm not sure yet."

There was the sound of footsteps behind them and Cilla turned to see Artur, the manager, standing there.

"Mr Haugr would like to see you in his office," he said,

nodding at Cilla. She stubbed her cigarette out on the windowsill and flicked the butt onto the grey paving below.

As she walked out of the kitchen Nancy called after her.

"Hey, do you want to go to a party tonight?" But Cilla didn't respond.

"I'd like to remind you that there is a no smoking policy in this kitchen," she could hear Artur saying sternly to Nancy behind her.

Vlad's office was a small room dominated by a large desk and a large leonine man seated behind it. There was a single low wooden chair in front of the desk. Cilla sat down without being asked.

"I was in seven hearts," Vlad remarked. "It was a good contract but the trumps broke five fucking nil."

"That's unfortunate," Cilla replied impassively.

"I can make it if I finesse the ten of hearts at trick two. But it was completely against the odds so I went down instead. Fucking odds. I should have trusted my gut. Cost me two and a half grand," he growled.

Vladimir Haugr: Haugr the Ogre: Vlad the Impaler: known for his short temper and his medieval appetites. There was something almost feudal about the man and the way he organised his domain. Much as his spiritual ancestor had done before him, Cilla suspected that Vlad truly enjoyed impaling his enemies, watching them, quite literally, squirm on the end of his hook. Of course the rate of impalement had decreased somewhat since Cilla had been in his employ. This was not merely because she favoured less conspicuous methods; the fact was that you could only impale so many people before the authorities began to get involved. MI2 were interested, a dossier had been compiled. It would probably take just one more victim, left writhing on a railing, with links to Vladimir Haugr for the agency to make their move. To some extent the reality of this was to Cilla's advantage; it kept her safe. Even when Vlad was pissed off with her he still needed her particular set of skills.

"How did it go yesterday?" Vlad enquired.

"All good," Cilla replied. "Clean and dry."

"Where did you do it?"

"At the airport."

Vlad sniffed disapprovingly. "A lot of people at the airport," he commented.

"Yes," Cilla agreed. "And none of them saw anything."

Vlad drummed his fingers on the desk.

"I want you to go and babysit Smithy," he announced. "I need a new passport."

He slid a set of four photographs of an unknown man towards Cilla. She picked them up.

"Today," he added. Cilla nodded. "And don't accidentally slit his throat whilst you're there."

Vlad grinned at his own joke; he had been making these insinuations ever since the incident with Jacob.

Babysitting Smithy constituted the subsidiary part of Cilla's contract with Vlad. Smithy was short for the Blacksmith, which itself was a play on words. Smithy was in fact a master forger and counterfeiter. He provided Vlad with illicit documentation: passports, birth certificates, driving licences and such. Since Vlad employed a steady stream of undesirables, Smithy was kept quite busy.

"Find out how he's getting on with the Mint."

Smithy was also working on a separate project creating a portable printing press for the production of the perfect ten pound note. This was known as the Mint. Smithy knew everything there was to know about counterfeiting; about holograms and watermarks, what type of paper should be used and how the end result was meant to look and feel. The

44

disadvantage of most counterfeiting operations was that they were cumbersome and stationary. The equipment could not be moved easily so if the police got wind of an operation that was the end of it. But if the press was portable, the operation could always stay one step ahead of the authorities. Vlad's controlling interest in various London casinos also provided him with the perfect entry point to put the counterfeit notes into circulation. The thought of it made him salivate.

But for reasons that were unclear, Vlad did not altogether trust Smithy. Since Cilla was also adept at forgery he had her take on the role of babysitter. Each time Vlad employed Smithy's services he sent Cilla to supervise. It was her job to observe and to make sure that Smithy did not take copies or retain any compromising information that could be used against his employer at a later date. The role was boring but restful. In Cilla's mind, the best part of the task was Smithy himself. She enjoyed watching him work; the dark eyes, the aquiline profile, his long delicate fingers manipulating their instruments like a surgeon.

"You like going to see that pretty boy?" Vlad commented as if reading her thoughts.

It was disconcerting how he could do this. Cilla had wondered, more than once, whether it was this intuitive ability that was in fact the source of his enduring influence, rather than his propensity for violence and mayhem.

It put her off poisoning him. She felt that Vlad might somehow sense the idea forming in her head and wipe her out before she could act on it. Or worse, he might take her down to the cellar. In any case, there was also the small fact that she was indebted to him. At the beginning of their association, when he had had both cause and opportunity to kill her, he had given her a chance instead. She could not easily forget this. But now that chance had turned into a burden; a heavy yoke. Cilla felt weary of death. It was a weight on her shoulders that would crush her sooner or later; and the hand on the yoke was Vlad's.

"Well, he's got a prettier face than yours," she said. There was a moment of tension between them; then Vlad roared with laughter.

"Just do as you're told," he advised.

Smithy lived in a bungalow at the end of the tube line in Amersham. The distinctive feature of the house was that it had a small disused indoor swimming pool in the basement which was where Smithy housed his equipment. As well as birth certificates and passports he also did a brisk trade in counterfeit first-class postage stamps.

Cilla loved travelling by tube. She liked the theory of it; the warren-like pattern of concentric tunnels linking all the parts of the city to each other. She liked the history of it; the classic station signs, the eau-de-nil metro tiles. She liked the actuality of it; the rumbling sound of a train as it roared into a station, the way the carriages shuddered and creaked as they travelled at speed. Most of all she liked the anonymity of it; the endless parade of faces, the constant flow of strangers around her. It never failed to astound Cilla that a carriage could be filled to the brim with people at rush hour and no violence would break out at all. Commuters were generally peaceful and well behaved, except for the odd predator like her.

It was mid-afternoon when she arrived at Smithy's address but he took a full five minutes to open the front door. Given his line of work he was very security conscious. There were various deadlocks and bolts that needed to be negotiated before the door could be opened. It was the only way in and out of the bungalow since Smithy had superglued the back

46

door and all the windows shut. When he finally appeared he looked dishevelled and his pupils were pinpricks in the centre of his eyes.

"Vlad wants a passport," Cilla announced and Smithy moved aside to let her in. It didn't really matter what sort of state he was in. If Vlad said "jump", Smithy's only viable response was: "How high?"

Over time Cilla had developed something akin to a friendship with Smithy. Perhaps friendship was not the right term but they had a bond, a mutual understanding. Not that there had been much choice. The alternative would have been for them both to sit in silence for hours as he worked. But over the course of the two years that Cilla had been babysitting Smithy she had learnt quite a lot about him. His story was one of reverse social mobility. He had started at the top of the pile and sunk steadily downwards. Too much money at too young an age had led to a crippling drug dependency. In fact Smithy had burnt through an entire trust fund to pay for his addiction. Once it was all gone he had to find some other way to support his habit. Fortunately he had discovered an unlikely talent for forgery which, frankly, was preferable to being a rent boy. None of his family would speak to him any longer since he had robbed all of them at one time or another. What they did allow him to do was to stay in the Amersham retirement bungalow where his widowed grandmother had lived out her final days once the family seat passed to her eldest son. All this Cilla had learnt during the course of their stilted conversations. He knew somewhat less about her, but he understood essentially what it was that she did for Vlad. She knew better than to go into too much detail and he knew better than to ask. What it all meant was that they were comfortable with each other, Smithy could bring out his lighter and foil, Cilla could take off her wig.

"Do you want a cuppa?" he said now. Smithy was one of the only people that Cilla would accept an offer of food or drink from. She had a natural distrust of ingesting anything that she hadn't prepared herself. But today she shook her head, reached into her back pocket and pulled out the strip of photographs.

"He wants it as soon as possible," she said, handing them to him. "Best get on."

It was an odd little house. All the rooms were filled with dark mahogany furniture apart from the hall, which was empty. Every conceivable flat surface was populated with photograph frames. Some of the photos were modern but a number of them contained black-and-white prints which looked as if they belonged to the Edwardian era; ladies in high-necked embroidered blouses wearing hats indoors, men with waistcoats and handlebar moustaches. There was one picture of eleven children lined up in order of age, each with their hand on the shoulder of the child in front. It was clear that all of the frames had belonged to Smithy's grandmother and that he had never thought to move them. Apparently he hadn't thought to dust them either. Cilla followed Smithy through the crowded lounge and down a cramped back staircase to the basement. He turned on the overhead strip lighting and began rolling back the pool cover. Once revealed, the small empty pool looked rather like a newspaper office. It was the cleanest area of the house. One corner of the deep end was partitioned off completely to form a mini dark room. The rest of the swimming pool housed a desk, several chairs, two filing cabinets, a photocopier and two printing presses. Cilla climbed down the metal ladder into the pool and went over to the smaller of these two.

"He wants to know about the Mint," she said.

"What does he want to know?" Smithy replied.

"When will it be ready?"

"I've still got some adjustments to make." Smithy had got into the pool as well and was examining the strip of photographs that Cilla had given him, holding them up to the light.

"This guy looks mid-thirties," he said. "I got a new batch in yesterday. Let's see if we can find a match."

Smithy did not actually create counterfeit passports. What he did was to buy stolen passports and adjust them. The fewer changes he had to make to the details, the more authentic the result.

He sat down at the desk and began to search through a pile of passports, examining the biographical page on each one and then discarding it for the next. Cilla took up her usual position on a nearby chair. After rejecting ten or so he held one up triumphantly.

"Got it. Emily Anne Jones; date of birth 2nd of March 1956. I can work with that."

Smithy put the chosen passport aside, stacked the others and placed them in two neat piles on the floor. He started collecting together the necessary tools for the job: a scalpel, ink, brushes, pens, solvent, titanium dioxide and his monocular handheld loupe. He opened the passport on its biographical page and fitted the burgundy cover into an aluminium frame to hold it steady. Then he began.

Smithy toiled with steady concentration and Cilla, from her vantage point, observed him. He was wearing a pale-blue shirt with a faint paisley design on it. His hair looked as if it needed cutting. A brown lock of it kept falling across his face and Smithy brushed it away unconsciously, tucking it behind one ear. When he moved his head it fell again. She wondered what it would be like to run her fingers through that hair, whether it would be soft to the touch; what it would smell like.

But there were other things on her mind. During the past few months Cilla had repeatedly tried to construct the idea of a new life for herself, one that did not involve murdering strangers, one that did not involve Vladimir Haugr. This was surprisingly difficult to conceptualise. She could not imagine herself leading some other sort of life. It was as if she were trying to locate the vantage point from the top of a mountain when she was in fact standing at the bottom of it. All she could do was to look upwards. What she had come to realise was that she didn't need to know what the view from the top of the mountain was going to look like, she just needed to trust that it was there. That trust would enable her to take the first step, and then the one after that, and the one after that.

The first step was to cast her skin. The second step was to create a new one; and for this she required Smithy.

"I'm going to need another passport," Cilla said tentatively. "There's no hurry with this one. You can do it in your own time."

Smithy nodded his assent and continued with his work; head bent, one eye close to the handheld loupe.

"And some A level certificates, and a degree," she continued.

Smithy stopped what he was doing and looked up. His eyebrows were raised.

"Vlad wants A levels?" he said.

"No, I do," Cilla replied. "Maths, English and Russian, that should be about right. And a degree – in Philosophy I think. I like Philosophy."

Smithy was silent. She could see him repeating her requests to himself internally, going over them, trying to make sense of what it was she was asking for.

"I need cash storage as well," she continued. "And a route

to transfer it to a UK bank account in the same name as the passport."

Still he said nothing.

"There's a 25K bonus for you above your usual fee if you keep your mouth shut about this," Cilla concluded.

Smithy looked away slightly; his expression was hard to read. He looked taken aback, shocked even and yet also somehow wistful and resigned.

"I'll see what I can do," he said.

5

Origins II

The car journey took some hours. Cilla wasn't sure how many because she slept for much of the time. She wanted to stay awake, to participate in every moment of this new experience, but a combination of the plush leather interior of the car and its steady rhythmic movement had a soporific effect and her eyes kept closing involuntarily. At one point she was woken by loud voices. The car had stopped and the driver appeared to be arguing with a soldier outside. It was clear that they were passing through a military checkpoint. Eventually the soldier waved them through and after a while Cilla fell asleep again.

When they finally arrived at their destination it was dark. The adults got out of the vehicle.

"Wait," the lady said to Cilla when she tried to follow them.

"Give her some food and assign her to one of the girls' dormitories," Cilla heard her saying to someone else. Then another woman, younger, fetched Cilla out of the car and before long she was sitting at a long table in a large hall eating bread and ham. The younger woman sat next to her.

"Are these your possessions?" the younger woman said, pointing at a rather sorry-looking bundle on a chair. Cilla nodded.

"You won't need them," the younger woman said briskly. "You'll be given a uniform in the morning."

When Cilla had finished eating the younger woman marched her out of the dining hall, back outside, and then into an adjacent building. It was very dark and the woman held a torch. After making their way down a corridor they stopped outside one of the doors. It had a metal plaque with the number six written on it. The younger woman knelt down so that her face was at the same level as Cilla's. She put her finger to her lips to indicate that Cilla should be silent. Since Cilla had not actually said anything up until this point, this gesture seemed unnecessary.

"This is your dormitory," the younger woman said in a low voice. "Everyone is asleep so you will need to be quiet." She pointed down the corridor. "Two doors down on the right-hand side is a girls' bathroom." The woman opened the door to the dormitory and shone her torch inside. Cilla could see three sets of metal bunk beds arranged in an L-shaped pattern. "All the top bunks have been taken," the younger woman continued, "but you may choose any of the bottom bunks as your own. There is an alarm at 6.30 a.m. The other girls will show you what to do. Follow their example."

Cilla lay in bed that night wide awake. After her extended nap in the car the last thing she felt like doing was sleeping. She had never slept in a bed of her own before; she had always shared with Tomas. Now she found that she missed his kicking and the little moaning sounds he made in his sleep. She missed Luna too, the feel of her fur, her warm doggy breath.

Cilla wondered what this new school actually looked like; it had been impossible to see in the dark. She had only a vague impression of several large imposing structures. Cilla's idea of what a proper school might be like was hazy. She thought about the village school: a damp ramshackle cabin with peeling paint and one leaking outside toilet. Clearly this institution was nothing like that. She thought about the old torn poster that had hung on the wall of her classroom promoting new Soviet schools. In the foreground was a young girl wearing a smart white dress and the red neckerchief of a Young Pioneer. She was holding a bunch of flowers and beaming. In the background other uniformed children were being shown into an impressive building by a benign-looking teacher. But somehow that didn't seem to fit either. There was something temporary about the structures here as if they were made of cardboard or fabric. Cilla contemplated getting out of bed and going to explore. She wasn't frightened of the dark. But she was aware that it would be easy to get lost and she might struggle to find her way back to the dormitory. It was probably best not to get into trouble on her very first night. There was nothing to do but wait for dawn to break.

In a sense, Cilla was right; the school buildings were temporary structures. The institution, known as Academy 43, was housed in a series of converted military barracks. There were five large prefabricated bunkers and groundworks laid for a sixth. One bunker housed the female living quarters, one housed the boys. A third bunker constituted the gymnasium which also doubled as an assembly hall, another was subdivided into classrooms. The fifth bunker contained the kitchens, dining hall and sick bay. The bunkers were surrounded by extensive grounds which were used for training, marching and parades.

Each morning the children were awoken at 6.30. They

washed, dressed and did fifteen minutes of invigorating exercise in the gymnasium before breakfast was served in the dining hall. The food was surprisingly good: simple, fresh, nutritious and, most importantly, there was enough of it to go around. No-one went hungry, except as a punishment.

After breakfast they went back to the gymnasium for half an hour in order to attend assembly. The subject matter for assembly was always the same: infinite variants on a single theme. That theme was devotion to the cause of Communism and loyalty to the Socialist ideal. Over and over again the children were taught that they were instruments of the State; their role was to enact the will of the Body Politic; their privilege was to sacrifice their individuality for the benefit of the Motherland. There could be no greater honour. Assembly usually ended with the singing of a patriotic song and the chanting of a slogan:

"To strive, to seek, to find, and not to yield."

It was many years before Cilla realised that this slogan was taken from the poem "Ulysses" and she often wondered how it was that Lord Alfred Tennyson had made his way into Socialist dogma.

For the first two months Cilla and the other children were assessed. These assessments were comprehensive and unceasing. Testing began after breakfast and continued throughout the day. Each child's entire academic history and potential was unravelled, laid out and scrutinised.

One of the first subjects that Cilla was examined on was literacy. In addition to completing several lengthy multiple-choice tests checking her grammar, spelling and comprehension she was asked to write a one-thousand-word essay entitled: "Who is your favourite family member and why?"

There was only one possible answer to this question. It was

Tomas. She could remember him as a baby lying squalling in his crib whilst she poked him. He didn't seem to hold the poking against her. As soon as he could crawl he followed her around. His first word was an abbreviated version of her name. Once he could walk he never left her side. In some ways Tomas's devotion was oppressive. It was based on a lie. Cilla knew that it was impossible for her to live up to his colossal expectations. But equally she liked the lie. It seemed to suggest that a better version of herself might exist out there somewhere. It would be easy to write about Tomas. She could describe how they had grown up together, all the games they had played, how she had taught him his letters when he was three years old. Cilla had enjoyed playing "teacher" and "pupil" with Tomas although, arguably, some of her methods were a little draconian. But something held her back. When the time came to put pen to paper Cilla found that she didn't want to mention Tomas at all. She knew that this must be the perverse, obstinate side of her character coming out again. The trait had been identified by her former elementary school teacher who had criticised Cilla for it repeatedly. But she couldn't help herself; she didn't want to write about Tomas. Her feelings about him belonged to her and her alone. She wasn't prepared to give them away.

But if not Tomas, who else would do? Cilla couldn't write about any of her sisters; she barely knew them. It would be ridiculous to write about her father. How could she come up with a thousand words about a man who spent most of his time either drunk or hungover? She would barely manage fifty. Cilla did consider writing about her mother. But the problem was that she didn't like her mother very much and this would mean that the essay was unlikely to be believable. If she was going to make something up then it had to be authentic. Cilla already understood that the best lies are usually those which are most closely aligned with the truth.

Then she hit on it; she would write about Luna. Surely a beloved dog could be considered to be a member of the family? The rest was easy. She wrote about how Luna had been given to them as a tiny puppy. She had been taken away from her mother too early and at first they had to feed her milk in an eye dropper. Nobody knew what sort of dog she was; Luna seemed to contain a little bit of every known breed. She was very smart. If you showed her a ball and then hid it in the next room she would search every corner, every cupboard, under every last bit of furniture in order to find it. By the end of a thousand words Cilla had almost persuaded herself that she preferred Luna to her brother Tomas after all.

As well as literacy Cilla was tested extensively in mathematics and reasoning. And the evaluation did not simply include academic subjects. All aspects of Cilla's mental, physical and emotional functioning were examined and re-examined. She underwent a thorough medical inspection. Her physical fitness was assessed. She was given repeated personality and intelligence appraisals. Cilla was even tested for psychic ability using dice and playing cards.

It was a bewildering time. Children seemed to come and go. There were frequently unfamiliar faces at breakfast. Cilla had only just got used to sharing her bunk with a tall pale girl called Katya when she disappeared one afternoon and was replaced by a fat blonde with plaits. After a while Cilla stopped bothering to ask other children what their names were. What was the point? Nevertheless she could see that the children around her were very different to the ones at her former school. Many of them were clever, like her. There were no cry-babies in the ranks although scuffles broke out frequently and displays of hostility between children were common. A couple of the most violent boys had dead flat eyes and everybody knew to stay away from them. At the same time, discipline within the school was vigorously maintained. Generally a child was given a severe warning for a first offence and it was explained to that child clearly and precisely what the penalty would be if they engaged in the prohibited activity a second time. If the offence was repeated punishment was meted out immediately and without exception. It was quite an effective system. Although there was a low undercurrent of aggression in the school, order was generally preserved.

At the end of the two-month period each remaining child was summoned to attend a meeting with a senior member of staff.

Once again Cilla found herself seated opposite the lady who had originally selected her out of all the children in the village school.

The lady had a large folder which she leafed through in a leisurely manner as Cilla waited for the meeting to begin.

"Do you know who I am?" the lady said.

Cilla nodded. Since arriving at the school she had learnt that the lady's name was Professor Kuznetsova and she knew that the lady was important. Cilla had not spoken to her again but she had seen her, on occasion, talking to other teachers.

"Do you know what my role is here?" Professor Kuznetsova enquired.

Cilla shook her head.

"I am the Director of Operations at Academy 43. My job is to oversee the screening of pupils and to make sure that they are suitable for this school. I chose you, didn't I?"

Cilla nodded.

"But do you know why I chose you?"

This time Cilla ventured an answer.

"Because I'm clever?" she said hesitantly.

"Yes, that's true in part," Professor Kuznetsova replied. "But intelligence is not the only attribute I am interested in. You, and all the other children here, have a special quality, something that sets you apart. This school will teach you to harness that quality and channel it in service to the State."

"What's my special quality?" Cilla asked. She had never been told that she was special before.

Professor Kuznetsova thought for a moment. "Do you ever cry?" she said.

Cilla shook her head. As far as she was aware she hadn't cried since she had been a baby.

"Do you ever feel anxious or nervous? Do you get homesick?"

Cilla shook her head again. She had been homesick once, but not after that. There wasn't all that much to get homesick about. Her previous life had been dull and boring. She had always seemed to be in trouble and there was never enough to eat.

"Do you feel sorry after you do something naughty?"

This time Cilla didn't react; she thought that it might be a trick question.

"You don't need to answer," Professor Kuznetsova reassured her. She held up the file. "I have all the answers I need about you in here. Now let's talk about your future."

The rest of the meeting was dedicated to finalising Cilla's personalised curriculum. The Academy had determined that she would study a wide-ranging academic syllabus and would specialise in English, Botany and Toxicology. She was also enrolled in the Academy's fitness, survival and weapons training courses but was exempt from the combat programme on account of her sex and small stature. It was all very well, but Professor Kuznetsova never explained to her what her special quality was and Cilla didn't like to ask again.

That first year at Academy 43 was arguably the happiest year of Cilla's life. Almost every waking moment was filled with something interesting. This meant that she was rarely bored and since she had little free time in which to get up to mischief it meant that she was rarely in trouble either. The Academy employed an excellent teaching faculty. Every member of staff was an expert in their field and dedicated themselves to making their classes as informative and interesting as possible. Most of the children at the Academy had IQs of 130 or above, so lessons moved at a tremendous pace and there was no need to wait around for the less able children to catch up since those children had already been weeded out and removed.

Cilla's favourite subjects were Maths, English and Botany. At the village school Maths had been taught by rote. The teacher would write sums on a chalk board as if they were part of some long list of laundry which the children were expected to wash, rinse and repeat. But now Maths became exhilarating. The Maths professor invented endless games and puzzles in order to instil the basic principles of the subject into his pupils. All of the children learnt to play chess and at least one Maths lesson a week was dedicated to improving their technique.

Cilla liked Botany because it involved an entirely different and contrasting set of skills. Although some lessons occurred in the classroom, much of the study was hands-on and took place in the lean-to greenhouses located on the south-facing wall of the Dining Hall bunker. Botany was calm and meticulous. It was impossible to force a plant to grow. If they were manhandled in any way they simply died. This taught Cilla patience. There was a considerable overlap between Botany and Toxicology. Cilla learnt how to make all sort of poisons from all sort of plants. She learnt that cyanide could be harvested from apple seeds and that belladonna berries contain atropine and hyoscine. She learnt the toxic properties of cherry laurel, laburnum and yew. She discovered that the pretty purple flowers of the corncockle contain a dangerous dose of glycoside githagin and agrostemnic acid. Some of the plants in the greenhouse were so dangerous that gloves had to be worn in order to handle them. Cilla's interest in the subject was encouraged by the young Botany teacher, Comrade Ivanova, who took something of a liking to the small stubborn girl. On the rare occasions that she had free time Cilla would steal away to the greenhouses hoping to find Comrade Ivanova in situ so that the two of them could tend to the plants together. Sometimes they chatted as well. It was the first time that Cilla had ever felt warmly disposed towards an adult.

But Cilla's favourite subject was English. When Professor Kuznetsova told Cilla that she was to specialise in English what Cilla hadn't understood was that this did not simply mean learning to speak and write the language fluently. It entailed immersing herself in British heritage and culture. Cilla studied British history, politics and current affairs. She read week-old copies of English newspapers and magazines. She listened to pop music. She had access to the Academy's English Library, the *Spetskhran*, which contained a comprehensive History and Philosophy section full of old politically incorrect material which had been confiscated from elsewhere. It even housed a Bible. Best of all she was expected to watch English television for an hour a day, six days a week. The programmes were selected from a huge collection of VHS video cassettes which archived the past twenty years of British television. Occasionally each child on the English Specialisation Course was allowed to choose a programme from the library. When it was Cilla's turn she tended to pick variety or comedy. Over time she succeeded in watching every single episode of *The Liver Birds*.

After watching English television programmes there was always an obligatory debriefing session. Whilst it was felt necessary that these hand-picked children should familiarise themselves with the Western Capitalist lifestyle the school authorities did not want their tender minds to become contaminated by the ideas they had been exposed to. Pupils were reminded that although such television programmes might be amusing, colourful and superficially attractive, they were simply opiates designed to lull their citizens into a comatose state. In reality the vast majority of citizens in the West were slaves because they did not control the means of production. Only in the Soviet Union were the working class truly free. Generally Cilla accepted this version of events although deep down she still wanted to meet John Lennon.

There were no school holidays as such. Pupils were allowed to go home twice a year for a few days to celebrate May Day and the 7th of November, the most significant holidays in the Socialist calendar. But returning home for these occasions was not obligatory; children could stay at school if they preferred.

Cilla elected to go home for May Day. She was excited about the May Day celebrations in her village which always involved parades, dancing and flag waving. But somehow the reality of this did not live up to her expectations. The village seemed even smaller and bleaker than she remembered; the family home more dilapidated. Her parents seemed ambivalent towards her presence and even the "Welcome Home" sign which had been hung on the gate to celebrate her return looked crude and clumsy. Tomas and Luna were, of course, overjoyed to see her. They danced around Cilla for the first hour after her arrival vying for her attention. Luna barked and jumped. Tomas chattered at breakneck speed about all the events that had occurred over the last six months since he had seen her. Cilla did her best to match their enthusiasm but it was as though she were putting on an act. She played pirates with Tomas, she slept in bed with him at night. She waved her little flag in the village square on May Day and joined in with the clapping and the singing. But it all felt fake. Once again, when it was time for Cilla to leave, Tomas began to howl. She gave him a hug and told him to be a good boy but the reality was that it was a relief to walk away from his blotchy tear-stained face.

When Cilla got back to school she discovered that the Academy had conducted May Day celebrations of their own. There had been a big party with chocolate bars and helium balloons. Cilla had always wanted a helium balloon of her own; to hold it on a long string and make it dance in the air and then eventually to let it go and watch the brightly coloured orb sail away into the sky. A couple of the balloons were still left in the dining hall but they had lost their buoyancy and floated pathetically along the floor. Cilla stamped on both of them, one after the other, until they burst.

Several children did not return after the May Day weekend. It was unclear whether they had voluntarily chosen not to come back or whether they had been deemed unworthy. It was impossible to find out this information because there seemed to be some sort of an unwritten rule that once a child was removed from the school they were never to be spoken of again.

Time passed; spring turned to summer. The pupils of Academy 43 spent more and more time outside. The school organised camping trips during which the children were taught how to survive in the wild, to forage for food, to shoot game with bows and arrows, to skin and gut their kills and roast them over an open fire.

Cilla even made a friend. The fat blonde with plaits who now resided in the bunk above hers was called Anya and she also attended the English Specialisation Course. It meant that their timetables were identical. Sometimes they did their homework together as well. By practising in front of the bathroom mirror repeatedly Cilla also discovered that she could do a passable impression of a Liverpool accent and she would make the other English speakers laugh by impersonating Beryl and Sandra from *The Liver Birds* or doing sketches of Ken Dodd and the Diddy Men using her socks as puppets. Anya always laughed the loudest of all.

As the 7th of November approached Cilla decided not to go home. She didn't want to miss another party. Very few of the other children went home either.

Two other events of note took place towards the end of the year.

The first was the arrival of a van-load of labourers who began working on the sixth bunker. They came every day to lay foundations of reinforced concrete. Whatever it was that they were building, it did not look like a temporary structure.

The second event, and the one which was more relevant to the pupils of Academy 43, was the Renaming Ceremony.

6

Parties

Including Smithy in her plans was a calculated risk. There was always the possibility that he would betray her. But it was a chance that had to be taken. Utilising Smithy's talents represented Cilla's best chance to create a new life. Without the proper documents she would have few choices. True, there was a substantial sum of money but unless she could legitimise the funds they were of limited value. All she would be able to do with them would be to hole up somewhere in the sticks and relocate periodically to avoid detection. She would talk to no-one, trust no-one; what sort of life would that be? How would it be any different from the life she led now, apart from the absence of killing? And eventually the money would run out and Cilla would be left with nothing. She did not relish the idea of nothing. She had walked away from that life when she was ten years old. What would have been the point of all those intervening years if all she did now was to walk right back towards it again?

By the time Cilla got back to the Bridge Club it was nine o'clock in the evening. There were at least eight tables in play and the club was heaving with people. A few of the big fish had turned up. Zia Mahmood, the great Pakistani player, was holding court at a game in the corner. She could hear him telling one of his stories as she walked past; something to do with the Pakistani national team going shopping before the final of the Bermuda Bowl. He was one of the few experts who could play bridge and talk loudly at the same time. Whenever he competed in a tournament Zia drew a crowd. Even now at TGR's, in a private money game, there was an entourage sitting behind his chair, watching his every move, hanging on his every word. If he farted one of them would probably attempt to bottle it.

Daniel Crawford was also there. He was sitting at the bar chatting to a couple of the young Scandinavian house players. He nodded to Cilla when he saw her. She wondered if he knew about what had happened to Maurice Malinowski? Probably not. His father regarded him as highly strung and he wasn't often kept in the loop. Vlad himself was nowhere to be seen so Cilla left the playing area and knocked on his office door.

"Come," came the response.

This time Vlad was not alone. Two of his senior lieutenants were standing in front of his desk receiving instructions. They eyed Cilla warily; it was common knowledge that she had been responsible for Jacob's execution. Stories abounded about the precise details of his death. The fact that Cilla was small and slight did nothing to diminish speculation. If anything it made them more nervous. One rumour had it that she had ripped out Jacob's throat with her teeth.

Vlad smiled broadly. He enjoyed their discomfort.

"Cilla," he said. "I'd almost given up on you. Do you have it?"

Cilla placed the passport on the desk. Vlad picked it up and inspected it.

"Frank Alan Jonson." He sniffed. "What sort of a name is that?"

"It's what you get when you amend Emily Anne Jones," Cilla replied. "Is there anything else?"

"No." Vlad waved his hand dismissively. "You can go." He turned his attention back to his men.

As Cilla exited the basement and walked up the stone staircase to street level she could not avoid tripping over the new girl, Nancy, who was sitting on the top step smoking a cigarette.

"You came back," Nancy said. She sounded pleased.

"Yes," Cilla agreed for want of anything better to say.

"So are you going to come to this party?" Nancy asked.

Normally Cilla would have said no. She didn't go to parties. She didn't really go anywhere. But she had a dissatisfied, gnawing feeling in her gut, the feeling that always descended on her after spending time with Smithy. There was something about being with him which made her feel restless and frustrated. Perhaps it was just the result of sitting on a wooden chair in his dank swimming pool for too long.

"What party?" she said.

"It's a warehouse party."

"A party in a warehouse?"

"You know, a rave. Haven't you ever been to a rave before?"

Cilla shook her head. Nancy laughed.

"Oh you'll love it. This one's very small, very elite. I've only just got hold of the address. It's near where I live. Look, I've got an hour left of my shift. If you come and give me a hand I can probably get off a bit early. Then we could go back to mine and change."

"But I don't have anything to change into!" Cilla protested.

"Borrow something of mine."

There was something infectious about Nancy's enthusiasm. Cilla was twenty-two years old, as far as she knew. She had no friends, except for Smithy, if you could call him a friend. She'd never been to a rave. She'd never really been to a party except for the May Day celebrations at school. If she was planning to reinvent herself perhaps it would be as well to try one new experience, something age appropriate, to dip her toe in the water, as it were.

"OK," she said. "I'll come."

Nancy lived in a flat share in Wandsworth. It wasn't very clean. There were bottles and glasses all over the living-room floor and the kitchen sink was overflowing with washing-up.

"Sorry about the mess," Nancy said breezily. "Let's go into my room and sort out some clothes."

Twenty minutes later Cilla was staring at herself doubtfully in Nancy's full-length mirror. She was wearing her own black jumper coordinated with a pair of silver sequinned shorts over fishnet tights.

"That looks fantastic," Nancy cooed. "You've got great legs. You have to let me do your makeup as well."

So Cilla sat on a chair whilst Nancy attended to her and applied considerable quantities of viscous black liner and eye shadow. The factor that Cilla had not taken into consideration was that she had removed her wig at Smithy's for a couple of hours and then put it back on again. This took its toll on the double-sided adhesive tape that was used to keep the wig in place. When Nancy put her hand on Cilla's head to tilt it back slightly the wig slipped off to one side.

Nancy snatched her hand away as if she had been burnt.

"Oh my God, you're wearing a rug!" she announced.

There was an awkward silence. Cilla did not have any of her kit with her so she took stock of the room. Discarded items of clothing lay everywhere. Perhaps she could use the green silk scarf lying on the floor to strangle Nancy. It wouldn't take long. Cilla glanced stealthily at the other girl, whose mouth had formed a tight round circle of surprise. Nancy was taller than Cilla but not by a lot. She didn't look as if she'd put up much of a fight and Cilla would have the advantage of surprise. But what to do with the body? This was more problematic. Cilla considered the option of going down to the street, hotwiring a car and transporting the corpse to the railway line. Or she could leave it here and make it look like suicide, or a sex game gone wrong. It all seemed like an awful lot of effort to go to when she was supposed to be having the night off. Then Cilla had another idea.

"I had cancer," she said speculatively.

"Oh my God," Nancy repeated. "You poor thing. Is that why you've never been to a rave?"

"Yes," Cilla agreed. "I've spent a lot of time in hospital."

"Take it off properly," Nancy requested, pointing at Cilla's head. "I want to see what you look like."

Cilla slowly removed her wig and held it in both hands on her lap. She felt slightly vulnerable, which was a curious experience.

"You look great," Nancy said. "You've got a really nicely shaped head. I think you should go out like that."

"Really?" Cilla responded. "Won't I stand out like a sore thumb?"

"I don't know. Maybe. Who cares? It's a great look."

The warehouse party took place in some empty studios just off Parsons Green which meant that it was within walking distance of Nancy's flat. Cilla had never gone outside with her shaved head on display before, not even into her own garden. She had always been concerned that one of the residents on the upper floors of the house might look down and see her "in the buff" as it were. The night air felt cold on her naked scalp but also liberating.

"Hey," said Nancy as she tottered down the road several steps behind Cilla. "Wait up. Do you want to drop an E before we get there?"

Both of them stopped and Nancy held out one of her hands to Cilla. In her open palm were two small white pills.

As an expert on drugs and toxins Cilla knew what Ecstasy was; it was the street name for Methylenedioxymethamphetamine. She knew that MDMA acts primarily by increasing the activity of serotonin, dopamine and noradrenaline in parts of the brain, giving the neurotransmitters a little happy boost. In fact Cilla had helped run an MDMA experiment for the Toxicology department at Academy 43, testing it as a truth serum on some of the poor sods from Bunker 6. The conclusion of the experiment had been that it was unreliable. She also knew, from reading, about its recreational usage. She was aware that, in all likelihood, the little white pills in Nancy's hand had been cooked up in some filthy basement by an amateur chemist who barely knew what he was doing and had probably used bath salts as a bulking agent. She knew that a bad batch could cause hyperthermia, dehydration and occasionally death. And of course all this reasoning was based on the assumption that the two pills were actually MDMA. It was quite possible that they weren't Ecstasy at all but something much more dangerous and unpleasant. Accepting one of the tablets would be like playing a form of oral Russian roulette. On the other hand, as Kant had written:

"Experience without theory is blind, but theory without experience is mere intellectual play."

Which was probably his way of saying: in for a penny, in for a pound.

Cilla took the nearest pill, popped it into her mouth and swallowed it quickly before she could change her mind.

At first nothing happened. They arrived at Fulham Studios, queued, paid money and had their hands stamped with a luminous yellow smiley face. The studios consisted of one colossal ground-floor space, most of which was given over to a dance floor, with a series of first- and second-floor metal galleries encapsulating it. Nancy seemed to know a lot of the people around them. She kept trying to introduce Cilla to strangers but Cilla was not one for small talk even at the best of times. But then, as the minutes ticked past, Cilla became aware that a change was taking place. It wasn't sudden or momentous, more of a slow transformation. In normal life there were two Cillas who co-existed in relative harmony. There was the base Cilla with all her urges and appetites: Cilla the predator, anticipating the hunt and the kill. Then there was the check and balance: Cilla the gatekeeper, whose role it was to supervise and restrict the other Cilla, to keep her shut in a cage and only let her out for short periods when it was appropriate and necessary. Usually Cilla the gatekeeper was in charge. She kept base Cilla under lock and key. But as the effects of the drug kicked in, the space between these two Cillas seemed to contract; the balance of power shifted. Or maybe it was just that gatekeeper Cilla felt tired and left the cage door open. Cilla the predator emerged from her enclosure whilst Cilla the gatekeeper slept. This strange mood was matched by the lasers, the lighting and the music, the heavy throbbing beat. Cilla wasn't necessarily in the mood for killing; she was just in the mood for something, even though she didn't know what that something was. Nancy had disappeared into the throng of people but that didn't matter. It felt good to be relaxed, to

71

wander around, unrestrained. After a while Cilla's attention was caught by three boys on the dance floor. They didn't dance like anyone else. Sometimes it almost looked as if they were running or skipping on the spot, moving their feet so fast that it was impossible to follow them. Then they would stand still for a moment making bizarre shapes with their arms. Everyone made space on the floor around them. Cilla threaded her way through the crowd to take a closer look. One of them was smaller than the other two. His hair fell almost to his shoulders. He wore a funny little hat and a long-sleeved top with vertical stripes on it which shone luminous under the lights. There was a raw primitive energy about him and periodically he spat on the floor as he danced. Cilla stood there watching him, oblivious to the heaving bodies around her. After a while it began to feel as if he were dancing for her, putting on a show for her and her alone. She bared her teeth at him slightly; somewhere between a smile and a snarl. He grinned back. As one song flowed into the next he stopped dancing and moved closer to her.

"Do you want a smoke?" he said softly in Cilla's ear. She nodded. He took her hand and led her through the crowd up one of the metal staircases to the second floor, through a door and out onto a balcony overlooking the street.

"What's your name?" he said as he took out a Rizla and laid it on the flat wooden top of the balustrade.

"Cilla," she replied.

"I'm Keith." He was sprinkling tobacco onto the paper in a straight neat line. He covered it with a delicate layer of hashish. "Where you from?"

"Nowhere you'd have heard of," Cilla said.

"Try me."

"Well, I grew up mostly on the outskirts of Kaliningrad," she admitted.

"OK you got me, where's that then?"

"The Soviet Union."

"You don't sound Russian. You sound English."

"Yes I do, don't I."

Cilla was beginning to regret coming out onto the balcony. She wasn't sure why she was there or what it was that she wanted. She didn't like all these questions. But then Keith lit the cigarette and took a step towards her, taking a long drag as he did so. He offered it to Cilla. As she put the cigarette to her mouth she could feel the damp imprint of his lips on it.

"Your eyes," he said. "They're weird, so pale and so black all at the same time."

She took a step towards him so that their noses were nearly touching. It felt strange to have her face so close to another human being who was still alive.

Without really thinking about it she turned her head slightly and brought her mouth up to meet his. Soft lips met soft lips. At first she wasn't kissing him so much as smelling him and tasting him. She caught the sharp fresh scent of his sweat and he tasted salty and good. Then he met her tongue with his own and began to kiss her back. Cilla dropped the cigarette, put her hands around his neck and pressed herself into his body. It was hard and unyielding, but the feeling of it crushed against her own was like nothing she'd ever experienced before. He kissed her with more intensity and slid his hands up the back of her jumper. She could feel them on her bare skin, warm and exploratory. He moved one of his hands around to the front of her torso, cupping her small breast through the bra and stroking her nipple with his thumb. That same hand descended downwards and slipped into her shorts, feeling its way around the contour of her buttock and extending further so that the tips of his fingers were between her legs. The sensation of his fingers stroking her was so intense that it made her dizzy, as if she were experiencing vertigo, falling from some great height into a velvet abyss and hoping that the fall would never end.

There were noises in the background, from the street level. At first Cilla tried to ignore them and concentrate on the kissing and the touching and the being touched, but gradually the commotion grew louder and by some silent mutual consent the two of them disengaged from each other and leant over the balcony to identify the source of the disruption. Five police squad cars had pulled up outside the studios. Uniformed officers were already making their way into the building.

"Fuck," said Keith. "Look, I've got to go and get my friends. Will you be OK?"

Cilla nodded. "I'll be fine," she replied.

As Keith left, Cilla the gatekeeper awoke. She took a deep breath and looked cautiously over the balustrade again to assess the situation. There were now four officers at the entrance to the building which probably meant that a score were already inside. There was no viable way off the balcony. It was too high for her to jump from and there were no drainpipes or other projections for her to climb down. In any case, if she were to attempt to scale the outside of the building she would simply attract the attention of the waiting officers below. There was no option but to go back inside.

Predictably, it was mayhem. People were running backwards and forwards trying to evade the police. Cilla kept to the walls and the shadows. There were two staircases down to the ground floor. Both were blocked with people attempting to descend. There were officers at the bottom taking IDs and carting off anyone who gave them trouble. It was like shooting fish in a bucket. There were also partygoers crowding through another set of external doors on the second floor.

This probably led to the fire escape, but in all likelihood there would be police waiting at the bottom of that as well.

Cilla retreated to the darkest part of the second-floor gallery and leant over the handrail. The distance between the second-floor gallery and the first-floor gallery looked to be about three metres. She climbed over the handrail, gripped on to the supporting posts and lowered herself down until she was hanging. The space between the two floors was such that her feet did not reach the handrail below. This was unfortunate. Cilla collected her thoughts for a moment and began to swing backwards and forwards. When she had sufficient momentum on an inward swing she let go of the posts. She hated making that final plunge but she had done it before and knew that she could. She landed awkwardly on the first-floor gallery and rolled towards the wall, winded but otherwise unhurt. Cilla gave herself a minute or so to regain composure, then crawled towards the handrail and peeped through the posts. The potential descent from the first floor to the ground floor looked more problematic. To begin with it was at least four metres in distance. And there were too many people running around down there. If she lowered herself down from the first-floor gallery and let go there was every chance she would land on some hapless partygoer. Although this would break her fall it would also attract attention. Cilla reconsidered the nearest staircase. She went to the top of it and began to edge her way down the far side. There was a landing halfway down at which point the staircase deviated at a ninety-degree angle to the right and continued to the ground floor. Once she had pushed past enough people to make it down a couple of steps she climbed over the banister and continued moving downwards on the outside of the staircase, placing her small feet carefully between the posts as she made her way down. She did this swiftly because she knew that once others saw what she was doing they might be liable to follow her example. When she reached the landing she eased her hands down two posts until she was in a semi-crouching position with the heels of her feet tipped over the edge. She could see Keith wedged on the landing but he didn't see her. She slipped her feet off the side, hung for a moment and let go.

It was relatively quiet and dark under the staircase. Cilla's shoulders ached, her fishnet stockings were torn in three places, her heart was racing. She shut her eyes and breathed in deeply through her nose and out through her mouth, counting to ten for each breath. Her heart rate began to slow down.

When she was certain that it was below eighty beats per minute Cilla stepped out from under the staircase. She walked across the dance floor and made her way towards the main doors. She kept herself as insignificant as possible, sidestepping police and civilians alike, hiding in plain sight. It was a simple matter of mathematics really. There were five hundred partygoers and perhaps twenty officers. When she got to the entrance she waited until the four uniforms all looked as if they had their hands full and then she slipped through the middle.

Once outside she walked loosely in the direction of the Fulham Palace Road. From there it was almost a straight line to Shepherds Bush and home. She still felt slightly euphoric; whether this was a response to the drugs, the kissing or the escape, she wasn't really sure. Perhaps it was a combination of all three. It didn't really matter. Something more important had occurred. Base Cilla had come out of her cage and she hadn't killed anyone. Perhaps there was hope for them both.

7

Metamorphosis

"The history of all society is above all the history of class struggle. You are fortunate indeed to have been born into the epoch of history during which humanity has begun to realise its full potential, has embarked on the journey to become fully civilised. You have been born into the era where the Proletarian movement has overthrown the Bourgeois supremacy. You have been born into the era of Communism. But great fortune is also accompanied by great responsibility. All of you have an obligation to make sure that humanity continues on this path. All of you have a duty to fulfil your roles as heroes and heroines of the Socialist State. There is no greater honour.

"We all know the story of Pavlik Morozov: the thirteen-year-old boy who denounced his father to the authorities for forging documents and selling them to enemies of the Socialist State. He placed the interests of the Motherland above his own ties of kinship. How was he rewarded for this act of patriotism? He was murdered by his family. Do we mourn for him? Do we pity him? We do not. We celebrate his nobility and his selflessness. Pavlik Morozov placed the interest of the State, of the Socialist People above his own feelings and for that he should be admired and esteemed. He was a martyr. He was a true Socialist Hero."

Morning assembly constituted the least interesting part of Cilla's day. After three months of endurance she avoided it once by going to hide in one of the greenhouses. Her absence was noted and afterwards her form teacher, Comrade Guseva, took her aside and explained the purpose of the assemblies and what would happen to Cilla if she failed to attend a second time. The consequence would be no food and only water to drink for twenty-four hours. The penalties for misdemeanours were not uniform within the school. Each punishment was personalised to the child. There was very little corporal punishment at Academy 43. Children like Cilla did not respond to physical chastisement. It was meaningless to them and did almost nothing to alter or improve undesirable behaviour. Instead the school created tailor-made disciplinary measures based on the information they had compiled about each individual child during their initial assessment period. It was an effective system. Cilla missed one more assembly. She suffered her punishment. After that she didn't miss it again.

"By attending this school you have already taken that first step in placing allegiance to the Motherland above all other loyalties. You are no longer living in the bosom of your families like other children; you are being raised by the State. The State is your mother and your father. You are soft wax, a malleable substance to be moulded by the guiding hand of Communism. You are the vanguard from which the Academy will forge a new generation of Communist men and women."

78

It went on in this vein for a while. Cilla began to fidget. She poked Anya who was sitting cross-legged next to her but Anya didn't respond and continued to look resolutely towards the front of the hall. Cilla poked her again.

"Stop it," whispered Anya. "It's about the Renaming Ceremony. You need to listen."

"All of you have now been at Academy 43 for a year. This represents an important milestone. It is time for you to formalise your allegiance to the Socialist State. You will do this by giving up your family name and taking on a new name. A new name symbolises a new beginning. It is the dawn of a new era in your lives. You will take on a new first name and a new surname. Your surname will be given to you by the Motherland. It will represent the bond that binds you to the Communist ideal. But you will choose your own first name. Mind that you choose carefully. By making this choice you pledge yourself to the Socialist State. Your new name is not your identity. It is your disguise. It is your promise. It is the oath that you take to sacrifice yourself for the greater good of the Soviet Union."

And so it was that Cilla decided to become Cilla.

"Cilla." Professor Kuznetsova rolled the name around on her tongue experimentally. "I've not heard the name before. You really feel that this constitutes an appropriate English sobriquet?"

Cilla nodded. One of the parameters for selection was that each child had to choose a name that was fitting for their specialist subject. Not all of the pupils were language specialists. Some of the boys were undergoing dedicated military training. They were encouraged to choose the first name of a war hero.

79

"Not Rose or Elizabeth or Victoria?"

Cilla shook her head.

"Why not?"

Cilla thought the question over. "Those are bourgeois Christian names. I wanted to choose a name that reflects my proletarian origin and allegiance." Cilla had not necessarily digested all the rhetoric she had been fed, but she had learned to imitate it effectively. What she omitted to disclose was that she had actually chosen her name because of her deep and abiding fondness for Cilla Black.

"What is your surname to be?"

"Wilson," Cilla replied.

"Cilla Wilson," Professor Kuznetsova repeated. "I suppose it will do. In any case that is not the reason why I have asked to see you today. Do you remember when you first came here? Do you remember the assessments you underwent?"

Cilla nodded.

"Do you remember that you wrote an essay about your favourite family member?"

Cilla nodded again.

"You wrote about a dog. Why is that?"

"She is my favourite," Cilla replied.

"I find that hard to believe." Professor Kuznetsova looked sternly at Cilla. "I think you are trying to hide something from us. Why did you not choose your mother or your father or your brother or one of your sisters?"

Cilla shrugged her shoulders. "I don't know," she said. "I suppose I don't like them very much."

"You don't like your father?"

"No."

"And your mother?"

"Not really."

"And your siblings? What about the youngest one? He is nearest in age to you."

"He was annoying," Cilla said stubbornly. "He followed me around all the time. And he was a cry-baby."

Professor Kuznetsova grimaced with frustration.

"I am going to ask you one question and I want an honest answer," she said. "Do you understand?"

Cilla nodded.

"All of your family members are drowning. You can only save one of them. Which one do you choose to save?"

"Can I choose Luna?" Cilla asked.

"Is that the dog?"

"Yes."

"Then no."

Cilla considered the question for a moment.

"But I can choose any of the others? It's my choice?"

Professor Kuznetsova nodded.

Cilla hesitated. She allowed the scene in her head to play itself out. There was Tomas; his small squirming body. He was struggling for breath. His hands were waving in the air. Water was closing over the top of his little head.

"I choose to let them all drown," she said.

The Renaming Ceremony was an elaborate affair. The gymnasium was decked out with the red-and-gold flags of Russia; the iconic hammer-and-sickle design to symbolise the union of workers and peasants; the gold-bordered red star to represent Communism itself.

A makeshift stage had been erected at one end of the hall. On it were chairs, a lectern and a large metal bucket. The benches from the canteen had been brought into the hall and were set up in rows.

At the appointed time all of the pupils filed into the hall. Each one was holding a piece of paper on which they had written their old name in capital letters.

All the senior members of the teaching faculty were present on the stage. Once the children were seated Colonel Dubrovsky, the headmaster, stood up and leant over the lectern to give a speech. It was about the Gold Star medal and how it was awarded for heroic feats in service to the Soviet State and society. He spoke at length and with great reverence about General Secretary Leonid Brezhnev who had received the medal multiple times.

At the end of this speech the headmaster took a candle and lit it.

"Each of us is a spark, together we are a flame!" he declared. At this point Professor Kuznetsova and Comrade Guseva stood up and approached the front of the stage. Comrade Guseva stood on one side of the headmaster, Professor Kuznetsova on the other. Each of them held a list of names. Professor Kuznetsova proceeded to read out the first name on her list.

"Maxim Adamovich," she announced.

A tall boy in the fifth row stood up and walked solemnly to the front of the hall. He mounted the steps to the stage and stood in front of the lectern. Colonel Dubrovsky leant over and handed him the candle. The boy took it for a moment, held up his piece of paper and lit the bottom right-hand corner. Within moments it was engulfed by flames. He dropped the burning paper into the metal bucket. Comrade Guseva consulted her list, leant forward and whispered into the headmaster's ear.

"Your new name is Philippe Blondeau," Colonel Dubrovsky proclaimed.

"I am Phillipe Blondeau," the boy repeated to the audience.

"I am a citizen of the Soviet Union. I dedicate myself, my life and all that I am to the greater good of the Socialist State."

The hall erupted into cheering and clapping. Some of the audience stamped their feet.

Each child went through the same process. Cilla watched as Anya took her turn. She approached the stage as Anya Federova and was reborn as Amelia Fleming. Her eyes were shining as she returned to sit on the bench next to Cilla.

Finally Cilla's old name was announced.

She felt no sense of affiliation to the name. It was like an old piece of clothing that she had grown out of; something to be discarded and left behind. Cilla approached the stage proudly, excited at the prospect of her new persona. But a strange thing happened when she came to burn the piece of paper on which her old name was written. She didn't let go of it, she just held it as it burnt. There was something mesmerising about the yellow flame with its blue base. Even as the pain in her thumb and forefinger became excruciating and she could smell the bitter scent of her own charred fingernail mingling with the odour of scorched paper, she continued to hold on. No-one noticed that she was doing this because she did not react to the pain. Eventually the flame went out and she was left grasping a minute piece of paper. It was a simple matter to hold on to this rather than throwing it into the metal bucket. Nobody saw. They were more interested in cheering at the proclamation of her new name.

When the last child had been baptised the congregation stood to sing a patriotic song. Finally a girl in the front row went up onto the stage and recited a short poem to mark the occasion:

Here we stand.
Shoulder to shoulder,

For the Motherland.
Hand in hand.
Brothers and sisters,
Of the Motherland.
Grains of sand.
We form the bedrock,
To the Motherland.

After the Renaming Ceremony was complete all the children helped carry the benches back into the canteen and there was a special celebratory lunch to commemorate the event. Even though her hand still hurt, Cilla tucked into the three courses with gusto. There was her favourite chicken broth followed by fried meatballs with sour cream and, as a special treat, pirozhki buns filled with jam.

The atmosphere in the canteen was loud and raucous. The pupils took great pleasure in announcing each other's new names repeatedly, trying them on for size. There was a considerable amount of shouting and laughing and, for once, the teachers on lunch duty did not attempt to remonstrate or restrain. All in all it was a joyous affair.

To mark the occasion the children were given the afternoon off from their normal commitments. As usual Cilla slipped away to the greenhouses. She found Comrade Ivanova in the kitchen greenhouse repotting tomato seedlings. Cilla stood quietly in the doorway until the teacher looked up and saw her.

Comrade Ivanova smiled. "Hello Sachenka," she said. "How did it go?"

Cilla glared at her and clenched her fists. "You can't call me that anymore," she said. "My name is Cilla now."

Comrade Ivanova shook her head. "I'm sorry, it was just a slip of the tongue. Maybe I can call you Cillenka instead."

Cilla considered this proposal. "I don't think so," she responded. "I'm supposed to be an English girl."

"Yes of course you are," Comrade Ivanova replied soothingly. "Would you like to come and help me with these tomatoes?"

They worked in silence for a few minutes filling plastic pots with compost. Each pot was left with a furrow in it so that the new tomato plant with its delicate root system could be transplanted intact. When Comrade Ivanova handed Cilla the first of these plants she saw the two blackened fingernails and the livid blisters around them.

"What happened to your hand?" she asked quietly.

"Nothing," Cilla replied.

"It doesn't look like nothing. It looks painful."

"I don't really feel pain," Cilla said nonchalantly. "I never have. And now we're having lessons on it."

"Lessons on pain?"

"No, on controlling pain. And lots of other things too. It's a new course I've started. It's called Impulse and Behaviour Regulation. Last week I learnt how to slow down my heartbeat. I was the best in the class."

"That's excellent," Comrade Ivanova said carefully. "But I don't want that hand to become infected. We're going to give it a wash and I have some salve which will help it heal. You can carry on repotting the tomato plants afterwards but you must wear some gloves."

Cilla allowed Comrade Ivanova to lead her over to the tap and to run her hand under cold water. Afterwards the teacher dried it with a clean towel and applied some sticky ointment.

"I'm a proper citizen of the Soviet Union now," Cilla said.

"I know you are," Comrade Ivanova replied.

"And I have pledged myself to the Socialist State," Cilla stated proudly.

Comrade Ivanova continued to apply the salve, stroking Cilla's fingers gently as she did so. She didn't say anything.

"Aren't you happy for me?" Cilla insisted.

"Oh yes, very happy," Comrade Ivanova agreed. She kept her head bent over the hand so that Cilla could not see the expression on her face.

"You don't sound happy," Cilla said accusingly. "You sound sad."

Comrade Ivanova raised her face to Cilla's.

"It is a glorious day and I am happy for you," she said. "I just hope that they know what they are doing. Every ant knows the formula of its anthill. Every bee knows the formula of its beehive. Only humankind does not know its own formula."

But this didn't make much sense to Cilla. She certainly wasn't an ant or a bee and she had never heard of Dostoyevsky.

8

Jobs

A new freelance opportunity had presented itself. After checking out their credentials Cilla arranged to meet the prospective clients at the Queen Victoria gate of Kensington Gardens. From there it was only a short distance to the Round Pond where the initial meeting could take place.

As usual she arrived early and stationed herself next to the King William statue where she had a good view of the gate. Some days had passed since her escapade at Fulham Studios and she still had the silver shorts in her possession. She kept them in her bag. Cilla wasn't sure whether to try and return them to Nancy or keep them as some sort of memento. She had spent most of the last week organising material for the Amy Levine project. All the photographs and relevant documentation had been pinned on to several large mood boards. She had spent one day doing fieldwork which mainly consisted of traipsing around after Mrs Levine as she went to the gym, shopped in Westbourne Grove and met a friend for coffee. None of this had been very productive. In truth, Cilla was grateful for the diversion that a potential new contract provided. Even if this meeting turned out to be pointless it was at least a distraction.

The prospective clients arrived five minutes early and stood at the gate waiting. They were a good-looking well-dressed couple in their late fifties. The husband was rather handsome with a full head of grey hair which he wore brushed back and bouffant. He appeared to be dressed for some sort of period drama in a three-piece tweed suit complete with waistcoat and cravat. His wife was still pretty in an overblown sort of way. Rather incongruously she had brought along a large wicker shopping trolley. They didn't look like murderers, but then again, who did?

Cilla approached them from behind. "Hello," she announced.

The wife started and spun around.

"Oh," was all she said when she saw the voice's owner. Cilla was accustomed to this sort of reaction. She knew that she did not fit most people's expectation of a paid mercenary.

The husband displayed more control and held out his hand. "Malcom Taylor," he announced. "This is my wife Barbara." It was as if he were introducing himself at a cocktail party. Cilla did not accept the proffered hand.

"Walk," she replied and led the way into the park.

The husband approached the subject matter of the meeting with a certain degree of bravado.

"It's my mother you see. She's over ninety. She's had a good life and, well, we feel that it's time now, you know, time to call it a day. She's in a care home. It's very expensive. She doesn't have much quality of life and we think that perhaps, enough is enough. She's had a good innings and all that. I know that she doesn't want to be a burden. We would very much appreciate it if you could help us with what we're trying to do here." It was peculiar the way in which Malcom Taylor circled around the issue of doing away with his mother repeatedly without actually mentioning the act by name. It was as if he were trying to pick up a large turd with a pair of tweezers.

"We're not bad people," Barbara chimed in.

"No, no, certainly not," Malcom agreed. "We just want what's best for her. If you think about it, what we're really asking for is euthanasia."

"Euthanasia." Cilla repeated the word slowly.

"Yes," Malcom agreed. "A mercy killing, to put her out of her misery as it were."

"And you've consulted your mother about this?" Cilla enquired. "Am I to take it that she is aware of your plans?"

Malcom and Barbara looked aghast.

"Of course not," Malcom replied. "We thought that, I mean we were told that you could manage this sort of thing discreetly."

"But why?" Cilla enquired. "Your mother is over ninety; she will die of her own accord soon enough. Why not let nature take its course? Why do you need me?"

Malcom Taylor looked sheepish in response to this question. "There are certain financial considerations," he admitted in a slightly pompous manner. "Nothing that you need to concern yourself about."

Cilla ceased her probing. Their motive was clear enough. Instead she began to recite her speech: her price, her requirements, her usual terms and conditions.

"Oh no, we can't wait three months," Barbara interrupted suddenly. "We need it done right away. We've brought all the money. Not just the deposit, all of it. It's in the trolley."

The three of them stopped for a moment on the north side of the pond and stared at the wicker shopping trolley which Barbara had been dragging along behind her. Its semi-circular raffia lid was fastened shut with a wooden toggle.

"Where did you get it from?" Cilla asked calmly. If they informed her that they had taken the cash out of their joint bank account that morning she would turn around and walk away.

"John Lewis," came the timid response.

"Barbara!" Malcom spoke sharply, but when he turned to Cilla his pompous manner had vanished. "It's everything that we could raise at short notice. I sold the car, for cash. We pawned some jewellery and my Patek Philippe watch. All our liquid assets are in that trolley; fifty thousand pounds. It can't be traced."

What a pair of jokers the two of them were, Cilla thought to herself. Did these people think that they could order a Dry Job as though it were a takeaway? No finesse, no fore-thought, no preparation. On the other hand, there was fifty thousand pounds for the taking in a shopping trolley and the proposed victim was a ninety-year-old sitting target. There would be no need to invent a script. The Story had already been written.

"Why do you need it done so quickly?" Cilla asked.

"I have a bridging loan that I can't repay," Malcom responded quietly. Now that the pomposity had gone there was a dull monotone edge to his voice. "We haven't paid the mortgage on our house for over a year and the bank is threatening to foreclose in three weeks. I will go bankrupt."

"How will your mother's death help?" Cilla persisted. "If she has any money you won't be able to get hold of it immediately."

"I'll have a list of her assets. I'll have the will, which will confirm that I am the chief beneficiary of her estate. It will be enough to provide a stay of execution. That's all I need."

"Please help us." Barbara sounded tearful. If there was one thing that Cilla couldn't stand, it was other people's tears.

"This is the information I will need," she said.

The old lady lived in a residential nursing home in Tunbridge Wells. She was ninety-one years old. Considering her age, she was in relatively good health although her eyesight was very poor. She was still lucid and could walk a few steps with the aid of a Zimmer frame.

The obvious antagonist to use in this case was diamorphine. A dose of thirty milligrams would likely achieve the desired result by causing the central nervous system to slow down and suppressing the respiratory response. Liquid would collect in the tissues and air sacs of the lungs. This would lead to respiratory failure. Effectively the old lady would drown in her own fluid. It wasn't as bad as it sounded. The analgesic effect of the drug would remove any discomfort. She wouldn't writhe around in agony, she'd just float away. Not that this mattered very much, but it had to be admitted that floating was easier to watch than writhing, and quieter too. But the important thing was that the official cause of death would be attributed to pulmonary oedema. There would be no murder and therefore no murder investigation. So far, so neat and tidy.

The first problem was that Cilla didn't have any diamorphine. She had used up the last of her supply on one of Vlad's customers a year earlier. If she'd had more time Cilla would have probably elected to break in to a hospital pharmacy so that she could replenish her stock. But this would add another layer of complexity and preparation to the job. It was probably simpler and easier to use heroin instead; which meant paying a visit to Smithy.

"I need some smack," she said when he answered the door. Smithy looked worse than usual. There were black shadows under his eyes and his hair, lank at the best of times, hung in a greasy curtain.

"Hello to you too," he replied sullenly.

"I need some smack," Cilla repeated.

"Well I don't have any."

"When are you getting some?" she persevered.

"Hopefully never." Smithy looked very much as if he wished to shut the door in Cilla's face.

"Can I come in?" she said. Smithy didn't reply, he just walked away, but at least he left the front door open. She followed him into the kitchen. He lit a cigarette; his hands were shaking visibly and he was sweating.

"So you're clean?" she asked.

"I wouldn't exactly say clean, I don't feel clean, I feel like death," he replied in a matter-of-fact tone.

"But you've stopped using?"

"Yes."

"Why?"

"Why what?"

"Why have you stopped using?"

"Why do you want a new passport and a degree in fucking Philosophy?" It was the first time that Cilla had ever heard Smithy sound angry.

"How many days?" she persisted.

"Four days, seven hours and approximately fifty-three minutes," Smithy replied. His face was an odd colour, somewhere between yellow and pale green, as if he were suffering from jaundice. He threw his cigarette into the sink and turned away.

92

"What you're experiencing is normal," Cilla advised. "The nausea should pass in a few days; you need to make sure that you stay hydrated."

"Thank you for the advice, Doctor. Would you be able to give me a prescription as well?"

Since Cilla didn't really acknowledge sarcasm she took the question at face value and looked thoughtful for a moment.

"I can mix you up something that will help," she said. Smithy looked sceptical. "It won't get rid of the cravings altogether but it'll take the edge off." He was silent. "I just need one thing in return."

"What?" said Smithy irritably.

"Your dealer."

After a certain amount of persuasion Smithy gave up the name and location of his supplier. He only lived a few streets away. Cilla knew that she couldn't go and see the dealer herself. She was a stranger and he would never answer the door to her. It was Smithy who would have to make the purchase. But Smithy didn't want to go. Smithy refused to go, repeatedly. In the end the only way that Cilla could coax him to do so was to promise that she would take the heroin off his hands immediately and then go straight home to concoct an elixir which would ease his suffering.

An hour and a half later Cilla was examining a gram of heroin in the privacy of her potting shed. She was trying to assess its strength. It looked and tasted as if it had been cut with baby formula. She considered trying to purify it to an approximate medical grade by using a drowning-out crystallisation method but there was always the possibility that she might ruin it during the process and be left with no heroin at all. It was probably more sensible to work with what she had and simply double the dosage. If sixty milligrams didn't finish off the old lady Cilla would just keep on injecting the stuff until it did.

She had solved the problem of supply but unfortunately in doing so Cilla had created a second problem: the elixir that she had promised to Smithy didn't actually exist. There was nothing that she knew of which could alleviate the discomfort of heroin withdrawal. Cilla had made it up; it was a lie. It wasn't even one of Plato's noble lies, which might have some sort of utilitarian justification, it was just a lie. She told the lie because she had wanted something and lying was the means of getting it. She told lies because she could and because she was very good at it. The reason that she was so good at it was because she saw very little difference between lying and telling the truth. The distinction was meaningless to her. Bizarrely, this also meant that Cilla was proficient at identifying lies told by others. It wasn't the act of lying in itself that tended to give some-one away but the distinction they made between lying and telling the truth. She could always discern the change of gear involved with the shift from honesty to dishonesty; it was just obvious.

But none of this solved the problem of what to do about Smithy's elixir. All Cilla could do was hope that a couple of crushed sedatives mixed into a bottle of two parts bronchial cough medicine and three parts brandy accompanied by a hefty dose of placebo would be sufficient to turn this particular lie into some sort of weak truth. She hoped it would. She also hoped that Smithy would start washing his hair again.

Having addressed the second problem, at least theoretically, Cilla turned her attention to the third problem. This was the issue of access.

The easiest method to gain admission to the nursing home where Mrs Taylor lived would be to pose as a care worker or nurse. In order to do that Cilla needed to get hold of the appropriate uniform. The best way to do that was to find out how they did their laundry.

One telephone call and a helpful receptionist later, Cilla had established that the nursing home outsourced their laundry to a local firm. With the final piece of the puzzle in place Cilla could formulate her plan.

She would go to Tunbridge Wells and book into a cheap hotel for three days.

On day one she would scope out the nursing home. She would watch staff arrive and leave; taking note of uniforms, shift hours and any other relevant information. Towards the end of the day she would deliver a bunch of flowers to Mrs Taylor. It would be interesting to see whether she was expected to leave the delivery at reception or whether she would be allowed to take them to the old lady's room. If the latter, she would use the opportunity to assess the internal layout of the building looking for points of entry and exit and observing staff. That night she would return in full blackout gear to examine the external building and calculate her route in and out. She would check whether the entry codes that Malcom had given her still worked at night and whether reception was manned. Once this was completed she would spend the rest of the night in a covert location observing patterns: who came and left the building, what lights went on and off.

She would return to the hotel by 6 a.m. and sleep for seven hours. On the afternoon of day two she would investigate the laundry service with a view to returning that night and stealing an appropriate uniform. Ideally this would be a below-radar break-in and Care 'n' Clean Ltd would never even know that someone had been there.

On day three she would tie up any loose ends and finalise her costume: wig, makeup, clothing, accessories. She would also prepare four hypodermics, each loaded with a sixty-milligram dosage. That would be enough heroin to kill a horse. On the evening of day three she would return to nursing home to finish the Job.

It was a simple and straightforward operation; Cilla was reminded of the old days. She still looked back on that time with a certain degree of nostalgia. At least then she had had a place and a purpose in the world. What did she have now? The only thing she was any good at was the very thing she would have to give up. And how would she fill the void that was left behind?

The first two days of the mission went like clockwork. Security at the nursing home was non-existent and Cilla was ushered towards the lift carrying her delivery of flowers without even being asked to sign in. She passed two nurses when she came out of the elevator. Both were dressed in blue overalls with a white trim. Neither of them paid any attention to her. Mrs Taylor's room was at the end of the corridor on the first floor next to a fire exit. Cilla knocked on the door but there was no response so she turned the handle and went in. The room was empty, but Cilla knew that she was in the right place because the first thing she saw was a photograph of young Malcom simpering at her from the bedside table.

It was a large corner room with windows on two sides and an en-suite bathroom. There were several vases on the floor beside the bed so Cilla filled one of these with water and placed the flowers inside it. She made a mental note of the position of the furniture and left.

Her reconnaissance visit later that night established that the reception was not manned after 5 p.m. but that the entry codes continued to operate seemingly all night. Cilla observed that the last member of staff punched himself in at 10.30 p.m. Noting the direction of finger movement through her binoculars she could see that there was only one code rather than separate codes for visitors and staff. There was very little activity after eleven. For seven hours the building was quiet. 6 a.m. appeared to represent the end of the night shift at which point there was a flurry of staff leaving and arriving.

Obtaining the correct nursing uniform was even easier. The laundry service was located on an industrial estate nearby. Having scoped it out during the day Cilla returned in the evening and was in and out within the space of half an hour. She took one clean size eight nurse's uniform from a large folded pile. It seemed unlikely that anyone would ever notice it was gone.

By 10 p.m. on day three Cilla was putting the final touches to her outfit. The uniform was a reasonable fit but the trousers were slightly long so Cilla cut off six centimetres of each leg and hemmed what remained. She had brought several wigs with her: ginger, curly brown and short blonde. Curly brown seemed to balance best with the pale blue overalls. A pair of glasses completed the costume. Cilla smiled at herself in the mirror. She looked sincere, eager, kind even.

In many ways it was an advantage to have an unremarkable appearance. Apart from the colour of her eyes there was nothing memorable about Cilla's face. It was like a smooth slab of clay ready for her to mould. With the right hair and makeup she could age up ten years. Or she could remove all the slap, add a plait and still pass for a schoolgirl. The fact that she was small in stature also had its compensations. She was unthreatening; people weren't afraid of her. Well not at first anyway.

When she was ready Cilla sat down on the bed and checked the contents of her black medical bag. Then she ran through the details of the operation one last time.

1. Enter the nursing home through the main doors using the code that Malcom had given her.
2. Make her way directly to Mrs Taylor's room. If she encountered any members of staff or residents smile politely and confidently but keep moving.
3. Once inside Mrs Taylor's room pause to allow her eyes to achieve partial dark adaptation.
4. Kill Mrs Taylor.
5. When the corridor was clear leave via the fire exit.

Everything went as planned. Cilla saw no-one from the moment she entered the building to the point that she reached Mrs Taylor's room. She opened the door, entered silently, and shut it behind her. At that precise moment the bedside light flicked on and the room was bathed in a low soft light.

"Oh aren't you clever. I haven't even managed to ring the bell yet. How did you know I needed you?" The old lady was sitting up in bed, awake and alert.

Cilla did not flinch. "I was doing my rounds and I thought I heard a noise," she replied evenly. She assumed the smile that she had been practising in the mirror earlier.

"I need the pot," the old lady said. Cilla looked at her blankly. "The lavatory, dear. Ever since my last fall I daren't go by myself."

The old lady began to extricate herself from her bedcovers. She was clearly expecting assistance and there was nothing that Cilla could do for the moment except help her.

"Now who are you?" Mrs Taylor enquired as she leant on Cilla's arm and they walked slowly towards the bathroom. "I don't recognise your voice. What's your name?"

"Cilla."

"I can manage this bit by myself," the old lady said as she shifted the burden of her weight from Cilla's arm onto the handle of the bathroom door. She edged inside the room and towards the toilet. "You just wait there."

Cilla did as she was instructed; it gave her time to think. She was trying to work out how to fit this new development into her plan.

When Mrs Taylor was done Cilla guided her gently back to her bed and settled her under the covers.

"Thank you dear. You're very kind. You know some of the other nurses can be a bit rough." The old lady sighed. "I suppose you've got to go now."

"Not really," Cilla replied. "I can sit with you for a little while, if you like."

"That would be nice." Mrs Taylor shook her head. "I don't sleep well anymore. Sometimes it feels as if I barely sleep all night and then I drop off constantly during the day."

"I've got something that will help with that," Cilla offered.

"Really?" Mrs Taylor replied. "Is it a pill? I'm not very good at pills anymore. I find them difficult to swallow."

"No it's not a pill, it's just a little injection," Cilla said. She picked up her black medical bag which she had left on the floor beside the bed. "It will give you a wonderful night's sleep, I promise."

The old lady did not have good veins. They were buried deeply beneath the mottled skin. Cilla massaged the inside of Mrs Taylor's left elbow and got her to drop her arm and make a fist as she tied the tourniquet to her upper arm. She guided the needle in at a twenty-five-degree angle in the direction of the heart. When Cilla thought she'd hit the vein she pulled the plunger back into the body of the syringe. The blood that accompanied it was dark and slow moving. Cilla emptied the dose into the old lady's arm. It was a strangely intimate moment.

"Oh you're very good," observed Mrs Taylor. "That

didn't hurt at all. Goodness, what's in this stuff, I feel quite lightheaded."

"Lie back," Cilla said. "Let's get you comfortable."

She rearranged the pillows and Mrs Taylor lay down on them, her thin white hair fanning out around her head.

"What did you say your name was again?" the old lady asked sleepily.

"Cilla."

"Oh yes. I remember now. That's not a name you hear very often. It reminds me of Cilla Black."

"I was named after her."

"That's nice, I like Cilla Black." The old lady's eyes were closing. "I saw her once at the Royal Variety Show in London. My husband took me. He always thought . . ." Mrs Taylor's voice tailed off into silence.

Cilla sat down on the edge of the bed to wait. The old lady didn't float away. She sank, like a small stone into a very deep well. After ten minutes her colour began to change and when Cilla checked her vitals, she had gone. Cilla looked at the smiling photograph of Malcom.

"Happy now?" she said.

9

Metamorphosis II

A subtle but prevailing change took place at Academy 43 during Cilla's second year of tenure. It was as if the Renaming Ceremony represented the end of childhood. The joyous uproar of that day was never repeated. Instead the atmosphere amongst pupils slowly became more sober and disciplined. They were competitive with each other. More was invested in them and more was expected of them accordingly.

Cilla was enrolled into a number of new courses. She was required to master methods and disciplines which were unlike anything she had encountered before. Some of these she enjoyed, some she found extremely demanding.

The Impulse and Behaviour Regulation class was a good example of this new mode of learning. It combined both the theoretical and the practical. Cilla was taught about the fight or flight response and the physiological principles behind it. Sometimes known as the acute stress response, it is primarily a survival mechanism that is triggered when an individual is placed in danger. The release of hormones leads to the production of adrenaline which prepares the body to stay and deal with the immediate threat or to run away. The problem with the fight or flight response is that it is an imperfect mechanism. The point of the Impulse and Behaviour Regulation course was to perfect it.

She learnt that in crisis situations people divide broadly into three types. About ten percent are so cognitively impaired under acute stress that their judgement and actions turn bizarre and unreliable. This is the person who runs up and down the aisle screaming as the pilot of an aeroplane is attempting to crash-land: the headless chicken type. In crisis situations such individuals are best avoided. They almost always end up dying and will take others with them if given the opportunity.

Approximately eighty percent of people suffer some degree of cognitive impairment under stress. This often results in partial and temporary judgement paralysis. These are the people that continue to sit in their seats after the aeroplane has successfully crash-landed, but is now filling with smoke. Some of them live, some of them die: the rabbit in headlights type.

Finally, ten percent of people are unaffected in moments of crisis. In fact their judgement is often enhanced under stress. This is the person who is most likely to survive the crash: this person is the fox.

The Academy did not want chickens or rabbits in its midst. There was no place for them at the school. There was only room for the fox.

All pupils were taught a myriad of techniques to encourage fox-like responses. They learnt how to regulate their breathing and slow down their heartbeat. They were taught how to control fear, panic and anxiety. Cilla was good at this. She was a natural fox in the first place so these techniques came easily to her and merely served to hone and enhance the skills she already had.

But she struggled with aggression and impulse control. She often made up her mind too quickly and took the wrong decision. One of the exercises that everyone participated in was Fight/Flee/Chase. This was effectively a game and took place in a sparring ring in the gymnasium under the auspices of the headmaster Colonel Dubrovsky. The rules of the game were rather like a physical version of rock/paper/scissors. Two children's names would be drawn at random. Each of them had a choice of three options: to fight the other contestant, to chase them, or to run away themselves. They wrote their choice down on a piece of paper and entered the ring. But the beauty of the game was that its outcome depended on what the other child had written down on their piece of paper.

If both children wrote fight then combat would begin. Fights lasted a maximum of five minutes or until one side surrendered. If there was no clear outcome then the Colonel declared the victor. The winner received two points.

If one child chose chase and the other chose flee then the absconder received a three-second head start and the chaser had five minutes in which to apprehend them. Neither contestant was allowed to leave the gymnasium and no-one else was allowed to aid or obstruct. Once again, the winner received two points.

If both children chose chase or both children chose flee there was no score.

If one child chose fight and one child chose chase then fight automatically won two points.

If one child chose fight and one child chose flee then flee automatically won two points.

It took Cilla three fractured ribs, a broken collarbone and

repeated and extensive bruising to understand that she should choose fight more judiciously, especially against those larger and stronger than herself. By contrast her friend Amelia (who had once been called Anya) was exceptional at the game. She rarely engaged in one-to-one combat but she was remarkably skilled at anticipating the choice her opponent would make. She won a lot of automatic points this way. But then again Amelia experienced other difficulties. She admitted to Cilla on more than one occasion that although she very much wanted to dedicate her life to the Socialist State she still missed her home a great deal and often dreamt about her mother.

Fight/Flee/Chase was just one of a number of physical and mental challenges that pupils engaged in as part of the Impulse and Behaviour Regulation course. Occasionally a child would break down under pressure. If it happened more than once they weren't seen again and nobody asked where they'd gone.

The Weapons Training courses also took up an increasing amount of time.

Some of the boys seemed to spend most of their day outside using heavy artillery. A large section of the school's grounds were now set aside for different forms of target practice and for military exercises. Since Cilla was exempt from the Combat programme on account of her size and sex she received only cursory instruction in the use of small sniper rifles and pistols. She wasn't allowed to handle the larger, more powerful guns because the kickback was too intense for her small frame. But she had a good eye and quick reactions and this did not go unnoticed. As a result she was entered into the Cold Weapons Training course where she received extensive tuition in the use of bows and arrows, crossbows, catapults and blowpipes. Target practice took place in groups of five on the archery range several times a week under the tutelage of Captain Antonovich, an elderly war veteran who was deaf in one ear. Cilla loved target practice. She didn't simply aim for the bullseye but took great pleasure in using her arrows to split or dislodge the shafts of others. Archery soon became her new favourite hobby and what little free time she had was equally divided between the archery range and the greenhouses.

Not only was Cilla taught how to use cold weapons, she also learnt how to make them in the metal and woodwork classes that the school organised. In fact pupils were encouraged to experiment with designing and constructing their own weapons. Cilla's contribution was a covert miniature crossbow that could be worn on the arm covered by the sleeve of her shirt. The release mechanism was in the palm of her hand and was triggered by clenching her fist. It wasn't very reliable, or very accurate for that matter. There was as much possibility that you would fire a small arrow straight through your own foot as there was that you would hit an actual target. Nevertheless the school was impressed and Cilla received an honourable mention from Colonel Dubrovsky during morning assembly for services towards the Defence of the Motherland.

She was also required to participate in Tactics for Retreat and Evasion. At first Cilla did not enjoy this course at all. There seemed something shameful about being taught how to escape and hide. She found herself envious of the big dead-eyed boys who could use their fists so effectively on her in the sparring ring and didn't have to learn how to run away. But as time went on she began to see the value of the strategies she was learning. Finally the day came when she faced Alexei in a round of Fight/Flee/Chase. He was one of the oldest boys with large ham-like hands and a wrestler's build.

He was known for his love of torturing small animals. If you ever found a cat strung up in a tree or a bird's nest of chicks stamped on the ground you could be sure that it was Alexei who was responsible. Cilla didn't really understand why he was at the Academy in the first place. She doubted whether his IQ was much above 90. But Alexei appeared to be on a specialisation course all of his own and was not required to attend any academic lessons. In any case, his low IQ had not prevented him from breaking Cilla's collarbone during their previous encounter.

Her only option was to choose Flee. Cilla reminded herself that this was not a dishonourable choice, it was the clever choice. If Alexei chose Fight (expecting her to do the same) she would automatically win the round. If he chose Chase then at least she still had a chance.

He chose Chase. Cilla's heart sank. She should have chosen Fight after all. She took her three-second head start and then Alexei jumped out of the ring and was after her. He was surprisingly fast for his heavy build. She dodged him this way and that, sidestepping groups of children, but Cilla doubted that she could outrun and outmanoeuvre him around the gymnasium for the full five minutes. But then she had an idea. She pretended to trip and fall; Alexei dived after her. She rolled out of the way and he hit the wooden floor hard. For a few moments she was outside of his field of vision and a few moments were all that she required. As if by magic, Cilla disappeared. Alexei stood up and brushed himself down. He looked one way and then the other, scouring the gymnasium in his attempt to find her. At one point he even looked up at the ceiling as if she might have flown away. The problem was that Alexei was looking in the empty spaces of the room. But Cilla wasn't in one of the empty spaces, quite the reverse. All she had done in those few precious moments was to melt into the nearest group of children. She was hiding in plain sight. After a while Alexei cottoned on to the idea of where she might be and started grabbing children, staring hard at them, and pushing them out of the way in his desperate bid to find her. But it was too late. The five-minute bell rang and Colonel Dubrovksy signalled that the round was over.

"Congratulations Cilla," he said. "That was impressive. I think we're all done for today." He walked over to where Alexei was standing, red-faced and seething with fury. "Come on Alyosha." Colonel Dubrovsky put his arm around the boy's shoulders. "You come with me now. Let's see if we can't put that anger of yours to a good use."

One afternoon in autumn Cilla was dividing some aconitum plants in one of the greenhouses. She had persuaded Comrade Ivanova to allow her to grow her own personal supply. It wasn't the tall spires of violet blue flowers that Cilla was interested in but the toxin aconitine that could be created from crushing and distilling the plant. She had read that the Ancient Greeks applied it to the tips of their arrows and she was interested in harnessing its properties for use with her miniature crossbow.

Cilla valued her time spent with the plants whether Comrade Ivanova was there or not. It always provided her with a few minutes of calm and a chance to restore some sort of equilibrium. But that afternoon her peace was shattered by Amelia bursting through the greenhouse door.

"I've been looking for you everywhere," she said breathlessly.

"Here I am," Cilla replied.

"I know what it is," Amelia said. She sounded tense and excited.

107

"What what is?" Cilla continued with the intricate task of teasing the aconitum plants apart from each other without breaking their fragile stems. She wore gloves to do this since even casual skin contact could be harmful.

"I know what the sixth bunker's going to be. I know what it is that they're building."

Cilla looked up. Amelia's eyes were wide and troubled; she was biting her lower lip. It was a problem, this anxiety of hers. Most of the time she disguised it well but occasionally Cilla could sense that beneath the layers of intellect and intuition Amelia was, not weak exactly, but soft. Cilla wondered if the school authorities knew about Amelia's softness; her anxiety, her longing for home, her dreams.

Probably not was the answer, and that was the weakness of the school. They thought everyone showed them everything, whereas in fact everyone was hiding something. The trick was to bury it so deeply that even you forgot it was there. Then the school could never find it.

"Go on then, what is it?" Cilla said.

"It's a prison," Amelia burst out.

"How do you know?"

"I've been thinking about it for ages. It's bricks and mortar, it's a proper structure, not prefab like ours, but there are no windows. Then I saw some of the fixtures being delivered today. They were these metal doors with little grates in the middle and when Comrade Guseva saw that I was watching she told me to go away. I know it's a prison, I know it is. I can feel it."

Cilla did not doubt her. Amelia's extrasensory perception abilities were undisputed even if they were not understood. It was what made her so good at Fight/Flee/Chase. If you threw a dice the probability of being able to predict the number that the dice would land on should be one in six.

Amelia's consistent record was one in three. The school had tested this over and over again. If Amelia sensed that Bunker 6 was going to be a prison she was almost certainly correct.

"But who is it for?" said Cilla, mystified.

"I don't know," Amelia replied. "Maybe it's for us, but that wouldn't make any sense. Do you think it's for us?" Her tone was shrill and uneven.

"No," said Cilla firmly. "And I'm not going to worry about it either. Nor should you. It's probably just for some stupid test that Professor Kuznetsova has dreamt up. You know how she loves her tests."

"Shh Cilla, you can't talk about her in that way. You'll get in trouble."

"No I won't. You're the only one listening and you won't tell." Cilla proceeded to put on her on her best overbite and launched into a Ken Dodd impression. "I'm going to get her with my tickling stick. I'm going to tickle her pink."

The anxious look in Amelia's eyes abated slightly.

"Then I'm going to make her sing 'The Song of the Diddy Men'." Cilla began to chirp in a high-pitched voice, "We are the Diddy Men, Doddy's dotty Diddy Men. Kuznetsova is a Diddy Man, she comes from Knotty Ash."

It was irresistible. Almost against her will, Amelia began to giggle and the issue of Bunker 6 was forgotten.

It took three further months before they found out the purpose of the new building. Amelia's prediction was nearly right, but not quite. Bunker 6 wasn't a prison, it wasn't a forced labour camp either, but it was something very similar.

Early one morning, before the alarm had rung, Carla-Rose, a girl from one of the neighbouring dormitories, erupted into Cilla's room to make an announcement.

"Come and see," she shouted. "There are trucks outside."

Cilla, Amelia and the other girls in the dormitory scrambled into their clothes and rushed out. Sure enough there were six trucks on the forecourt and they arrived just in time to see the occupants of the third transport emerging from the vehicle. Dawn had not yet broken and the headlights of each of the six trucks blazed into the darkness.

Ten men came out squinting and blinking. They were pale and unshaven, dressed in grubby white boiler suits. Two armed guards were ushering them in the direction of Bunker 6. The men didn't look like prisoners as such. They weren't handcuffed or shackled. But at the same time there was something downtrodden and vacant about them. They walked in single file staring at the ground. As they reached the entrance of the new building the front doors of the fourth truck opened and two more guards got out. Then Cilla heard a sharp clap behind them.

"What do you think you're doing?" It was her form teacher Comrade Guseva. "Get to your exercise session immediately."

"Who are all those men?" Amelia said quietly to Cilla as they scuttled off towards the gymnasium.

"I bet they're scum," Carla Rose replied, keeping pace with the two of them.

"What do you mean scum?" Amelia enquired.

"You know, politicals," Carla Rose replied dismissively. "Enemies of the State, dissidents, scumbags. Where did you grow up, under a stone?"

Amelia and Cilla exchanged a look. Carla Rose had spent her early childhood in Leningrad and laboured under the illusion that growing up in a city made her more sophisticated than her country bumpkin compatriots.

They didn't have to wait very long before Carla Rose's description of the new residents was substantiated. At assembly that morning Colonel Dubrovsky did not give one of his lengthy speeches about devotion to the cause of Communism or loyalty to the Socialist ideal. Instead he introduced a guest speaker, Dr Turgenev, from the Serbsky Institute in Moscow.

"Good morning everyone." Dr Turgenev produced a large toothy smile. "I am delighted to meet you all. I have heard a great deal about you and about this school and I am looking forward to finding out more. My name is Dr Turgenev and I am a psychiatrist. Do any of you know what that means?"

Nobody answered or put their hand up. All questions posed during assembly were purely rhetorical.

"It means that I am a doctor of the mind." Dr Turgenev tapped his forehead. "I come from the Serbsky State Scientific Centre for Social and Forensic Psychiatry but I will be stationed here for the next year, maybe for longer. All of you have seen the new building that our comrades have been working so hard to construct for the past year. This building is a psychiatric hospital and today I want to talk to you about the patients who will be treated in that hospital. They are most unusual. All of them, without exception, are responsible for contravening Article 190–1 of the penal code: the dissemination of fabrications known to be false which defame the Soviet political and social system."

The doctor paused for a moment to allow the weight of this wrongdoing to be fully acknowledged by his audience.

"Yes, it is a shocking thing that these men and women have done. They have told lies about the Soviet State. They have betrayed the very system that has given them life, given them hope, given them opportunity. They are traitors. But they are not simply criminals. Each and every one of them suffers from a mental disorder. All of the patients who will be treated at this hospital have been diagnosed with sluggish schizophrenia."

111

He paused again. "Sluggish schizophrenia is a difficult illness. It is slow, it is progressive, sometimes it is intractable. Such individuals often show symptoms of pessimism, of poor social adaptation and conflict with authorities. As the illness develops they may display signs of philosophical intoxication or religious mania. They may reject the Motherland altogether. My staff and I will do our utmost to help those that can be helped, to guide them back to the true path of Communism so that they can be re-integrated into normal society and lead useful lives. But amongst these unfortunates there are many who cannot be helped, who cannot be saved from the mental disintegration that consumes them. But this does not have to mean that their lives are lived in vain. Here, at Academy 43, we will make sure that those who cannot be cured can still dedicate themselves to the greater good of the Socialist State. And all of you, with your talents and your training, you will play a role in ensuring that this is so."

Dr Turgenev turned towards Colonel Dubrovsky to indicate that his speech was complete and the Colonel began to clap enthusiastically. Everyone else followed suit.

This speech seemed to exist in isolation. It didn't lead to anything. As time went on there was no indication to Cilla how she or any of the others would play a role in making sure that the psychiatric patients in the hospital could dedicate themselves to the greater good of the Socialist State. She rarely saw any of the doctors, nurses or guards who worked there and the patients, not at all. There appeared to be complete segregation between the pupils in the five bunkers and the inmates of the sixth. No wonder that the schizophrenics had looked so pale when she caught her brief glimpse of them; it would appear that they spent all of their time indoors. After a while Cilla almost forgot about the hospital completely, it had so little bearing on her life.

But then as she was making her way to the greenhouses one day after lessons she realised that Alexei and two other boys were walking together in front of her. They were pushing and shoving each other as usual but there was a purpose and direction to their stride which intrigued her. Instead of cutting right to the greenhouses she followed them to see where they would go. She was too far away to hear anything they said but it was clear that they were in high spirits. They marched in the direction of Bunker 6. When they got to the hospital they ignored the front entrance and went around to the far side of the building. Alexei knocked on a small black door. The door opened and in they went. Cilla waited for a few minutes but they didn't come out again.

"But why?" said Amelia when Cilla told her about the incident later that evening in the dormitory. "We're not allowed anywhere near the hospital. Comrade Guseva is always reminding us."

"Maybe they're outpatients receiving treatment," Cilla suggested. "Perhaps Alexei has been given a diagnosis of sluggish stupidity."

The following morning they were booked in for target practice on the archery field. The weapons in use were medium-sized crossbows with a range of approximately fifty metres. The problem was that there was no target. The dartboard had been removed and all that was left was the post to which it was usually attached. Cilla, Amelia and the three others milled around uneasily. One of the boys tried to ask Captain Antonovich what was going on but he was being particularly deaf that day and ignored them. Cilla was considering abandoning the activity and going back to her dormitory when she realised that a prison guard from the hospital was walking slowly towards them. The reason that he was walking slowly was because he was accompanied by a patient. Cilla nudged Amelia and nodded in the direction of the two men. The patient did not walk as such; he shuffled and shambled alongside the guard. His head wasn't bowed, he was looking straight in front, muttering continually as if involved in deep conversation. Gradually the others became aware of the approaching figures and they fell silent. The guard escorted the patient all the way to the wooden post, forty metres distance from where they were standing. When they reached their destination the guard stood the patient in front of the post so that he was facing them and tied his hands behind the post with a length of rope. At no point did the man resist. He was like a giant life-size doll except for his mouth which never stopped moving. Once the guard had determined that the knot was properly tied he walked nonchalantly away lighting a cigarette as he left. The man muttered; the children stared; no-one was quite sure what to do next.

"What are you waiting for?" barked Captain Antonovich. "Prepare formation."

The staccato sound of his voice galvanised the archers into action. They formed a line and waited.

"Well?" said the Captain tersely. "You have your target. Get on with it."

Four of the children loaded their crossbows, all except for Amelia. She just stood there holding her weapon limply, she didn't even put her foot in the stirrup. She appeared to be in some sort of trance.

"Raise your weapon," instructed Captain Antonovich. "Fire at will."

Four bolts were loosed from four crossbows. Not one of them hit the target.

"Pathetic," was the Captain's assessment. "Again."

Still Amelia just stood there. So far Captain Antonovich appeared to be unaware of her failure to participate, but it could only be a matter of time.

"Amy," hissed Cilla. "Snap out of it. You have to do this. You don't have to hit him but you have to take your shots." Amelia ignored her, so Cilla kicked her hard on the ankle.

"Ow!" said Amelia indignantly but at least she woke up from her stupor and began loading her weapon.

Cilla turned her attention back to the target. The man was considerably larger than a dartboard although more narrow than the widest part of the dartboard's diameter. All five children were decent shots and yet their bolts just whistled past him.

"Concentrate," she said to herself as she raised her weapon and put her eye to the scope. The man's face was magnified through its lens. He was still talking to himself. Cilla wondered what it was that he was saying: prayers, curses, apologies. It didn't really matter. They were all just abstract nouns.

"Relax." She tried to let the tension fall from her shoulders and her arms as she placed her fingertip on the trigger. She took a deep breath and as she let it out she pulled the trigger.

Cilla's aim was still slightly off but her bolt hit the man on his right thigh. He raised his head to the sky and screamed. It was a horrible sound, piercing and raw. A deep red stain appeared on one leg of his white boiler suit. A pale yellow one began to spread on the other.

Two more arrows hit him almost simultaneously, one in the shoulder and one in the stomach. He yelped in pain and began to make a high-pitched keening sound like an animal.

This time Cilla aimed for his throat; anything to stop that dreadful noise. She must have nicked one of his carotids with the tip of her bolt because as the arrow lodged in his neck, blood started pouring from the wound. It was all over now.

Cilla waited for Captain Antonovich to order them to lower their weapons before moving in to take a closer look. She walked over to the post where the man hung lethargically, held up only by the rope which still tied his hands. What she could see of his face was ashen. His boiler suit had turned more red than white and there was a crimson pool at his feet. She felt awed by the quantity of blood contained in a human being. It seemed strange and invigorating to think that hers was still pumping furiously around her body whilst his was congealing on the ground. Apart from that she didn't feel much of anything at all. She wondered how he had felt in those last moments. If you could strip out the pain, what would be left: fear, rage, sadness, relief? Was he one of those who were suffering from philosophical intoxication or religious mania? Was that why he was muttering? It didn't matter now. None of it mattered now. All the thoughts and feelings he had ever experienced had been erased by the final bolt from her crossbow. And what did they amount to anyway? They were all just abstract nouns.

10

Changes

Haugr the Ogre was in a bad mood. His booming voice reverberated around the playing area at TGR's. He had a captive audience.

The henchmen were seated at two of the playing tables clustered together as though they might find safety in the pack. Vlad was shouting at them. He was complaining about product quality, sales and margins. They all looked thoroughly miserable.

Cilla sat alone at the bar. She was not sure why she had been invited to attend this little get-together. She had nothing to do with the distribution side of the business and she was bored. Boredom was and had always been one of Cilla's biggest stumbling blocks. On a bad day, and today was a bad day, she felt as if she had been bored for the whole of her life. Give her pain, horror, fear and misery any day of the week, but not boredom. If boredom could be visualised Cilla thought that it would look like a blanket of cinders that had settled on the earth. It tainted everything. Even the things that normally interested her began to lose their appeal once that grey snow began to fall.

Cilla glanced towards the clock on the back wall. It was 11.15 and the club did not open for punters until midday which meant that Vlad could hold this motivational meeting safe in the knowledge that they would not be disturbed. At least the kitchen staff would be arriving soon. That should put an end to his tirade. He was so angry that white fragments of spittle were collecting in the corners of his mouth as he roared.

Apart from the fact of being forced to attend this pointless meeting there were two other reasons why Cilla was having a bad day. The first was that her head itched. In anticipation of living a civilian life she had decided to grow her hair. This meant that she was sitting with a centimetre of hot uncomfortable stubble beneath her wig. The second reason was because she had woken up that morning with the realisation that she was no closer to resolving how to kill Amy Levine than she had been three weeks ago. It wasn't for lack of trying. Cilla had spent more than a week following the woman around West London. She had gone to see *White Fang* at the cinema with Mrs Levine and her two children. She had stood outside countless cafés whilst Amy chatted with friends and drank coffee inside. She had even spent two uncomfortable nights lying prostrate with a pair of binoculars staking out the Levine residence from a vantage point in the private square opposite their house. But nothing gave; nothing revealed itself. Amy Levine seemed to lack any sort of idiosyncrasies that could be exploited in the cause of her death. The final blow occurred when Cilla discovered that the stockbroker's wife drove a Range Rover which meant that brake tampering, always a reasonable last resort, was unfeasible. Cilla felt weary and disheartened.

As Vlad thundered on Cilla found herself seriously reconsidering the possibility of killing him instead. He would probably be easier to dispatch than Amy Levine. At least he smoked and drank and whored and gambled. It wouldn't be that difficult to write a convincing story for Vladimir Haugr although, having said that, it was difficult to imagine an ending for him that did not involve extreme violence. He lived by the sword after all, could he really die any other way? It was hard to envisage him keeling over with a cup of poisoned coffee in one hand or dying in his sleep. As if catching her train of thought Vlad turned sharply towards her.

"You have something you'd like to say?" he demanded. Cilla shook her head. "You think maybe I should hand one of these clowns over to you? Make another example." Vlad turned back towards his lieutenants. "Is that what you want? Do you remember what happened to Jacob? Do you? This little vixen drained the blood from his body. She did it on my orders. Maybe I get her to do it again to one of you, but this time I say to her, do it slowly, very slowly. Is that what you want?"

There was an uncomfortable scraping of chairs and various murmurs of "No Boss."

The door from the hallway to the playing area opened and Nancy skipped into the room wearing headphones and humming loudly. It took a few moments for her to register that the room was occupied. When she did, she pulled the headphones down around her neck and fumbled in her jacket pocket to turn off her Walkman.

"I'm so sorry Mr Haugr. I didn't mean to interrupt," she said awkwardly.

"Don't worry darling," Vlad replied in a friendly voice,

"you are here to do your job. That is good." This was another disconcerting aspect of his persona. Vlad could flip between moods in an instant: fury one moment, calm the next, then back to rage. It was as if he were some sort of elemental force, like the weather.

He turned back to the room and started shouting again. "I just wish you fuckers would do the same," he roared. "Now get out of my sight."

Nancy winced as he raised his voice.

"Sorry darling," he said, patting her arm. "Nothing for you to worry about, just men's talk. You go do your work."

It was only when Cilla stood up from the bar stool that Nancy realised she was there. Nancy didn't say anything. She just gave Cilla an odd look and backed out of the playing area towards the kitchen. But before Cilla could follow, Vlad stopped her.

"Wait," he said. "You and I need to have a little chat."

Cilla went back to the bar stool and sat down again. Vlad waited until the heavies had left before he came to the point.

"Several weeks ago I asked you to go and check on the Mint. You remember?"

Cilla nodded.

"You come back to me, you tell me – pretty Smithy says he's still got some adjustments to make." Vlad spoke the latter part of this sentence in a cringing falsetto voice. He was looking for a response.

Cilla didn't flinch; she sat impassively, her hands in her lap. Never react was one of the very first rules that Colonel Dubrovsky had taught her.

"Several weeks ago," Vlad repeated in a slow angry tone. "And since then, nothing. I bet that little fucker is printing ten pound notes like they're confetti. You tell him from me

120

that he's got until the end of the month to get the Mint up and running or I'll shove a fucking railing up his asshole."

Even now after everything that she had seen and everything that she had done it still mystified Cilla that people could think up such unpleasant things to do to each other. A railing up the asshole was simply not a form of execution that would occur to her. Yet clearly it occurred to Vladimir Haugr. Moreover it was quite possible that, in the past, he had actually shoved a railing up some poor sod's asshole. And if he had, it wouldn't be the first time that this had happened. Go back a few hundred years and thrusting a red-hot poker up someone's rectum was a notorious form of covert murder because it didn't leave any outward marks on the body. You could even say it was the original Dry Job.

And what about Vladimir Haugr's namesake, the original Vlad the Impaler, ruler of Wallachia in the fifteenth century. He was notorious for skewering his enemies onto stakes via their anus. The stake would be oiled and inserted vertically so that eventually it would exit via the mouth. Cilla had even seen a photograph of a German woodcut which showed him dining amongst the dead and dying corpses of his victims.

She did not mention any of this to her employer. She merely noted the historical coincidence. But perhaps it wasn't a coincidence at all, perhaps Vladimir Haugr was just a copycat killer inspiring fear and awe by adopting the practices of his ancestor.

"I thought you didn't do that anymore," she said quietly as she stood up.

"Do what?"

"Kill people with railings. I thought that's why you employed me, so that you could adopt a more subtle approach and stop drawing attention to yourself."

The two of them stood facing each other. Vlad was precisely twenty-eight centimetres taller than Cilla and almost twice her girth. She looked like a child beside him.

"Oh Cilla," Vlad sighed. "Cilla, Cilla, Cilla. Sometimes I wish my guys had half your fucking balls. And sometimes I don't. You just go and deliver my message. Understand?"

❧

Nancy was in the kitchen emptying the industrial-sized dishwasher. She glanced up when she saw Cilla standing in the doorway, set her mouth into a thin straight line and went back to the task of putting away cutlery.

"I've got your shorts," Cilla said. Nancy didn't reply. "They're in my bag. Do you want them back?" Still no response. On their previous encounter it had been Nancy who had done most of the talking. Cilla wasn't quite sure what to do with this new silent Nancy. She waited for a moment and then turned to walk away.

"What were you doing in there?" Nancy blurted out.

"Mr Haugr called a meeting," Cilla replied. "I had to attend."

"But why?" Nancy demanded. "I thought you were a waitress, like me. But you're clearly not a waitress are you? I never see you pull any shifts. Why were you at a meeting with all those thugs? What is it you actually do for Mr Haugr? And why did Artur tell me to stay away from you if I knew what was good for me?"

For a moment Cilla considered telling her the truth.

"Well Nancy, Artur probably told you to stay away from me because I am in fact a hired assassin. Despite my perfect accent I'm not English at all. I grew up in a Soviet State-sponsored boarding school which trained children to become executioners. For some years I worked for the government as a spy and a hit man. When the State cut me loose Vladimir Haugr was kind enough to offer me a position in his organisation. I kill people for him. But lately I have come to realise that there is no future in doing this. It's a dead-end job – pardon the pun. So I'm trying to give it up. As soon as I've saved enough money I'm going to disappear and start again. I'm going to be normal. But when you come along and start sticking your nose where it's not wanted this creates a problem for me. And the solution to that problem is that I poison you in your sleep, write your name on a headstone and add it to the graveyard inside my head. So, Nancy, can I suggest that you stop asking awkward questions, please, for your own good?"

This was the longest speech that Cilla had ever made. It was almost a pity that she only said it inside her head. What she actually came out with was: "I never said I was a waitress. I occasionally help out when we're short-staffed but actually I'm Mr Haugr's P.A."

"Oh." Nancy looked crestfallen. "But why did Artur tell me to stay away from you?"

"Because he resents me. He's the manager here so he gets to order everyone around but I only answer to Mr Haugr."

"Oh." Nancy was beginning to look more cheerful again. "Hey, do you want to come to another rave this weekend? The venue hasn't been confirmed yet but I reckon it's going to be at the Casino Club. I know it's a bit of a trek but it will be worth it. They'll be playing happy hardcore."

Quite a lot of this speech didn't really make any sense to Cilla but she nodded anyway. She felt better for saying yes. If nothing else, going out with Nancy would provide another opportunity to practise being normal; whatever that meant.

❦

When Smithy answered the door he looked different. For a start, he'd had a haircut. The lank greasy locks had disappeared. He looked younger, almost boyish. It wasn't just the hair; Smithy's skin had visibly changed. He was still pale but the scabby addict's complexion had almost completely cleared up and his lips, usually colourless, were a deep rich red.

"Who are you?" Cilla enquired. "I've come to see Smithy." They both smiled. It was the first joke that Cilla could recall making in many years.

"What do you think?" Smithy said shyly. "Better?"

"Much better," Cilla agreed. Without really thinking about it she reached her hand out towards the side of his head and stroked his hair. It was as soft and as smooth as she had always imagined it would be. Smithy took a step back.

"Don't tell me you want more gear," he said. "I won't do it for you. I'm done with that shit."

Cilla shook her head. "Vlad sent me," she said. "He wants to know when the Mint will be ready. He's pissed off."

"Come and see for yourself," Smithy replied. "I'm working on it now."

The interior of the bungalow looked different as well. It was clean and tidy. The cushions on the sofa were plumped and someone had hoovered the carpet. There was a fresh bunch of daffodils on the dining table in the lounge and some of the mahogany furniture and all the old photograph frames had gone. Cilla followed Smithy down to the basement. The Mint lay in pieces on the swimming pool floor.

"That doesn't look good," Cilla commented.

"There's a glitch," Smithy admitted. "Florence Nightingale's nose isn't coming out right. I've taken it apart to find out what's going wrong. I know it's not the plate. The plate is perfect. But something isn't right with the transfer and I don't know if it's the transfer from the plate to the blanket or the transfer from the blanket to the paper."

"Vlad wants it ready by the end of the month."

"I'm doing my best. That's always the problem with an offset lithograph press like this one. It's great when it works. You've got the four colours, you get the result you want, but when there's a problem it's hard to identify. There are so many components."

"He says that if it's not ready by the end of the month he's going to kill you."

"You mean he's going to get you to kill me?" It was the first time that Smithy had ever made a direct reference to Cilla's line of work. It gave her an unpleasant feeling in the pit of her stomach. It wasn't the reference as such but the fact of him saying it.

"No," she replied. "He said he'd do it himself."

"Bullshit," Smithy announced. "He can't kill me and he knows it."

"Why not?"

"Because the Mint has no value without me. I'm the only one who can finish it. I'm the only one who can make it work. And you can tell him from me I've run out of rag paper. I told him I was running low and he said he could source some. If he wants tenners that don't disintegrate on contact then I need that rag paper."

Cilla absorbed this information carefully. She was unused to the current version of Smithy. It wasn't just his appearance that had altered; it was his range. Smithy the addict had only two settings; he was high or he wanted to get high. Smithy the addict did not have agency or emotion; he just did what he was told. This new clean version of Smithy appeared to function on a different, more complex level. It was unsettling.

"Why did you stop using?" she asked (again) and this time

Smithy did not bite her head off. Instead his face coloured slightly and he looked away.

"You," he said, refusing to make eye contact.

"Me," Cilla replied thoughtfully. "In what way, me?"

"Well, you've decided to stop haven't you? I'm assuming that's what the new passport and the A levels and a degree in Philosophy is all about, isn't it? You're going to stop, you're going to walk away, aren't you? If you can do it, why can't I?"

Smithy was asking questions but none of them seemed to require an answer.

"I don't want to spend my life as an addict," he went on. "It's just become boring. There's no room for anything else and I want to do something else."

Cilla didn't say anything. She just stared at him with her pale glittering gaze.

"What is it you want to do?" she asked eventually.

"I don't know, not forgery that's for sure. Something legitimate; something where I don't have to worry about spending the next decade in jail." Finally he looked at her. "Do you know what you want to do?"

"I want to be normal."

Cilla said this so earnestly that it made Smithy smile.

"What does that mean?"

She shrugged. "It just came to me when I . . ." she stopped short. Cilla didn't want to tell Smithy about her encounter with Jacob; his hands around her neck; the view into the abyss; the blood; the fish; her epiphany. She tried to explain it in another way. "I just realised that if I do what I've always done then the best I can hope for is that I'll get what I've always got. And that's the best I can hope for. What's more likely is that the thing I do will be done to me."

"Do you feel guilty?" Smithy asked. It was something that

126

he had always wanted to ask. "About all the people you've killed?"

"No," Cilla replied. "I don't feel guilty about anything. Everyone dies, I just speed up the process. What I feel is that I've been asleep for a long time and I'm waking up."

But now that Smithy had asked the question he couldn't let it go. "Of course everyone dies. That's not the point. You cut people's lives short. Imagine if you added up all the years that you took away from them. It might come to hundreds."

"Or thousands."

Smithy looked aghast. "And you don't feel guilty about that?"

"No," Cilla repeated firmly. "A soldier doesn't feel guilty for killing enemy troops during battle. A farmer doesn't feel guilty for sending his cattle off to slaughter. I just do what I've been trained to do. But now I want to stop doing it and do something else. I want to be normal. I want to live in a normal house and have normal hair and do a normal job."

"A normal job? And what might that be?"

"I was thinking that I might become a teacher."

"You want to become a teacher? You've killed all those people and now you want to become a teacher? Do you have any idea how insane that sounds?"

It wasn't so much the words coming out of Smithy's mouth as the expression on his face. He looked almost disgusted with her. Cilla felt something flood her system; it was akin to an adrenaline response but much less tolerable.

"What the fuck do you know?" she spat back at him. "You're just a fucking addict."

"That's right," Smithy replied. "I'm an addict. Every day is hard. Even if I never take heroin again, I'll always be an addict. It something that I have to come to terms with. But so do you. You can't just walk away and pretend that none of

127

it happened. You have to come to terms with it. You have to come to terms with yourself."

"And how do I do that?" Cilla demanded.

"How the fuck should I know?" Smithy replied. "That's your stuff, I've got my hands full dealing with my own stuff. In any case, it probably doesn't matter."

"What?" Cilla said indignantly. "You say all this shit and then you tell me it doesn't matter?"

Smithy smiled sadly. "Don't you understand?" he said. "You can get yourself a new identity but he'll still come after you. You're too valuable to him. I'm too valuable to him. He'll never let either of us go."

11

Metamorphosis III

Everything looked the same. The front gate was still missing
one hinge. The small house was as shabby and peeling as
she remembered it. The yard was still full of rusty broken
machinery. Could this really be the same lawnmower sat
waiting for its cutter blade to be replaced? The hen house still
occupied the back right-hand corner of the yard. It had five
scrawny residents. Presumably these were not the same five
chickens that had been there when she had last come home
for May Day. Those chickens and probably the ones that came
after that would have been dead and gone by now, consumed
with relish by a local fox. These must be different chickens.
But they looked the same.

Her mother was still wearing the same faded blue smock
that she had always worn. She still wrung her hands in the
same nervous way when she spoke. Her father was still hungover. Her older sister, Marta, had left home in order to work
in a factory in the city but this barely counted as a change.

Everything was the same. The only thing that was different was Tomas.

Tomas had grown into a big strapping boy. He had a low hairline and ruddy cheeks. He was now the same height as Cilla and his calves were considerably broader than hers. He seemed to have adopted a new masculine posture and stood with his feet planted wide and his arms folded in front of his chest. All the babyish charm and appeal had evaporated.

Tomas did not seem particularly pleased to see Cilla this time. He had become used to being an only child. During their first supper together he made no effort to engage with her. In fact he barely spoke at all and as soon as the meal was over he excused himself and retreated to his bedroom leaving Cilla and her mother to clear up.

"Where shall I sleep?" Cilla asked as she scraped the plates into a bucket. Her mother looked mildly flustered.

"Where you've always slept, with your brother," she replied.

"I don't think the bed is big enough for the two of us anymore," Cilla observed. "Why don't I take Marta's place on the sofa?"

"As you wish," her mother responded blankly.

The best and the worst thing about coming home was Luna. She frolicked and capered around Cilla's ankles, delighted that her young mistress had returned after so long away. Every time Cilla so much as glanced in her direction, Luna's tail thumped with joy. When they went to bed that night Luna refused to go up with Tomas, preferring to stay downstairs with Cilla. Tomas shot an ugly scowl in her direction but said nothing and trudged back upstairs.

There was very little to do during the day. Tomas went off to the same village school that Cilla had once attended. Her mother left early to work at the farm collective. Her father

130

never appeared downstairs before lunchtime and then, as far as Cilla could work out, spent rest of the day in his tiny shed preparing, fermenting and flavouring the moonshine that he both drank and sold to their neighbours. At least he was now earning a few kopeks from his alcoholism. That was different.

Cilla walked around the village a couple of times but there was very little to see. Everything was falling apart, as it had always been. During one of their rare conversations her father told her that he had heard there was a plan to "systemise" the whole area. This would involve razing all the villages in the region to the ground and replacing them with vast agro-industrial centres. He didn't seem to be very enthusiastic about the idea.

The village was set in a valley surrounded by higher ground on three sides. When she was younger Cilla had been forbidden to wander outside its perimeter; not that this edict would have actually stopped her had she really wanted to break it. But in the old days she generally had Tomas in tow and the little boy had refused to stray beyond the village boundaries. Now there was no-one to tell her where she could or could not go. After two days of tedium, hanging around and getting bored, Cilla decided to spend the rest of her two weeks at home exploring the local terrain. Each day she made a packed lunch of boiled eggs, cheese, bread, and a few meat scraps if there were any available. She put Luna on a long rope lead and the two of them left the house shortly after breakfast. They rarely returned home before nightfall.

Her newly acquired knowledge of plants and Botany was put to good use. On the first day Cilla found a couple of interesting specimens that would be worth taking back to school with her. She marked the places where she had found them with stones and branches and that evening she ransacked the house for anything she could use as makeshift plant pots. By

131

the following morning she was fully equipped with a series of cut-off cartons and plastic bottles with holes punched through the bottom for drainage. There was no gardening equipment in the house but she found an old wooden spoon and honed the ladle to a point so that she could use it to dig out plants. By the end of the first week there were nine transplanted specimens carefully arranged in the sunniest part of the backyard. Cilla was particularly excited about a patch of conium maculatum that she had found. They were young plants which hopefully meant that the presence of y-coniceine in their stems and foliage would be at its peak. She couldn't wait to take them back to school and show Comrade Ivanova. Tomas inspected the growing collection of plants each evening but he never asked Cilla anything about them.

Flora and fauna apart, spending her days with Luna climbing hills and descending into dells felt almost idyllic. The sun shone and the scenery was breathtaking. From the peak of the highest elevation the entire valley was stretched out before her. She could see not just her own village but a couple of other hamlets located nearby. The idea of demolishing these communities seemed rather sad. What would happen to all the villagers? Where would they live? Would they be expected to inhabit huge new concrete blocks like their city-dwelling proletariat brethren? And all this in the name of progress.

Luna was in her element. After the first day Cilla didn't bother with the rope lead anymore and Luna roamed at will, rushing this way and that, chasing rabbits, barking at squirrels, sniffing and digging to her heart's delight. On one occasion she nearly chased a rabbit over the edge of a small precipice. The rabbit dived over but Luna managed to stop just short of the edge. Cilla peered over the verge, interested to see if the animal had survived its suicidal leap. There was a drop of twelve metres or so to rocks and vegetation below but she couldn't see any sign of the rabbit. Perhaps its small body lay concealed amongst the bushes. Perhaps it had survived and run away. Cilla took note of the location of the precipice. It would come in useful later on.

No matter how absorbed Luna was in her new and exciting surroundings she always came when she was called. After a few hours of walking the two of them would take a rest and eat lunch together. Cilla divided up the rations equally but Luna always bolted hers down in seconds and then sat with her head on Cilla's lap staring up at her mistress with imploring soulful eyes. It was impossible to resist giving her titbits. After lunch Cilla would fill up Luna's water bowl and take a long cool draught from the bottle herself. Sometimes the two of them were so content that they fell asleep under a tree together lulled by the sound of insects and the breeze rustling through leaves.

The two weeks passed quickly; far too quickly. And still the deed was not done. All too soon it was the morning of the thirteenth day, the day before Cilla would return to school. She made a packed lunch as usual and left the house early with Luna skipping at her heels. That day Cilla brought the length of rope along with her again.

It had come as a complete surprise to everybody when Colonel Dubrovsky announced that there was to be a two-week holiday. Pupils would return to the homes of their families for a fortnight so that Academy 43 could be "refurbished". No-one was sure how to react to this news. Cilla felt ambivalent at the prospect of such a holiday. She had not been back to her place of birth for over two years. She no longer thought of it as home. Colonel Dubrovsky also instructed them to use their former names for the duration of the two weeks. They were strictly prohibited from revealing their new names to their families. None of this seemed to make much sense.

The day before she was due to leave Cilla was summoned to an interview with Professor Kuznetsova.

"How are you getting on?" Professor Kuznetsova enquired. As usual she was browsing through a file as she spoke. The file looked thicker now. Some of the pages were typed up, some were handwritten. What Cilla wouldn't give to be allowed to take a long look at this file herself.

"Well, I think," she replied cautiously.

Professor Kuznetsova nodded. "The reports from your teachers are positive. That's good. Are you looking forward to seeing your family?"

"Not really," Cilla replied.

"I see." Professor Kuznetsova closed the file and turned her full attention towards Cilla. "You have been set an assignment to complete during the two weeks that you are on holiday."

"Yes," said Cilla expectantly.

"You are to kill the dog Luna."

"Excuse me?"

"You are to kill the dog Luna," Professor Kuznetsova repeated.

"But why?" Cilla was bewildered. "What purpose does it serve?"

"It is a test of obedience, of loyalty and of discipline."

"But why Luna, why did you choose Luna?"

"I didn't choose Luna," Professor Kuznetsova replied. "You did."

A cold chill passed through Cilla: it seemed to start in her jaw and radiate internally like a pond freezing over. She could feel the hairs standing bolt upright on her arms and the back of her neck.

"This is your first mission as a Citizen of the Soviet State," Professor Kuznetsova continued, "and there are some parameters to this mission that I must make you aware of. Firstly, you are not to discuss your mission with anyone except me. Secondly, the target, which in this case is the dog Luna, is to be dispatched efficiently and discreetly. At this school you have been given the tools to perform such a task. Now it is your responsibility to put those tools to use. Thirdly, you must complete this mission without being identified as the perpetrator. The death must be perceived as an accident or due to natural causes. Do you have any questions?"

There were a thousand questions filling Cilla's head to the point that she thought it might burst but she limited herself to three.

"Can I change the target; perhaps I could kill my father or my mother instead?" she suggested desperately. "Surely that would provide better proof of my loyalty?"

"No," Professor Kuznetsova replied curtly.

Cilla moved on to her second question: "What happens if I refuse to do this?" she said.

"Then your life and the life of the dog Luna are forfeit," the Professor replied simply.

Cilla was silent for a moment, digesting the indigestible. There was just one more thing that she wanted to know.

"Has everyone been set an assignment like this?" she asked.

But Professor Kuznetsova merely shook her head.

"Oh Cilla, you know better than to ask that," she responded. "It is not your business. There is no fixed agenda at this school; no two pupils are treated the same: from each according to his ability, to each according to his need. That is one of the tenets of our great Socialist State. Do not concern yourself with the assignments of others. Concern yourself with completing the assignment that you yourself have been set. It is time to prove, once and for all, that you are worthy."

❦

It was a crisp bright day. Cilla chose a path that she and Luna had taken before. It loosely followed the course of a stream and was fringed with early wildflowers blooming under a canopy of birch and alder. Two hours of walking would bring them to a small glade where they could stop to eat. The glade was located not far from the precipice where Luna had nearly leapt off a week earlier.

When it was lunchtime Cilla gave Luna a smaller portion than usual and watched her gobble it up greedily. Then Cilla sat down with her back against the trunk of a tree, her bag by her side, her legs stretched out long and sure enough Luna came over and laid her head in Cilla's lap, gazing up at her mistress lovingly and expectantly. Cilla had prepared Luna a special treat. She had stolen some of her mother's raw sausage mix, not too much, not so that anyone would notice; just enough to divide into five small pellets. Into each of these pellets she had inserted two of the ten milligrams of diazepam that she had been allowed to bring home with her. It wasn't enough to kill Luna, but it would put her into a deep sleep. Cilla fed them slowly to the dog, lingering over each one. Then she scratched behind Luna's ears, stroked the top of her head and crooned nonsense at her. After half an hour the dog felt heavy in Cilla's lap. She called her name a couple of times and flicked Luna's nose but the dog did not stir. It was time. Cilla took the length of rope out of the bag beside her. She wrapped it twice around Luna's neck and began to tighten her hold. Luna's body twitched a few times but this was probably just a reflex reaction. Cilla maintained her grip for a count of two hundred as she had been taught. Then she placed the rope carefully on to the ground and continued to sit stroking Luna's head. Cilla sat there for a long time until the day and the corpse began to turn cold. Then she fashioned the length of rope into a harness around Luna's chest, stood up and began to drag the dog's body towards the precipice.

It was dusk by the time Cilla reached the verge. She untied the rope from Luna's body and rolled the corpse over the edge. It hit the ground below with a heavy thud. When Cilla leant over she could just make out the shape of the carcass in the fading light. She turned and began to walk back to the village.

When she arrived at the house the others were already eating dinner in the small low kitchen. Her mother had made dumplings filled with sausage.

"You're late," her father noted wiping his mouth with the back of his hand. "We started without you."

"Where's Luna?" Tomas asked trying to adopt the same gruff tone as his father.

"There was an accident," Cilla replied.

"Where is she?" Tomas repeated.

"She was chasing a rabbit. It went over the edge. She couldn't stop. She went over after it."

"What are you saying?" Tomas demanded. He had stood up and was clenching and unclenching his fists repeatedly.

"Luna's dead," Cilla said.

"No I don't believe you," Tomas yelled. Even though he wasn't crying, his face had started to turn blotchy.

"I'm sorry Tomas. Luna's dead. She chased a rabbit over a verge. She couldn't stop."

Thomas charged at Cilla and pushed her back against the wall. He began landing flabby punches on her face and torso, shouting as he did: "You killed her! You killed her!" Cilla did not attempt to defend herself. "You're evil. I know you killed her."

She took the blows. They weren't very hard. It wasn't as if it were Alexei or one of the big boys beating down on her. There wouldn't be any broken ribs today. It was just Tomas; little baby Tomas; sobbing and wailing as always. Her father pulled him off. He put his arms around Tomas, half restraining, half comforting.

"You're leaving tomorrow," her father said giving Cilla a grim cold look. It was a statement rather than a question.

"Yes," Cilla replied. "The car will pick me up early. Before any of you are awake."

"Well then. Let's sit down and eat. I don't want any more fuss about the damn dog."

Cilla was up before dawn. It didn't take her long to organise her belongings. She found an old cardboard box in the kitchen and took it outside to pack up the plants. But someone had emptied them out of their makeshift pots and stamped on them all during the night. It was probably Tomas who had done it, but this was by no means certain. It might have been her mother or her father, and frankly, who could blame the culprit anyway?

She arrived back at school at lunchtime. The place was very quiet. Lessons did not begin formally until the following day and many of the pupils had not yet returned. As the day wore on they turned up in dribs and drabs but there were still lots of absent faces. One of these was Amelia. Cilla went to the greenhouses and to the target range but she found that she couldn't concentrate on any activity. She just kept wanting to return to her dormitory to check if Amelia had come back yet. Suppertime came and went but there was no sign of her friend. In the evening Cilla watched two episodes of *The Good Life* with one of the others from her English specialisation group. Still Amelia did not return. Instead of going to bed at the appointed time Cilla made her way to Comrade Guseva's room and knocked on the door.

"What is it?" Comrade Guseva said abruptly when she saw Cilla standing there in the corridor. "You should be in bed by now. Are you ill?"

"I'm sorry to bother you," Cilla began. She knew that she was likely to get more information out of her form teacher if she made an effort to be polite. "I just wondered if you knew when Amelia Fleming is getting back?"

"I'm not sure," Comrade Guseva replied. "Some pupils have a dispensation to spend an extra couple of days with their families."

"But why?" Cilla persevered.

"To attend funerals," her teacher replied. "Now get back to your dormitory immediately. You have an early start in the morning."

That made sense. It also answered Cilla's third question, the one that Professor Kuznetsova had ignored. Everyone had been set assignments when they went back to see their families and the assignments were all the same.

Cilla spent the next two days anticipating and preparing for Amelia's return. She knew that Amelia would probably be upset, maybe even distraught. Although these were emotive states of mind that didn't mean very much to Cilla she understood well enough that a person in such a state might cry and require comforting. Some of the other pupils had been behaving rather oddly since their return and at least three had been sent to the infirmary for bed rest. Cilla put clean sheets on the upper bunk for Amelia. After classes she made copies of her notes so that Amelia would not fall behind. She even put an illicit vase of wildflowers on Amelia's nightstand. But days passed, the flowers began to wilt and still Amelia did not return.

Eventually Cilla sought out Comrade Guseva again.

"Has Amelia attended the funeral yet? When is she coming back?" This time Cilla forgot to be polite.

Comrade Guseva was marking homework. She had a large pile of exercise books beside her, each open to the same page. She closed one book, took up the next and began decorating the page with a series of red ticks and crosses.

"Amelia Fleming isn't coming back," the teacher replied.

"But you said she was at a funeral."

Comrade Guseva put down her pen. "I said no such thing. I said that some pupils had dispensations to attend funerals. It turns out that Amelia Fleming was not one of these. She will not be returning to the Academy."

"Where is she?"

Now Comrade Guseva began to look irritated. "That's quite enough Cilla. I have nothing further to say. I'm extremely busy. If you want to know more then take it up with the Colonel, but I really wouldn't recommend doing that. He will not be impressed with you for asking questions about matters that are no concern of yours."

But Cilla wasn't listening anymore. About halfway through her teacher's diatribe she turned tail and walked away. She went outside to the greenhouses. There was no-one else there. Cilla went into the kitchen greenhouse, closed her eyes and leant her forehead against the glass frame. It felt cool against her hot skin. In her head she returned to the moment when she had rolled Luna's body over the edge of the precipice and it had landed with a dull thump on the ground below. In that instant she had seriously considered diving head-first after her. Now she wished she had.

"Cilla!"

She heard her name being called and opened her eyes. Comrade Ivanova was walking towards the greenhouse and waving. Cilla put her hand up to wave back but instead she clenched her fist and smashed it straight through the pane of glass.

❧

She woke up in a small single room in the infirmary. She was in a cot-like bed and her left arm was bandaged as far as the elbow. It hurt. Professor Kuznetsova was sitting on a chair on one side of the bed.

"Well you gave us quite a fright," she said. "How are you feeling?"

Cilla did not reply.

"You are very fortunate that there was no nerve damage. You should regain full use of your hand and arm."

Cilla said nothing.

"Now I want to talk about what actually happened."

Silence.

"Comrade Ivanova tells me that she saw the whole thing and that it was an accident. She says that you tripped and put your hand out to break your fall, that it went through a pane of glass. Is that correct?"

She paused. "Is that correct? Cilla, I need you to corroborate her version of events. Otherwise I'll have to launch an official enquiry."

Cilla opened her mouth to respond.

"Where is Amelia Fleming?" she said.

"That's not what I'm here to discuss. You need to confirm what happened in the greenhouse."

"Is she dead?"

"You know that I can't give you any information about

141

Amelia. She has left Academy 43. That is all you need to know."

"Where is she?"

"Cilla, I am not here to talk about Amelia. I am here to find out what took place in the kitchen greenhouse. Comrade Ivanova says that you accidentally put your hand through a pane of glass. Can you confirm this?

But Cilla merely shut her eyes and turned her face to the wall.

Professor Kuznetsova did her best. She coaxed, she cajoled, she wheedled and she threatened, but all to no avail. After a while she went out of the room and Cilla was left alone with her thoughts.

She no longer cared about what would happen to her. Although she was injured and helpless the fact of her indifference instilled in Cilla a sense of calm and power. Perhaps Colonel Dubrovsky and Professor Kuznetsova would decide that they had had enough of her. Perhaps they would send an armed guard to escort her to the target practice range and tie her to a pole. It really didn't matter anymore. Nothing mattered. As long as she kept her arm still it didn't hurt too much and she could just float away in her mind.

"I have been given permission to provide you with some information about Amelia Fleming." The sound of Professor Kuznetsova's harsh voice intruded on Cilla's reverie. She flicked open her eyes and turned towards the professor.

"She has been sent to a school in Moscow that has links with the Serbsky Centre. If all goes well she will train to be a doctor."

Cilla mulled over this information for a moment. "I don't believe you," she said. "I think she's dead."

"Why would she be dead?" Professor Kuznetsova sounded exasperated.

"You told me my life was forfeit if I didn't kill Luna. I am assuming that you told Amelia the same thing. Except in her case her target was her mother. But I know perfectly well that Amelia isn't capable of killing anyone, least of all her mother. Which means her life is forfeit and she's dead." It was difficult to refute Cilla's logic.

"What you say is true," Professor Kuznetsova admitted. "But in Amelia's case a degree of leniency was applied."

"Why?"

"Because of her particular capabilities. It was decided that it would not be in the State's interests for her talents to go to waste because of one mistake."

"I want to talk to her."

"Cilla, you know that's impossible."

"I want to talk to her. I want to know that you're telling the truth."

It took Cilla two more days of blank shut-eyed silence to persuade the powers that be to fulfil her request. But eventually she found herself sitting in Professor Kuznetsova's office holding a telephone receiver for the very first time. It was a short conversation. Amelia was well. She liked her new school. Her mother was alive. There wasn't much else to say.

Afterwards, when things were more normal, Cilla wondered how it was that the school authorities had allowed her so much licence. In the past children had been removed for much lesser misdemeanours. But looking around the classroom during an English lesson she suspected that she knew the reason why. The class was half-empty. Over fifty percent of the children who had been on the course had not returned from their "holiday". Apart from Amelia, Cilla didn't know where any of them were, she didn't know if leniency had been dispensed towards each of them. The school had miscalculated; it had not anticipated the loss of so many students.

143

It was the good ones that had been lost as well. Alexei and his bovine compatriots had no difficulty in completing their assignments, but all the Amelias were gone. That's why the school had pandered to Cilla's requests. They couldn't really afford to lose another one.

And after all, she had completed her mission successfully.

12

Truth

Amy Levine. Age: 35. Height: 1 metre 70. Weight: 57 kilos. Colouring: Fair. IQ: 125 (estimate). Education: Degree level. Family: Married to Paul Levine, 2 Children: Michael, (age 7) Samantha (age 5). Hobbies: Tennis, yoga, reading. Congenital problems: None. Ailments: None. Vices: None. She didn't even take sugar in her coffee.

How do you kill someone like that?

Over the next few weeks Cilla's life settled into an odd sort of pattern. During the week she continued her research into the life and works of Amy Levine. She had compiled so much information on the woman she could have written her biography. Not that any of it helped. At the weekends she went to raves with Nancy and worked out some of her frustration on the dance floor. Her hair grew. One Saturday, on a whim, she shaved it all off again, leaving two tufts on either side of her head. These she sprayed gold and fashioned into small horns. Nancy loved it. Cilla saw Keith a few more times at various warehouse parties. There was always a pull between them. Sometimes they would end up kissing and touching. On one occasion they had sex in a rather dirty toilet cubicle. She didn't let him know that it was her first time; what would have been the point? Perhaps he could tell. Cilla wasn't sure if her lack of experience was apparent and whether sex was something you got better at with practice, like archery. Keith was nice enough afterwards but somehow it was never quite the same as it had been on the balcony at the Fulham Studios. The velvet abyss stayed closed.

Even though the Mint wasn't yet ready Vladimir Haugr did not fulfil his promise to impale Smithy on an iron railing via his rectum. There were negotiations between the two of them and an uneasy truce was reached. Cilla acted as the go-between and managed to broker an extra month's extension for Smithy. When he wasn't working on the Mint Smithy peddled large quantities of counterfeit postage stamps in an attempt to accumulate some savings of his own. He was still clean so the money that had previously been used to fund his habit could also be stashed away. Perhaps he was building up a getaway fund of his own.

"I've got something for you," he said one day when Cilla was sitting in his kitchen drinking tea. She often came round to see him now, and not just on the orders of her employer. Smithy handed her a passport. It was burgundy red, crisp and new. She ran the tips of her fingers over the golden lion and unicorn on the front cover, read the inscription below: "Dieu et Mon Droit" and flicked through to the data page. There was her photo, insipid, unsmiling, looking like anybody. And there was her new name, or rather her old name, at least a part of it anyway.

"Sorry it's taken me so long," Smithy said. "It was difficult to find a match with the name you wanted."

"No matter," Cilla replied. "How are you getting on with the other things I asked for?"

"Still working on them," Smithy admitted. "You just need to give me a bit more time."

Time, always an issue; there never seemed to be enough of it. Two months had passed since she had fed the ducks with Paul Levine in St James's Park and the fact of the matter was that Cilla was no closer to writing The Story and creating a viable, believable ending for his wife than she had been when Paul Levine had first handed her his white plastic bag. Cilla had done her research, she had examined all the options. She had even sifted through the contents of the Levine residence in her quest to find a suitable method to kill Amy Levine. She didn't have to break in, Paul had given her a set of keys. Once Cilla had identified the family's routine it was merely a case of letting herself in through the front door and turning off the burglar alarm when she knew that they would all be out for at least a couple of hours.

It was an early Victorian townhouse, white, terraced, set right onto the street and separated from the pavement by three steps, a wrought iron gate and a set of black shiny railings. The house was situated on the west side of a private square. There were four storeys to the building. The basement housed a TV room and a large kitchen diner. The most interesting aspect of the kitchen, from Cilla's perspective, was the contents of the larder and of the fridge. There were all the usual middle-class staples: muesli, organic chicken, wine, hummus. The challenge was to find some delicate morsel with which she could poison Amy Levine. But there were two difficulties with this plan. The first was that Cilla needed to identify an edible that was consumed by Amy Levine and only Amy Levine. It would be embarrassing and unprofessional if the wrong person died or if all of them died. The second was that it would be necessary to use a toxin which would induce fatal symptoms that could be attributed to a natural cause. If Amy Levine ate an olive, started vomiting green bile and dropped down dead there would be an autopsy which might then lead to a murder investigation.

What about an accident instead? Perhaps Amy Levine could fall down the stairs. It was a four-storey house, there were a lot of stairs. But such a fall might not kill her. OK, so if she fell down the stairs and if it didn't kill her Cilla would break her neck in such a manner as would be consistent with the fall. But this was a tricky manoeuvre to pull off. If she got it even slightly wrong a good pathologist would identify the anomaly. No, the stairs were out.

How about electrocution, another common cause of domestic fatalities? Cilla was in the master bedroom now examining the contents of Amy Levine's wardrobe. She kept a hairdryer on the floor in there along with her collection of shoes. Could Cilla short-circuit the dryer so that it gave Mrs Levine a fatal shock when she next attempted to use it? It was an option, but again the shock might not kill her. And there was always the possibility that Samantha might come and play with Mummy's hairdryer before Mummy had a chance to use it. The electric shock would definitely kill a five-year-old and that wouldn't do at all.

The problem of trying to arrange a Dry Job within the confines of the Levines' home was that there were too many variables involved and it was impossible to control them all. As Cilla punched the code into the alarm, let herself out of the house and double-locked the door behind her she knew that she would have to think again.

There was also another issue that Cilla was becoming dimly aware of. The more closely she examined Amy Levine's life the more Cilla began to find herself experiencing an odd

sense of something; a something that she was not really familiar with; an inconvenient something. Was it possible that this
something was sympathy?

Sympathy: the act or capacity for sharing in an emotion
belonging to another.

Yes, Amy Levine was smug and entitled. She lived in an
urban middle-class bubble and was aware of nothing outside
her pampered little world. But Cilla sometimes found herself
experiencing a sense of rapport with her intended victim. In
her funny little way Amy Levine had a certain amount of
pluck, a quality which Cilla admired and approved of. Mrs
Levine took her tennis very seriously; she was part of a box
league at her club. At least a couple of times a week she played
singles, and frequently her opponent was a man. She was
fast and scrappy around the court and never admitted defeat
until she was shaking her opponent's hand over the net. She
spent no time whatsoever with Paul Levine. Their marriage
had clearly disintegrated but she held her head up high and
soldiered on. She never looked tired or bitter. And she was a
good mother. She took her children to school in the morning,
she picked them up most afternoons. She and Matilde, the au
pair, acted as a team; shopping, cooking and cleaning; fer-
rying the children back and forth to the various activities in
which middle-class children engage. Once a week Amy went
out in the evening to her book club. Occasionally she had
dinner with a friend. If the kids were going to lose a parent
it would be far preferable that they lost their father rather
than their mother. Paul Levine was hardly ever there. He left
the house before the children were awake in the morning
and returned long after they had gone to bed. He frequently
worked at weekends.

Cilla thought back to her first meeting with Paul Levine
during which he had confided that he was in love with

149

Matilde and planned to marry her once his wife was out of the way. At the time this scenario had seemed unlikely; now it looked like pure fantasy. The only evidence that Cilla had found of any sort of relationship between the two of them was in Paul Levine's study. A quantity of Matilde's underwear was stuffed into the lower drawer of his desk hidden underneath papers. Cilla knew it belonged to Matilde from the bra size and the Spanish labelling. Now it was quite possible that Matilde had given this underwear to Paul but from what Cilla had observed it seemed more likely that he had stolen it. Paul was clearly sleeping in the study as well. The little sofa bed in there was made up and the rumpled duvet and sheets bore testament to recent use.

It struck Cilla that nothing, so far, that Paul Levine had said had turned out to be true. His wife wasn't having an affair; nor was he. Were these lies that he was telling or were they delusions? The only way to find out would be to subject him to closer scrutiny. So Cilla decided to leave Amy Levine alone for a while and to concentrate on Paul Levine instead.

She started tailing him the following morning. In some ways he had a fairly predictable routine. He left home at 6 a.m. and took the District line tube to Mansion House. He stopped off briefly to pick up breakfast and entered the Gerrard building by seven. After that the day became less predictable. He was forever popping out from the office, always to meet someone and rarely the same person twice. He would have coffee with one individual, lunch with another. Sometimes a meeting would simply consist of a two-minute conversation in the street and a handshake. All of the people that he met looked much like him: city boys in expensive suits. When he left the office at the end of the day he never went straight home. There were drinks and dinners with more associates followed by strip joints and nightclubs. There was something odd and suspicious about the continual rendezvous but nothing that Cilla could really put her finger on. This went on for about a week and Cilla was beginning to lose heart until finally, one evening, events took an interesting turn. On that day Paul Levine made his way to Covent Garden after work. He went into a pub and sat nursing half a pint of lager at the bar. He was clearly waiting for someone. When that someone finally turned up Cilla recognised him. It was one of Vlad's boys, which could mean only one thing: Paul Levine was buying cocaine.

It fitted: the twitching, the bad temper, the paranoia. When Cilla thought about it Paul Levine came across as a fairly typical coke fiend. But the strange thing was that no exchange took place, nothing was passed. The two men just sat and chatted for a while. Then they went their separate ways, that was all.

Paul Levine proceeded to take a route through Chinatown towards Soho. He lingered outside some of the sex shops and girlie bars but he didn't go in. It looked as if he was just killing time. Finally at about nine he cut down Dean Street and started walking with more purpose. When he hit Oxford Street he turned right and Cilla realised that she knew where he was headed. Paul was going to pick up a package. He wasn't a coke fiend, or he wasn't just a coke fiend, he was a dealer as well.

Sure enough he turned left on to Rathbone Place and ducked into the private car park that Vlad owned there. This was a regular pick-up point. Cilla lurked in a doorway and ten minutes later the stockbroker came out again carrying a familiar-looking black holdall. Cilla had seen these holdalls a hundred times. Vlad bought them in bulk. She had even been given a guided tour around one of his packing operations where the product was neutralised, tried and tested, cut with

151

a combination of caffeine and laundry detergent and packed into the black holdalls. Each holdall contained four kilos. If Paul Levine was buying four kilos then he was a serious player. He wasn't just some City street dealer supplying his friends on the exchange floor, he was a major customer. In turn this meant that Vladimir Haugr knew him personally. Vlad didn't just sell a black holdall to anyone, he would have vetted Paul Levine himself. This was interesting. It revealed a direct link between the two men.

Now the constant meetings and the rendezvous began to make sense. They were just drugs deals. The reason that Cilla had failed to identify them as such was because although it was obvious now that the coke was being passed via the handshakes, she had never actually seen any money change hands. Paul Levine was distributing nose candy but he wasn't getting hard cash in return. What was that all about? What was it that he was getting instead?

Cilla followed the stockbroker to Tottenham Court Road station. He boarded an eastbound Central line tube towards Epping. He clearly had no intention of going home anytime soon. He got off the train at Woodford and Cilla tailed him to a lock-up garage. Now she had seen enough. The lock-up must be his storage facility, the place where he would cut and carve. Given that he had four kilos in that holdall he might be there all night. She doubled back to the tube station with the intention of heading home. She could take the Central line all the way to Shepherds Bush. But as she sat on the tube, watching strangers board and depart, enjoying the resonance and the reverberation, she was struck with a sudden urge to get off at Holland Park. From there it was only a ten-minute walk to the Levines' house.

The square was dark and quiet. It was nearly midnight now and all the lights in the house were off except for one burning in the kitchen but it was impossible to see into the basement from the street level. Cilla looked up and down the street; there was no-one around. It was a fairly simple matter for her to climb over the railings and lower herself down. She backed into the shadows and edged out cautiously so that she had a clear view of what was going on in the basement.

What she saw was worth the effort. Amy Levine sat alone at the kitchen table absorbed in an intricate task. To all intents and purposes she was hulling a bowl of cherries. She put the flesh of the cherries into one bowl and the stones into a second bowl. But it was clear that her interest was in the stones rather than the fruit. One after another, she placed each stone on a large thick chopping board and crushed it with a hammer. She examined each result. Some of the crushed stones were discarded back into the bowl but occasionally she found a pit to her liking. When this happened Amy picked out the pieces of shell with her fingernails and began to chop and crush the remaining contents of the pit with a small sharp implement, possibly a razor blade. She chopped and crushed until the contents of the stone had transformed into a grainy paste. This she scraped up with the side of the razor blade and deposited into a small glass jar.

Just as interesting as the activity was the look on Amy Levine's face. The bright eager countenance that she usually wore for interacting with the world had gone; the mask had been removed. And beneath it was an expression of pure fury.

Cilla thought back to Amy Levine's Filofax and her enigmatic resolutions for the year: "Hold it together", and "Keep to the plan".

She smiled to herself; now she understood. She quite liked Amy Levine's plan. It was simple and straightforward. Perhaps, with a little thought and consideration, it could be incorporated into Cilla's own plan.

153

"You shall know the truth and the truth shall make you free."

Philosophy was all well and good, but it was hard to beat the Bible for summing up those really epic moments.

13

Missions

Academy 43 was never the same after that first mission. There were significant changes. Someone had to take responsibility for the loss of so many able pupils and the obvious scapegoat was the headmaster. Like so many children before him one day Colonel Dubrovsky just disappeared and no-one spoke of him again. Professor Kuznetsova also lost her position as Director of Operations and was reassigned elsewhere. Cilla wondered to what extent she had been responsible for the Professor's demotion. It felt like a victory of sorts. She hoped that the Professor had been stripped of her title and was just plain old Comrade again. Cilla liked to imagine Comrade Kuznetsova in some dingy office, somewhere cold and depressing, performing some boring clerical task for a job that never ever brought her into contact with children.

Not all of those pupils who had successfully completed their first mission remained at the Academy. There were further absences and losses. One boy committed suicide. He crept out during the night and hanged himself from a tree with his bedsheet. This was not officially acknowledged by the school but everybody knew what had happened.

Cilla kept herself to herself. She did not try to make any new friends. She didn't believe in friendship any longer, she didn't believe in anything. It was hard to even accept the existence of other people. Everyone around her seemed to have become somehow hollow and unreal; walking, talking automatons without density or substance. They didn't matter. She didn't matter either. It was as if she carried a vast expanse of emptiness insider herself, a ruined wasteland of nothing. She told no-one of this; she simply continued with her usual routine. She attended assembly, she did her lessons and spent the rest of her time on the target range or in the greenhouses with the plants. The broken pane in the kitchen greenhouse was replaced. The only evidence of the incident which had taken place there were the long thin scars which ran from wrist to elbow on Cilla's left arm. Comrade Ivanova tried to talk to her a few times about what had happened but Cilla resisted her overtures. She didn't know why Comrade Ivanova had lied about the "accident" with the glass and she didn't want to know. She didn't care anymore, about that or about anything else. After a while Comrade Ivanova gave up trying to draw Cilla out but she still welcomed her presence and her help with the plants. All conversation between them was strictly horticultural.

With so many children gone the bunkers seemed vast and desolate. There were only three girls left in Cilla's dormitory which had a capacity for six. The one next door was empty. After a couple of weeks she moved up to the top bunk where Amelia had slept. A few of Amelia's belongings had been left behind and these now became Cilla's. There was noth-ing very personal in the collection of clothes and trinkets but Cilla kept a couple of them. There was an old shirt of Amelia's that Cilla liked to wear to bed. The best item of all was a small green oval pendant which could be hung from a chain. Cilla didn't have a chain so she threaded it onto some string and wore it sometimes under her uniform. One day when she was fiddling with it, Cilla's thumbnail slipped into a crevice on the side of the pendant and it split. For a moment Cilla thought that it was broken but then she realised that the pendant was actually a locket and she had simply opened it. There was nothing inside. But Cilla knew exactly what to put in there. She had kept the tiny charred piece of paper from her renaming ceremony safe for nearly two years and now it had a home. The nail on her thumb where she had held the piece of paper and refused to let go had borne the worst of the burn. It was still scarred. The nail bed was deformed and the keratin that grew out of it was gnarled and thickened. The skin around the bed was hyper-pigmented; pink and livid. It wasn't very pretty. But Cilla wasn't bothered; she liked her scars. In her mind they were part of her collection of precious possessions. The locket, the piece of paper, her nail, the marks on her arms, these were all evidence of her identity, of the choices that she had made, rather than the ones that had been made for her.

The bunkers did not stay empty for very long. After several weeks, six truckloads of new occupants turned up without warning. But these were not children, nor were they psychiatric patients; they were military personnel. Academy 43 was no longer a school. It had reverted to its original purpose as an army barracks. Cilla and the other remaining children were simply absorbed into the new regime.

In a sense, when Cilla thought about it, Academy 43 had never really been a school at all. There had only ever been one intake of children. After the first couple of months

157

of selection no new children ever arrived. They only left. No, it wasn't a school at all. That was clear now. It was an experiment.

A new regime meant new leadership and Colonel Dubrovsky was duly replaced by Major General Barkov. The leadership may have changed but the rhetoric remained the same. Major General Barkov conducted Assembly each morning just as his predecessor had done. He made long fervent speeches about world revolution and its ultimate aim to construct a utopia of brotherhood and justice. He was particularly fond of the term "True Believer" which was sprinkled liberally into his discourse.

Some of the teachers remained at the Academy. But with fewer children the classes were smaller in size so all the classrooms were partitioned down the middle with plywood. The purpose of this was to improve the efficient use of space but in reality it had the opposite effect. The plywood did little to block the noise coming from the neighbouring lesson and Cilla found it hard to concentrate on Maths when she could hear some noisy Sergeant barking at his privates next door.

The English Specialisation group was particularly depleted; only four of the original cohort remained. But three years of intense tuition had served its purpose. Each of them spoke English fluently with no trace of Slav in their intonation. They knew far more about British culture, politics and current events than their genuine counterparts in the UK. Not only could they identify Margaret Thatcher as the British Prime Minister, they could name all the members of her cabinet as well. They read British newspapers, usually a week out of date, and English literature. They had their favourite television programmes and their favourite pop bands. In short, they were ready.

158

At the end of six months Cilla was invited to an interview with Major General Barkov and found herself seated in the waiting room outside his office listening to the rhythmic clicking of his secretary's typewriter. A buzzer sounded and the secretary stopped typing.

"You can go in now," she said pleasantly to Cilla.

Cilla opened the door to the adjoining office and entered. She was not entirely sure how to greet the Major General so she gave a tentative salute and clicked her heels together, standing straight with her chest thrust forward as she had seen the privates do on parade.

It was the same office that Colonel Dubrovsky had occupied but it looked different now, more elaborate and ornate. Major General Barkov had brought his own desk with him: a huge piece of furniture constructed from a rich dark wood with a rectangle of green leather embossed with gold stretched over the flat surface of its top. He had adorned the walls as well. There were photographs of Lenin, Brezhnev and other venerable men that Cilla did not recognise along with several framed certificates identifying the Major General's achievements in service to the Motherland.

"You may sit," the Major General announced.

Cilla took her place on the low chair in front of his desk.

"Cilla Wilson," he said slowly and awkwardly. "This is now your name."

Cilla nodded.

"You will address me as your commanding officer and respond accordingly when you are spoken to," Major General Barkov reminded her sternly.

"Yes, General Comrade General," Cilla replied.

"You completed your first mission successfully six months ago," he went on.

"Yes, General Comrade General."

"You killed a dog." The Major General did not sound impressed.

"I eliminated the target that had been assigned to me, General Comrade General."

"A dog," Major General Barkov repeated.

"Yes, General Comrade General."

"I did not approve the training programme for Academy 43." Major General Barkov declared. "In fact I spoke out against it. It was rash, foolhardy; trying to mould young reprobates to be Heroes of the Socialist State." He shook his head. "And it appears that my concerns were justified. The programme has not been a success." He shook his head again. "Here I am left with the stragglers trying to work out what to do with them."

Cilla was silent. There didn't seem much point in agreeing with him.

"What are your specialities?" the Major General enquired.

"English, Botany, Toxicology, Cold weapons and Evasion, General Comrade General," Cilla replied.

"How good is your English?"

"Fluent, General Comrade General."

"Can you pass for English?"

"I believe so, General Comrade General."

"You believe so. Well, I suppose that will have to do. I think it's time we put your training to the test. I'm going to assign you a second mission to complete," Major General Barkov stated.

"Yes, General Comrade General."

"It'll be a proper target this time. No animals involved. You are a covert agent for the Socialist State not a bloody butcher."

"Yes, General Comrade General."

The meeting was over. Cilla felt more energised and

160

positive than she had done in months. A second mission; it was an unexpected gift. She could think of nothing that would give her more fulfilment and satisfaction than the opportunity to complete a second mission.

The target was identified as a forty-five-year-old writer living in Cambridge. Since defecting to the West, Sergei Milov had been working as a journalist and broadcaster for Radio Free Europe. He had used this forum to conduct a vitriolic campaign against various incumbent Socialist regimes. One of his favourite criticisms was to rail against the hypocrisy of the Communist system by identifying the lavish lifestyles of those in power in comparison to the privations suffered by the ordinary worker. He had even made a short series entitled: *Mansions of the Inner Circle*, an entire programme of which had been devoted to describing the forty-room villa in Snagov, Romania, owned by Nicolae and Elena Ceauşescu. It was most embarrassing. The man was not important as such, but he was an irksome thorn in the side of the Motherland and her allies and it had been agreed that he should be eliminated. The codename for his file was: Architect.

As part of the mission Cilla was asked to plan the assassination in detail: access, method, mode of delivery and exit strategy. There was no guarantee that her proposal would be used at all but she knew that it would be examined closely by her superiors and if they liked it then this would be a feather in her cap, whether they used her suggestions or not.

It felt good to have purpose. Cilla spent all her spare time for the next week preparing and constructing her proposal. She studied maps of Europe, working out her route of travel. She consulted Comrade Guseva on toxins and mode of delivery. She spoke at length with Captain Antonovich about the pros and cons of various small weapons. After five days and very little sleep her plan was complete.

She would travel to East Berlin and cross to the West by road at the Helmstedt–Berlin autobahn as part of a legitimate Soviet military patrol. Once inside West Berlin she would assume her identity as Cilla Wilson and make her way over the border to Belgium. From there she would fly to the UK and travel directly to Cambridge.

The toxin she would use would be ricin. It would be inserted into a platinum/iridium pellet coated with a solid sugar crust designed to melt at 37 degrees Celsius, the human body temperature. She would use a retractable spring-loaded guiding pin as the mode of delivery, aiming for the back of the thigh or the buttock area. The pin would also contain a dose of anaesthetic which should mask the act of insertion, at least partially, and control localised pain for a couple of hours. Once the ricin dispersed the target would die in four to five days probably due to kidney or liver failure. The advantage of this slow method was that by the time the man was dead, even if the pellet was found during autopsy, the ricin itself would no longer be detectable, and Cilla would have returned behind the Iron Curtain.

Using a guiding pin would involve direct contact with the target. Cilla would spend a few days doing surveillance, study his routine and engineer a close-quarters encounter in the street. As a final touch Cilla suggested that she might pose as a schoolgirl in uniform. She hoped very much that the authorities would appreciate her attention to detail.

Waiting for a response from Major General Barkov was excruciating. Cilla kept running through the finer points of the proposal in her mind. Was ricin an appropriate agent? Had she planned her route properly? Was the suggestion that she dress as a schoolgirl ridiculous? All the time there was this nagging doubt, like toothache, that the plan wasn't good enough to bear scrutiny. And what would happen to Cilla if her superiors assessed her proposal as sub-standard, lacking in merit or, worst of all, unsound? Now that Cilla had received this gift, she was vested in it; she wanted the chance to unwrap it and keep it for herself. She also had a strong feeling that this mission represented her last chance. If she failed, at any point, it would be the end.

Two full weeks passed before she heard anything but then, jubilation, her proposal was accepted; but with one significant amendment. Since she was still only fourteen years old, Cilla would require an escort.

The person selected to accompany Cilla on her mission was Junior Sergeant Irina Petkovic. She was a forty-two-year-old career soldier who had spent the last ten years working at a desk job in foreign communication analysis. She was chosen for three reasons. Firstly, her record was exemplary, her loyalty beyond doubt; secondly, she spoke passable English and German; and thirdly, she fitted the physical requirements of the role. For the purpose of the mission she would be issued with a British passport in the name of Pauline Wilson. Cilla was instructed to address her as "Mum".

Cilla did not relish the prospect of an escort. She did not want some low-level sergeant muscling in on her proposal, telling her what to do and taking credit for the mission if it was a success. But once she actually met Mum she realised that her fears were unjustified. Mum was nothing more than a slightly sluggish office clerk, calm, phlegmatic, trained to do what she was told, to take orders not to give them. Even though Mum had never travelled outside the Soviet Union before she appeared to take the prospect of a covert expedition to Western Europe in her stride. She did not even sit in on the meetings that Cilla had with Major General Barkov and a couple of others as they thrashed out the details of the mission. Mum was just a subordinate, a fully paid-up Party member, a tiny cog turning repeatedly in the giant machine of Socialism. As an escort, she was ideal.

Except for one thing. Whoever had evaluated Mum's English as passable had, in Cilla's opinion, made a serious error. She understood the language well enough but she could not speak it competently. Her accent was heavy and guttural, her diction was laboured. In conversation her word order was unreliable. There was not enough time to try and improve Mum's English before the trip so Cilla concentrated on teaching her to say key words and phrases perfectly, like a parrot.

Mum mastered the proper pronunciation for "Yes", "No", "Please" and "Thanks" quite quickly. Then they moved on to some necessary stock phrases.

"Here you go."

"That would be lovely."

"I'd like a twin room please, paying cash."

"Cilla love, could you give me a hand?"

And the most important one of all, which was not a phrase as such but a collaboration between the two of them, to be initiated by Cilla when Mum looked as though she was in danger of getting out of her depth.

"Can I do it, Mum?"

"Go on then love." A small smile aimed towards the waitress, shop assistant, passport control officer, or any other individual involved in the interaction. "Do you mind if my daughter takes over? She does so love to be in charge."

Mum lay on one of the twin single beds, propped up with pillows, eating crisps and watching *Dallas* on the hotel television.

164

Cilla sat on the other bed writing up her notes for Sergei Milov in coded shorthand. Although she had attended a course on the subject she had never actually conducted live surveillance before. Mostly it just involved hanging around Sergei Milov's address during daylight hours and making sure that she remained inconspicuous. She didn't need to know where he was all the time, she just logged his comings and goings and followed him around a bit on foot. Now she had four days' worth of analysis and a pattern had emerged. As a freelance writer and broadcaster he mainly worked from home, a top-floor flat on Bateman Street, close to Cambridge station. But he appeared, fairly predictably, at least a couple of times a day. On three of the four mornings he had strolled to the local newsagents to buy a paper sometime between 8.30 and 10 a.m. On one day he had taken a train to London. Cilla hadn't bothered to follow him; instead she took the afternoon off. On two of the days he had appeared at lunchtime and crossed over Station Road to a café opposite. He had used his car twice that she had seen, once during the day and once in the early evening.

The paper run was the obvious opportunity. Cilla's preference was to intercept him on the way home from the newsagents since he liked to look at the headlines as he sauntered along the street. She needed to engineer direct contact with the man so that she could get close enough to use the guiding pin. Her plan was simply to bump into him and drop her bag, spilling the contents onto the pavement. It was a near certainty that he would bend over to help pick them up, at which point she would place the pin in position and insert the pellet. Sergei Milov would feel nothing more than a scratch, possibly not even that if he was sufficiently distracted.

"I've worked it all out. I'm doing it tomorrow," Cilla announced to Mum.

Mum nodded her assent. "That would be lovely," she replied. They were strictly forbidden to speak anything but English to each other whilst on British soil. It limited their communication and for that Cilla was grateful.

"You need to be packed and ready early. You will wait for me at the station with our luggage," Cilla went on. "Understand?"

Mum nodded again and put another handful of crisps in her mouth. She had a particular way of eating crisps. She didn't eat them one at a time, instead she stuffed four or five in at once, crunching them noisily and then masticating the mouthful at length as if she were chewing cud.

Mum also snored.

Travelling through Europe with Junior Sergeant Irina Petkovic had been a new experience for Cilla. She had always shared a room with somebody, her brother, Amelia, the other girls in the dormitory, but it was the first time that Cilla had lived in close quarters with an adult female. She didn't much like it. The hotel rooms always seemed to be dominated by Mum's underwear: her pants and girdles washed and dripping in the bathroom; her vast brassieres draped over furniture. And Mum herself, stolid and calm, her large calf-like eyes glued to the television.

Mum's lack of English meant that, for the most part, she was confined to whatever hotel room they were staying in. Mum didn't seem to mind. She liked watching TV. In fact, as far as Cilla had observed, there were only two other activities which elicited any sort of positive response in Mum. The first was food. Mum loved Western junk: crisps, chips, hamburgers, pizza, anything laden with salt and fat that she could ingest from the comfort of her bed. The second was shopping. A certain amount of capitalist consumption had been necessary for the good of the mission. When they

166

reached London the first thing that Cilla and Mum had done was to visit Peter Jones in order to buy a school uniform: a white shirt, striped tie, grey sweater and grey pleated skirt. Cilla also needed a school bag and some appropriate English language texts to go in it. The whole process should have taken no more than an hour. But once Mum had entered the hallowed halls of a department store it became impossible to make her leave. After the uniform had been purchased, Mum left the escalator at the Ladies' Clothing floor, without warning, and wandered slowly around the racks of garments, stroking them lovingly and sighing. Every time Cilla suggested that it was time to go she said loudly, "Cilla, love, could you give me a hand?"

Cilla had no choice but to let her continue. Once she had exhausted Ladies' Clothing Mum made a beeline for Beauty and Fragrance. She spent ages trying on perfume testers and then moved towards the makeup counters. After some time Mum picked out a coral pink lipstick, some matching nail polish and a mascara wand.

"It's time to go," Cilla had repeated through gritted teeth.

But Mum had just looked at her stubbornly, clutching the items in one of her plump hands.

"Buy for me," she had hissed at Cilla.

"And then we leave?" Cilla did not like to bargain in this unseemly manner in public, but what choice did she have?

"Yes," Mum had promised.

At 8.21 a.m. the following morning Cilla and Mum sat in the café on Station Road looking at menus. Cilla did not select the window table but seated the two of them one table back where she still had a direct view of the intersection between Station Road and Bateman Street. At 9.03 Sergei Milov

appeared on the corner walking away from them towards the newsagents.

Cilla reached across the table and took Mum's hand. She did not like touching Mum but she wanted to make sure that her message was properly understood and absorbed.

"Finish your breakfast slowly. Pay the bill. Take the luggage to the station. Wait for me there on the bench next to the ticket office. I will buy the tickets when I get there. Understand?" Mum nodded, but her mouth was too full to actually say anything.

Cilla stood up. She hoisted her school bag onto her right shoulder, walked outside and took up her position. She removed the guiding pin from an internal pocket of the bag and held it in the palm of her right hand so that the length of the pin was obscured by her wrist. All her senses were alert. She could hear the sound of her own heart beating methodically in her chest. She waited. Only when Cilla saw Sergei coming out of the newsagents did she cross the road and begin to make her way towards him.

He held the paper folded in half at chest height. His eyes were skimming an article on the front page. As he approached she concentrated on the rhythm of his motion from the corner of her eye. Time seemed to decelerate as if to allow her the chance to attune herself to him in time and space, the precise movements of his body; the apex of their slow fatal alignment. Just before they moved past each other she tripped, falling diagonally towards him, the dorsal side of her right hand flipping her school bag upside down so that the contents emptied themselves onto the pavement.

Sergei Milov stopped. Cilla was sprawled on the ground, surrounded by loose papers and a couple of textbooks. He stared at her speculatively. For a moment it seemed as if he might ignore her and just walk on. Cilla burst into tears.

"Are you OK?" he said. He bent over and began to pick up the papers. Cilla stood up and made a show of brushing herself down with her left hand. As she did so she edged close to him. He was wearing crumpled beige chinos made out of a thin material, cotton perhaps, easy to pierce at any rate. He was still collecting the loose papers together, bent over. His hind quarters were presented to her. It only took a moment to move the guiding pin into position and release the mechanism.

"Ow," Sergei Milov said, turning his head sharply. "What was that?"

Cilla began to cry again.

"I scraped my knee," she said, pointing to the red mark on her kneecap. It hadn't actually been caused by the fall. It was a friction burn that she had made herself the previous night in anticipation.

"You'll live," Sergei Milov commented. He picked up the two textbooks from the pavement and stood up. "*A History of Western Philosophy*," he observed as he handed the papers and books back to her. "That's a big book to be reading. Are you enjoying it?"

Cilla had purchased this text from the book department at Peter Jones for the purpose of filling her school bag. She could have gone for something boring like *Chemistry: A Practical Approach* which would have been appropriate reading for an English schoolgirl. But when she saw Bertrand Russell's opus for sale Cilla could not resist purchasing a copy. She very much wanted to read it and there might never be another chance to get hold of the book. Perhaps she wasn't so different from Mum with her penchant for lipstick and nail varnish after all.

"It's a bit heavy going," Cilla admitted with a shy smile. "I'm not really reading it. It's just for a school project." As she put the books back into her bag she dropped the guiding pin in there as well. "Thanks for picking up my things. Sorry I bumped into you."

"No problem," Sergei replied. He began to walk away. Cilla stood for a moment watching him retreat. Once the anaesthetic wore off his thigh would begin to hurt. A small red pimple would form. That evening he would have a fever. By tomorrow he would be in hospital. But there was nothing that anyone could do. Nobody would ever know that he had been poisoned with ricin. And even if they did, it was too late. There was no antidote.

Mum was waiting for Cilla on the bench in the station as instructed. Cilla purchased two single tickets and the two of them boarded the next train to London. In doing this Cilla made a slight miscalculation. The train they had taken was not one of the modern fast ones. By mistake they found themselves on a slow train stopping at every station between Cambridge and King's Cross. Not that it mattered very much. There was no hurry. It was quite restful to be seated in this strange old-fashioned compartment, with its plush plaid seats and manual doors. There was barely anyone on board and they had the whole carriage to themselves. The train ambled along slowly, undulating gently from side to side through the English countryside. Cilla could feel the tension of the last few days, of the last six months, slowly ebbing from her system. Her mind wandered in various directions and settled on the afternoon that she had spent walking around Cambridge. It was the day that Sergei Milov had departed on the London train. Cilla should have gone straight back to the hotel room, but the idea of spending the afternoon with Mum watching television had not inspired her. In any case she wanted to see Trinity College where Bertrand Russell had lived and worked. No-one would know if she went to have a secret look so she bought herself a tourist map and made her way towards the centre of town.

The Great Gate, the main entrance to the college, was located on Trinity Street. It resembled a castle with two turrets, battlements and a huge arched doorway. Above the doorway was a statue of what looked like a king. To the right was a smaller arched wooden door. The entrance itself was framed on either side with racks of bicycles and there was a steady stream of students arriving and departing. Cilla walked through the wooden gates into the Great Court. It was vast, a huge imposing rectangle of green enclosed by grey stone cathedral-like buildings on all sides. Cilla had never seen anything like it in her life. She spent ages wandering around the college, making her way through the different courts, examining the architecture, touching the stone, and staring up at the windows with their intricate stained-glass detail. It was all steeped in history and significance. Around her the students seemed to come and go, chattering, laughing, waving at their friends. They occupied the same physical space as she did but they existed in a different reality, one that she could not enter, she could only look in on, her awe and delight tinged with a sour edge of envy.

A sudden jolt of the train brought Cilla back to the present. It would not do to relax too much. The main objective of the mission was complete but there was still the return journey to consider.

"When we get to London we will go to the airport," she said to Mum. "We have open tickets, so we will take the next flight to Brussels with available seats." Mum had an odd expression on her face. It was similar to the one she had worn in Peter Jones when she had demanded that Cilla buy her makeup. "We can get something to eat when we get to

Heathrow. They have pizza there." Cilla didn't actually know if there was pizza available at Heathrow or not but she sensed that it was important to engage Mum at this precise moment, to give her something to look forward to.

"I don't want to go back," Mum announced. She wasn't speaking English.

"What do you mean?" Cilla replied.

"I don't want to go back," Mum repeated. "I want to stay here. I want you to give me my British passport so that I can stay here."

"You know that's impossible." These words sounded familiar to Cilla even as she said them. Then she remembered that it was exactly what Professor Kuznetsova had said to her when she had demanded to speak to Amelia.

"It's not impossible," Mum insisted. "If you give me the passport then I can be Pauline Wilson and I can live here. I won't go to the authorities; I won't get you in trouble. I'll just be Pauline Wilson."

Did Mum really believe what she was saying? Had she made this decision now, spontaneously, or had it been forming slowly in her mind during the previous few days as she lay in bed? Who knew that such thoughts could manifest themselves in Mum's brain; that she had these hopes and dreams? But how did she think that she could just be Pauline Wilson? It was merely a passport, not a golden ticket to the future. What would she do without contacts, without money, without a place to lay her head? How long would it be before "going to the authorities" would begin to seem like quite a good idea and what a story she would have to tell them?

"If I refuse?" Cilla said.

Junior Sergeant Irina Petkovic stood up. She was not a tall woman, but she was taller than Cilla and heavy set.

172

Something about her stance suggested that she could handle herself. She was a career soldier, after all, she must have some training and experience of combat.

"It's OK, just sit down," Cilla said. "If you want the passport I'll give it to you."

Cilla reached into her school bag. The two passports were in a zipped compartment inside.

"Nice and slow," Irina Petkovic advised Cilla as she returned to her seat. There was something in her tone which indicated that this was not a spur-of-the-moment decision. Cilla wondered if, every time she had left the hotel room, Mum had leapt out of bed and ransacked the place, searching desperately for the precious passport.

Cilla took out the two passports now and carefully handed one of them to Irina. The Junior Sergeant accepted it, maintaining eye contact. Cilla put her own passport back into the compartment. As she did so her fingers sought out one of the other items located in there. The train slowed down as it arrived at the next station.

If Irina Petkovic got off the train now, all would be lost. Cilla would never see her again and she herself would be faced with a classic Siberian dilemma: defect to a hostile country and, in all likelihood, be prosecuted for murder; or return home and face the consequences that would ensue when she took responsibility for the failure of the mission. She took her hand out of the bag and sat quietly, childlike, bewildered, and all the time she willed Irina Petkovic to remain in her seat.

The train came to a standstill. Irina Petkovic did not move. She held the passport firmly in one of her fat hands with its coral pink nails, her eyes still locked on Cilla. As the train drew out of the platform it entered a short tunnel and the displacement of air created a loud roaring sound. There would never be a better moment.

Junior Sergeant Irina Petkovic had not been at the meetings with Cilla, Major General Barkov and the other two gentlemen, the KGB operatives, as they finalised the details for the murder of Sergei Milov. Those meetings were beyond the Junior Sergeant's rank and her paygrade. If she had attended them she would have learned that State-sponsored assassinations always include a backup proposal, a Plan B if Plan A fails to work. In this case Plan B was the classic kill combination: sleep and stick. In the zipped-up compartment of Cilla's school bag was a plastic sachet of chloroform-soaked tissues and a single hypodermic syringe filled with Compound 146; fresh 146.

As the train passed through the tunnel Cilla raised her arm and brought her hand down in a stabbing motion whilst simultaneously launching herself from her seat and onto Irina Petkovic. She put her entire weight behind the lunge. As she landed on the Junior Sergeant's lap the needle penetrated her breast plate. Cilla was aiming for the heart. If she could empty the contents of the syringe into Irina's heart paralysis would ensue immediately. Irina Petkovic screamed but the sound was lost in the sonic roar of the train in the tunnel. Then she stopped screaming and started to convulse, her body jerking repeatedly as Cilla remained seated on her, straddling her lap.

Cilla got up. There was no time to lose. She took the sachet out of the compartment in her school bag and extracted a couple of chloroformed tissues. These she clamped over Irina Petkovic's nose and mouth until she was still and quiet. Cilla picked up Pauline Wilson's passport from the floor and put it back in her bag. Then she began the distasteful task of removing the Junior Sergeant's clothes and jewellery, anything that might identify her and where she was from. Once the Junior Sergeant lay slumped and naked on the tartan velour seat Cilla stopped for a moment. When she thought about it, the whole

174

episode that had taken place in the last few minutes on the train reminded her of a game of Fight/Flee/Chase.

Irina Petkovic had chosen Flee and she should have won. But when the opportunity to enact her choice came she had failed to act.

Cilla had chosen Fight. She should have lost. But when the opportunity came to enact her choice she took it. That was because she was a fox. She looked at Mum's pale body where it lay on the seat, slack and spreading. Mum wasn't a rabbit, and she wasn't a chicken. So what was she? Then Cilla had it. Mum was a cow. A big fat cow; and big fat cows get slaughtered.

Cilla moved over to the carriage door and looked out of the window. The ground below fell away from the train track. It was a thicket of buddleia, brambles and rosebay willow herb. It would have to do.

She opened the train door marginally. Then she turned back to Mum and rolled her body over towards the train door. She opened the door wider and heaved Mum's body through the gap. It fell like a large limp doll into the dense vegetation below.

By the time the ticket inspector came round ten minutes later Cilla was sitting contentedly in her seat reading Chapter 2 of Russell's *A History of Western Philosophy*. There was no indication of the carnage that had taken place. All of the clothes that Mum had been wearing had been packed into one of the holdalls and Cilla had placed the bags under her seat where they were not immediately visible.

"Shouldn't you be at school?" the inspector asked as he punched her ticket with a small hole.

"I've got the afternoon off," Cilla replied happily. "I'm going to the orthodontist."

"Well, be good," the inspector said with a wink. "And if you can't be good, be careful."

175

"I'm always careful," Cilla replied primly.

She knew there would be some explaining to do when she got home but she wasn't worried about it. She had done the best she could under the circumstances. Major General Barkov and the KGB men would understand; she would make them understand. Of one thing Cilla was certain: there would be no more escorts.

14

Routine

Routine: a sequence of actions regularly followed.

Cilla liked routine; not her own routine, she didn't really have a routine. She liked routine in her victims. It was her ally. It created pattern, predictability and opportunity. It helped her understand her target on the basis that, in the words of Aristotle, "We are what we repeatedly do."

To complete a Dry Job successfully Cilla needed to know her prey: their habits, their tastes, their loves and hates, their quirks and vices; but most of all, she needed to know about their routine: where they would be on a given day at a given time. Then she could make her move.

It was a good rule, one that applied to the wild just as much as it did in a domestic human setting. Take the cheetah in the Sahara, for instance. She leads a lonely nomadic existence feeding mostly on gazelles. She hunts during the day to avoid the larger nocturnal cats who would steal her kill. In the beginning she is taught to hunt by her mother who brings back live prey on which the young cat can practise her instincts and her abilities. She will begin to chase gazelles for herself when she is about six months old but she probably won't make her first successful kill for some time. After that it will be a hit-and-miss affair for several years whilst she hones her skills. To become a successful hunter the cheetah needs to understand her prey, to anticipate its location, its actions, its very next move. In other words, she needs to learn about its routine.

The Levine household had a recognisable weekday routine. Paul Levine left for work at 6 a.m. Amy Levine got up at seven, Matilde and the children at 7.30. They ate breakfast together and Amy Levine and the children left the house by 8.15 to walk to school. Each morning Matilde attended an English class from 9.30 until midday. On two of those mornings Amy played tennis. On the third she had a regular appointment with her personal trainer, the one she wasn't having an affair with. On the fourth morning she invariably drove off in the Range Rover to do a large family food shop. But on the fifth morning, Friday, Amy Levine almost always stayed at home. For three and a half hours she was alone in the house. That was her pattern; that was her routine. That was Cilla's opportunity.

Now that Cilla had a plan there was no need for any further delay. Early the following Friday she took up her position in the private square, the vantage point from which she had a good view of the Levines' house. Paul Levine left for work at 6.03. Mrs Levine and the children hurried out of the door, slightly late, at 8.22. Matilde departed at 8.53 and five minutes later, just before nine, Amy Levine returned home.

Cilla waited for a further fifteen minutes to monitor any further coming and goings but the house remained quiet. She scanned the square but it was empty so she got up, brushed

178

off the leaves and loose heather that seemed to have attached themselves to her clothes, adjusted her bag so that it sat snuggly on her hip, put on her gloves and made her way out of the gate. She crossed the road and quietly let herself in through the Levines' front door.

Cilla closed the door behind her with a click and stood in the hallway waiting and listening. She needed to locate the position of her prey. She took five silent steps towards the stairs and stopped. From down in the basement Cilla could hear the muffled sound of a radio. She took the blowpipe out of her pocket. It was already loaded. In Cilla's opinion the miniature blowpipe was a much underrated weapon: it was small, portable, easy to disguise, and had a range of up to five metres. Best of all it was inaudible. The only sound that occurred with its use was the single directed breath that it took to launch the dart. Cilla hesitated for a moment, trying to detect any further sounds but there were none. She crept down the stairs noiselessly and edged round the landing so that she could see into the kitchen below. Amy Levine was sitting at the kitchen table reading the paper and drinking coffee. Her blonde hair was tied back into a ponytail so that the whole of her neck was exposed. That was convenient. What was less convenient was the perpendicular angle at which she sat. It was unclear at what point Cilla would enter her peripheral vision and she needed to get close enough to be in range for the blowpipe. She edged down the last few steps. Amy Levine turned a page of the paper but she did not look up. Cilla estimated she was now ten metres away from her target. She kept moving forward slowly, stealthily. Amy Levine took hold of her cup and brought it to her lips. It was nearly empty so she raised her head to tip the last dregs of the coffee into her mouth. As she did so Cilla came into view.

Amy Levine had surprisingly fast reactions. She didn't say

179

anything, she just lifted the coffee cup up and back as if she was intending to throw it at Cilla. But by the time she did this the dart had already lodged itself in a soft nook at the base of her neck just above her collarbone. The cup clattered to the floor, breaking into several pieces. Amy Levine collapsed forward onto the table, one arm extended, the other dangling by her side.

Cilla acted quickly. She checked the location of the dart to make sure that it hadn't hit an artery. It needed to be left in place for a further couple of minutes. She examined Amy Levine's forehead and nose for damage and bruising; there was none; she put a cushion from the sofa under her head and turned her face gently to the side. Cilla picked up the broken pieces of cup, put them in her bag and cleared up the remnants of coffee from the floor.

She took a small wooden box from her pocket, opened it and placed it onto the table. There were two more darts in there and an empty space for a third. The box was specifically designed to hold its contents. The darts sat top-to-tail in velvet-lined indented grooves. Cilla carefully extracted the dart from Amy Levine's neck and put it back in the box. She took out the middle dart and reloaded her blowpipe. The darts all had hollow tips and this one was loaded with curare. She put the blowpipe back in her pocket. Finally she sat down at the kitchen table opposite Amy Levine to wait.

After a further ten minutes Amy Levine began to stir. She lifted her head groggily and leant back in her chair. When she realised that Cilla was sitting opposite her she started but her movements were disjointed and uncontrolled as if she were drunk. The cushion fell to the floor. It would be some minutes before the stockbroker's wife regained full control of her motor functions and Cilla hoped that this would be long enough.

180

"Try not to be alarmed," Cilla said in her calm even tone. "I'm not going to hurt you."

Amy Levine tried to respond but she seemed to lack the ability to move her mouth properly. Cilla reached into her bag and took out the black leather Filofax.

"I have something of yours," Cilla said and she placed the Filofax on the table between them. Amy Levine stared at it for a few moments.

"Why do you have this?" she said finally, her words slurred. It was an effort for her to speak. "I lost it; couldn't find it."

"You didn't lose it," Cilla informed her. "Your husband took it and gave it to me."

"Why?" Amy Levine said but Cilla suspected that she already knew the answer to her own question.

"He's hired me to kill you."

Amy Levine hung her head slightly. She looked sad, defeated even, but she didn't cry.

"But I have observed that you are also trying to kill him," Cilla continued.

Amy Levine's head jerked up again.

"What? No. That's not true. I haven't done anything."

This was a disappointing response. Even though Cilla lied as a matter of course, she found it tiresome when other people attempted to lie to her. They were just so bad at it. Maybe she would need to use the curare after all.

"So why have you been extracting cyanide from cherry stones?" Cilla asked her.

Amy Levine covered her face with her hands. She was regaining full control of her movements. Cilla reached into her pocket and felt for the blowpipe. If the stockbroker's wife tried to do anything foolish she would be prepared.

"I was desperate," Amy Levine admitted. "I still am." She took her hands from her face and placed them on the table, palms down, fingers splayed. Cilla could see how hard she was trying to remain calm.

"What exactly were you planning to do with the cyanide?" Cilla enquired, "Out of interest."

Amy Levine kept her gaze on her hands. "I don't really know," she murmured. "Poison him I suppose."

"You'd have been better off using arsenic," Cilla commented. "Small doses over a period of time. Eventually he would have died of renal failure."

Amy Levine looked up, a slightly horrified expression on her face. "Why are you telling me this?" she said. It was a reasonable question.

"Why are you trying to poison your husband?" Cilla countered.

"I've had enough," the stockbroker's wife replied. "Enough of the lies and the drugs and the debt." Now she had the same cold look of fury on her face that she had worn the night she had been hulling cherries. "He told our au pair that he loves her. How could he do that to me?"

"Why not divorce him?" Cilla asked. Another reasonable question.

"I don't want to be divorced," Amy Levine responded stubbornly. "I'd lose the house. I'd have to share custody of the children. I just want rid of him."

"He wants rid of you as well."

The fury faded and Amy Levine looked frightened again. "So what are you going to do?" she asked. Her voice was unsteady. What she meant was: are you going to kill me?

"I'm going to make you a proposal," Cilla replied.

The stockbroker's wife took a long intake of breath and looked directly at Cilla. It was interesting to observe Amy Levine's face up close like this. She was a rabbit, that was clear; a rabbit in headlights; alert, tense, but essentially incapacitated, not by the drug that Cilla had administered, which was wearing off, but by her own essential nature. She would never have gone through with poisoning her husband. The jar of cherry-stone paste would have sat on a high shelf somewhere gathering dust and going mouldy. But even so, she was quite brave, in her way, for a rabbit. And here she sat with the faintest glimmer of hope on her face.

"What proposal is that?" Amy Levine said.

"I am willing to change the target. I could kill your husband instead of you," Cilla explained.

Amy Levine said nothing but she gave an almost imperceptible nod.

"There would be a cost," Cilla went on. "The price would be seventy-five thousand; twenty-five to cover the loss of income that arises from not completing this job; fifty thousand for the elimination of the new target. That's my standard fee."

Amy nodded again.

"Can you get hold of the money at short notice without your husband knowing? It can't come from a joint account; it needs to be yours alone."

"I have some of my own savings," Amy Levine said. "And I can sell my engagement ring." She lifted her left hand from the table for a moment and the diamond on her fourth finger caught the light. "It's worth enough to make up the difference."

"Good," Cilla said. "We understand each other."

"But what about the police? If they look at my bank account, won't they question where the money went? Won't that incriminate me?"

"You will tell the police that you gave it to your husband. That he came to you, desperate, in fear for his life, and that you gave him seventy-five thousand."

Cilla was quiet for a moment. She was giving Amy Levine time to adjust to the new reality in which she now resided.

"There is something else," Cilla said. "Normally I am very discreet in these matters, but unfortunately, in this instance, that won't be possible."

"What do you mean?"

"Your husband will die a rather violent death. I'm afraid it's essential."

"How? How will he die?"

"It's best that you don't know. That way, when it happens, you will be as shocked as everyone else."

"Will he suffer? Will he be in pain? I don't want him to be in pain." Finally Amy Levine began to cry. Nothing else changed about her face; she didn't blotch up or grimace; the tears just fell from her eyes and formed two wet lines down her face like the silver trail from a slug. She didn't wipe them away.

"No. There will be very little pain."

"Why are you doing this? Why are you helping me?"

But Cilla merely shook her head. "You don't need to know," she replied gently.

"When will you do it?"

"Soon," Cilla replied. Her normal procedure was not to inform clients when the target would be eliminated, but this job was the exception to all the rules. It was special in another way as well; it would be her last job. "It will take place on a Saturday," she continued. "I will give you three days' notice that I need the money. Then, you will give it to me and take the children and Matilde to your parents for the weekend."

"My parents?"

"Yes. Richard and Margaret Sheppard of Saxbys Mead, Cowden, Kent. "

184

"How do you know where my parents live?"

"I know everything about you. I was going to kill you, remember?"

Cilla paused again. She did not want to overwhelm Amy Levine but at the same time it was imperative that her cooperation was assured.

"There is one last thing you must understand." Cilla leant forward across the table. She allowed the stockbroker's wife to look behind the flat pale surface of her eyes, to catch a glimpse of base Cilla who dwelt within. The soft coaxing tenor of her tone had disappeared. When she opened her mouth again Cilla's voice emerged as a low snarl. "This agreement is binding. You tell no-one about it, not now, not ever. If you do what I say you will live to see your children grow up. If you don't then I will come back. I will murder your husband. I will murder you. Your children won't be left as orphans because I will murder them as well. And I will make you watch before I kill you."

Amy Levine was trembling from head to foot now; the tears were running thick and fast and she couldn't make her hands stay still. They shook so much that the band of her engagement ring clattered repeatedly against the oak tabletop. Poor brave rabbit.

"But that's not going to happen, is it?" Cilla said, gentle again, "because we understand each other."

There was not much pleasure to be had by terrorising Amy Levine, but it was necessary. The predator was the predator; the prey was the prey. Usually the predator killed the prey; that was routine. On this one occasion Cilla was giving her quarry a choice, an opportunity, a chance to evade slaughter. But not for one single moment could this little rabbit be allowed to forget exactly what she was.

"We understand each other," Amy Levine repeated faintly.

"Good." Cilla stood up, picking up the Filofax and her box as she did so and returning them to her bag.

Plan A had gone as well as could be expected, Cilla decided, as she let herself out of the front door. There had of course been a Plan B. If there had been any doubt as to Amy Levine's willingness or ability to finance and cooperate with the murder of her husband, Cilla would have used the second dart, the one loaded with curare. Then she would have dragged Amy Levine's paralysed body up to her bedroom and staged an elaborate suicide. It would have been a dirty Dry Job but a Dry Job all the same. But this was better, this was preferable. Amy Levine would get to survive and Cilla felt good about that. And, more importantly, saving Amy Levine might just give Cilla the chance to save herself.

15

Ideals

Over the next five and a half years Cilla undertook thirty-two missions, an average of five or six a year. She was a lone operator, briefed and managed by her handler, Colonel Nikonov, one of the two KGB officers who had advised on Operation Architect, both of whom stayed on at Academy 43, now renamed the Turgenev Institute since it no longer functioned as a school of any sort.

Of those thirty-two missions, five were aborted before completion, on orders from above. The fast-changing political landscape meant that enemies of the State might find their dissident status rescinded at short notice. Two missions were aborted after completion. This was unfortunate but since the State did not acknowledge its role in any assassinations that took place overseas such oversights could be ignored and quickly forgotten about.

Of the twenty-five missions that counted, twenty-three were successful. This gave Cilla a completion rate of ninety-two percent, a record of which she was rather proud. She had been commended twice by Major General Barkov and had once been put forward to receive a Hero of the Soviet Union award although nothing had actually come of this.

Of the two unsuccessful missions or "incompletes" as they were known, one failed simply because pre-op research did not provide Cilla with the requisite information. The target had been Maxim Bitov, an elderly ballet coach who had defected to the UK during his company's tour of the country shortly after his sister had been purged. Really, the authorities should have known better; Maxim Bitov should never have been allowed to travel with that tour so soon after his sister had died. It was just asking for trouble. But somehow he had slipped through the net and defected during a performance of *Swan Lake*. At the beginning of Act Four when the swan maidens were trying to comfort a distraught Princess Odette, Maxim Bitov slipped out of the Royal Opera House and into the nearest police station.

Two years on Cilla was sent to eliminate him. She had become renowned, in KGB circles, for her subtlety and tact. Her methods were discreet and her persona, as a young English woman, was beyond reproach or suspicion. She had been to the West many times on covert missions and had never shown the slightest interest in defecting herself.

The removal of Maxim Bitov should have been a run-of-the-mill assignment. She had used aconitine, the alkaloid toxin produced by the aconitum plant, one of her favourite and most reliable poisons. Locating him had been relatively straightforward. Late one night she had broken into the small suburban residence that he had been allocated in Pinner. She had applied a sedative and then followed it up with a vial of the purified plant extract injected into the axillary artery in his right armpit. What was meant to have happened was that the poison should have interacted with the voltage-dependent sodium channels in the membrane of his cardiac cells. The end result should have been a fatal heart attack. Goodbye Maxim Bitov; your dancing days are over. But no-one had told her that the ballet coach was on medication to treat low blood pressure. That medication interfered with the pathway of the poison and what should have been a fatal heart attack turned into a mild one instead. Plan B could not be enacted because twenty-four hours after this happened Maxim Bitov was whisked into a British military hospital without warning.

There was no explanation as to how the British authorities had got wind of the fact that this was not your average, everyday heart attack. Perhaps they detected the aconitine in his system. Perhaps there were too many defectors dying of natural causes on UK turf. Perhaps there was a leak.

The second incomplete Cilla had to own herself, although in her mind it did not constitute a failure at all. The mission wasn't a Dry Job as such, and it wasn't in the UK. It was the routine disposal of an East German music student who had committed the ultimate act of political depravity: he had successfully absconded over the Berlin Wall. The East German authorities wanted to make an example of him in order to discourage other weak-minded undergraduates from following his lead. They had sent in two of their own operatives, one after the other, both of whom failed to return. Perhaps this disposal was not so routine after all. The head of the Stasi appealed to his KGB brethren for help. The KGB provided him with Cilla.

Clearly this music student was not your average dissident. Stefan Kuhn had made good his escape by using meat hooks to scale a steel-mesh border fence with his saxophone case strapped to his back. The guards claimed to have seen nothing, although it was always possible that they had been bribed. Then later he had dealt with not just one but two Stasi officers, each of whom had been sent to kill him. Presumably he had disposed of their bodies afterwards. Such acts demonstrated enterprise, guts and ingenuity.

But Cilla was not daunted at the prospect of killing Stefan Kuhn, of trying to succeed where other older, stronger, more experienced operatives had failed. In her mind the whole thing was just a maze to be solved. Clearly each of those Stasi officers had taken some sort of wrong path and found themselves in a blind alley confronting a victim-turned assailant. Cilla would not make the same mistakes. She would assess all the variables, she would examine the possibilities; she would find the algorithm. And her youth, her small slim stature, her still childlike face, all the elements of her which could be categorised as weaknesses were in fact her hidden strengths. She had seen photographs of the missing Stasi officers. One was a big burly man with a mean expression. The other looked arrogant. Stefan Kuhn would have identified each of them approaching from a mile away. But Cilla was different; he would never see her coming; she was invisible.

One of the reasons that the East German authorities were so incensed by the defection of Stefan Kuhn was that he did not run away and hide in some hole, never to be heard of again. Although he had entered the West German dissident protection programme he periodically came up for air and played his saxophone in Berlin jazz clubs. Consequently he had become something of a cause célèbre for the youth of West Germany and East Germany alike: a poster boy for free will, autonomy and artistic expression. Every time he performed it was reported in the national West German press, and copies of these articles always seemed to worm their way into East Germany. The GDR authorities found this intolerable.

Cilla sifted through the music student's files at length but in the end her plan was simple. She would take him out during one of his performances. She would use her self-cocking mini crossbow. In the subsequent mayhem she would leave. The beauty of this particular crossbow model, which she had helped to design, was that it could be dismantled and disguised. All of its constituent parts fitted neatly into a large makeup case. So even though there would undoubtedly be checks and a heavy State personnel presence at any club where he was due to perform, she should be able to pass through security with ease. Then it would simply be a case of reassembling the weapon in the privacy of a toilet cubicle. The sharp tips of her eyebrow tweezers would clamp together to form the bolt. She would have precisely one shot. There was no Plan B.

The East German authorities cautiously approved her proposal. What they liked most about the plan was that it was tantamount to a public hanging. They hoped that this act of Socialist retribution would crush the harmful and amoral surge in the popularity of jazz music amongst the young. There was only one question that the GDR asked. Given that advanced notice of Stefan Kuhn's performances was a well-kept secret how would Cilla know where he was going to play?

"I don't think it will be so hard," she told Colonel Nikonov. "He only plays at a few venues. I'll trawl each of them in the early evening before they open. When I find the one making preparations for increased security, that will be where he'll perform."

Cilla took her usual route into West Berlin, hitching a lift with a Soviet military patrol. Her German was fluent but she used her British passport and took care to speak German with an English accent and to wear English clothes. If by some misfortune, she was identified as Stefan Kuhn's executioner, the West German government would labour under the illusion that it was the British who had killed him. What a good joke that would be.

She booked into a cheap nondescript hotel. Apart from reconnaissance there wasn't much to do, but Cilla had prepared for this by bringing a number of Philosophy and History texts with her. She was currently making a study of Plato. She very much liked his theory of forms and ideals and the fact that his thinking evolved from Pythagorean philosophy, which held that mathematical formulas and proofs could accurately describe the essential nature of all things.

It took ten days and three false alarms to identify where and when Stefan Kuhn would perform. But once Cilla arrived at the venue, a small dark subterranean bar called the Treble Clef Café in the Zehlendorf district, she knew, from the goose bumps on her arms, that she was in the right place. She had scoped it out earlier and there was an obvious presence of plainclothes militia. As she stood in the queue to buy her ticket she could see that everyone was being patted down on entry. A bouncer opened her bag and even unzipped her makeup case but as everything was so carefully disguised, there was nothing for him to find. Once inside all that was left to do was to assemble the weapon, sit at the bar and wait for Stefan Kuhn to arrive. Two bands and three beers later he appeared on stage. Cilla didn't even need to turn her head to know that he was there, the rapturous applause informed her of his presence. He was part of a four-man ensemble. There was a pianist who sang as well, a guitarist, a drummer and Stefan on the sax. They didn't really play jazz, more of a soft jazz/rock fusion. Cilla let them perform a couple of songs. She wanted them to settle in and get comfortable. She wanted security to relax. When the opening chords of Gerry Rafferty's "Baker Street" reverberated around the bar she knew that it was time.

Cilla stood up and began moving gently through the crowd, edging forward slowly and artlessly, swaying to the music as the others were doing. She took the crossbow out of her bag and concealed it under her jacket. The venue was full but not heaving and she concentrated on picking her way through the throng, moving ever closer to the stage. There was a saxophone solo two-thirds of the way through the song and she wanted to be in place when it began.

It was only as she reached the barrier in front of the stage that she looked up and saw Stefan Kuhn for the first time. She had seen photographs of him but nothing could have prepared her for how handsome he was. He looked like some Greek god up there, his black hair slick with sweat, the moisture forming a golden sheen on his face reflected off his instrument as if he were lit from within. His eyes were closed and, despite the exertion, his skin was quite pale. All of his energy and his beauty seemed to be projected into the saxophone. He held it like a lover, with his knees slightly bent, pouring himself into the sound. All Cilla could do was stand there and stare, captivated by his beauty and the beautiful sound that he made. And in those few moments she decided not to kill him.

The authorities did it. They aborted missions, it was just that this time it was her decision to abort, rather than a directive passed down from above. Under cross-examination Cilla would have been hard put to explain exactly why she did not want to kill the musician. It wasn't that killing Stefan Kuhn would be wrong. Cilla had no interest in that sort of nursery morality, silly ideas of "good" and "evil" invented to maintain the social contract. What was more important was that Stefan Kuhn was exceptional. He embodied some-thing. His defection from East Germany and all that had ensued represented courage in its purest form: the choice to confront pain, danger, uncertainty and intimidation. And he continued to do this simply by performing on stage. He embodied the Platonic ideal of valour. To this he added beauty, not simply physical beauty but the exquisite sound he created with his skill. To execute him would be to desecrate an ideal, to violate an eternal truth. Cilla would not do this; she had no right.

She discharged the bolt into the base of the stage so that she could not change her mind and put the crossbow back into her bag. No-one saw. When asked, she would claim that someone had nudged her as she was taking aim causing her to miss. Then Cilla put her bag down on the floor, and gave herself up to the music, to Stefan Kuhn's golden presence, and forgot about everything else for a little while. The last thing she did, when the set was over and everyone was whooping and cheering, was to lean down, extract the bolt, and put it in her pocket.

Colonel Nikonov was furious. Cilla had expected him to be angry but she was still surprised by the extent of his outrage. What he appeared to be most unhappy about was not so much the failure of the mission as the fact that the KGB had been made to look foolish in front of the Stasi.

"But why did you miss?" he kept asking. "You've never missed before."

"I told you," she replied. "Someone bumped into me as I took the shot. There was nothing I could do."

Cilla was dismissed and assigned to domestic duties for two months as a punishment. But in truth she didn't mind this at all. Domestic duties meant working with Comrade Guseva and Comrade Ivanova perfecting new and better toxins; searching for those perfect poisons that imitated natural physical catastrophes and left no trace of their journey through the human body. When they created a new formula it would be tested on the ever-changing cast of human guinea pigs who still resided in Bunker 6. Now that Cilla was an adult she called her former teachers by their first names. Comrade Guseva was "Olga" and Comrade Ivanova was "Irina". It felt good to be on an equal footing with them.

Looking back, not killing Stefan Kuhn seemed rather foolish. She had besmirched her own near-perfect record and for what? But when she replayed events in her head, particularly the moment when she looked up and saw his face for the first time, she knew that she would always make the same choice; the choice to defend an ideal. Just occasionally she liked to extend the scene in the Treble Clef Café, to play out a different and prolonged version. In this alternative narrative, Stefan Kuhn was aware, and he saw her shoot her bolt into the stage.

After the set was over Cilla went back to the bar and ordered another beer. As the club began to empty Stefan Kuhn appeared beside her. He sat down on the bar stool next to hers.

"You were sent to kill me," he said.

"Yes," Cilla replied, taking a sip from her bottle as she spoke.

"You missed," he observed.

"On purpose," she corrected him.

"Why?" he demanded.

"It doesn't matter," she replied. "What matters is that you are not safe. You can't keep doing this. The next one they send might not miss."

"I'll deal with that when it happens," he stated.

"Like you dealt with those two Stasi officers?"

"Yes."

"But you don't understand," she remonstrated. "They will keep sending people until one succeeds."

"No, you don't understand," he countered. "I made it over the Wall. That means something. I have to show them that it means something. One day the people will decide to get rid of that fucking wall for good. They will destroy it and I will stand on the very top tearing it down brick by brick."

After this, things got a bit hazy. It was a very silly scene and Cilla did not indulge herself by thinking about it too much.

More often she allowed herself to imagine Stefan Kuhn's journey over the wall. One particular detail of his escape fascinated her. He had climbed the border fence using meat hooks. How did they know he had used meat hooks if no-one had seen him? Did he leave them behind in no man's land? Where did he get the meat hooks from in the first place and how did he know that they would work? Had he practised his ascent beforehand or did he go in blind, trusting his fate to chance?

So many questions; no-one to answer them. Cilla did consider talking to Irina Ivanova. She remembered, all those years ago, how she had punched her fist through the glass pane of the kitchen greenhouse and how Irina had covered for her and said it was an accident. Although Comrade Ivanova had long since given up trying to draw Cilla out, her eyes still seemed to invite confidences. But it was just too dangerous; and what would be the point? It would be impossible to make Irina Ivanova understand the importance of a Platonic ideal, that it was a principle, not just an abstract noun. So Cilla kept her own counsel and added the bolt to her small cache of possessions: a locket, a charred piece of paper, the deformed nail on her thumb, the scars on her forearm; and now a bolt made from the tips of a pair of eyebrow tweezers clamped together. All of the things that represented the choices that she, Cilla, had made for herself, as opposed to the ones that had been made for her.

16

Details

The Wet Job is a euphemism for an assassination that involves the spilling of blood. It doesn't pretend to be anything other than what it is: a murder. The perpetrator has two main objectives: to eliminate the assigned target and to return to base without being captured. The most important component for the completion of a successful Wet Job is probably speed. The operative wants to get in and out as fast as possible. To this end death is generally violent but quick. Weapons of choice include guns, crossbows, explosives, tall buildings.

The Dry Job is an entirely different affair. It disguises itself. The Dry Job does not want to be categorised as a murder at all, it poses as a death by natural causes. The most important element to the completion of a successful Dry Job is attention to detail. The weapons of choice are mostly poisons, although tall buildings can still be useful.

The hit that Cilla was planning was ostensibly a Wet Job.

But in many ways it felt like a Dry Job. There was so much planning, so much patience, so much precision.

In order to provide the necessary attention to detail, Cilla needed to spend more time at TGR's and in order to do that she needed a plausible reason to be there.

"By the way, would it be OK if I played some bridge at the club?" she asked Vladimir Haugr at the end of one of their meetings in his small office.

"You want to play some bridge?" Vlad observed her with a sceptical expression on his face. "Why is that?"

"There's not much going on at the moment and I have some time on my hands. I've always thought that it looks interesting," she replied. "I understand the basics; I've spent enough time watching the punters here play cards. And I read a book."

"You read a book?" This was a warning sign. Vlad had a habit of repeating statements as questions when he was suspicious. "What book would that be?"

"*Bridge is an Easy Game*," Cilla replied readily. She could feel Vlad trying to probe her thoughts with that powerful sixth sense of his. It was fortunate that she was quite interested in bridge. If she had been faking he would have found her out.

"Really," he said. "And what did you think of it?"

"I thought the title was misleading," Cilla replied. This made Vlad smile.

"OK," he said. "You can play some bridge. You start in the £1 game, understand? Then we will find out what you can do."

So Cilla started playing bridge at TGR's.

Bridge is a partnership game involving four players who sit at the four points of a compass. North is partnered with South and East is partnered with West. All the cards are dealt so that each player has thirteen of them, holding them up in a fan so that their cards are concealed. The play of each hand starts with an auction where the two partnerships bid to see which suit will be trumps. When the auction is over one player will end up as Declarer. Declarer will play the contract, trying to make as many tricks as possible. His partner will be Dummy; their hand is spread open on the table for all the players to see. The two players in the other partnership are the Defenders. The aim of Declarer is to make his contract. The aim of the Defenders is to defeat him.

This was how money was won and lost at TGR's. When Declarer made a contract it was worth a certain number of points. At the £1 table, each one hundred points translated into £1 worth of profit for Declarer and Dummy. When Declarer failed to make a contract, this represented points for the Defenders and money in their pockets instead.

Bridge demands a combination of logic, aggression and bluff. It is the king of card games, an enigma, a conundrum, an endless challenge for those who choose to take it on. But one thing Cilla learnt quickly; at the £1 table it was not a partnership game.

The £1 game was the lowest-stake game available at TGR's. It was populated by poor players and the elderly, neither of whom could be relied on as partners. They bid like idiots, played like morons and defended as if they had forgotten whose side they were on. In order to succeed at this level Cilla quickly realised that she would have to play a solo game.

This wasn't really a problem since she had been playing a solo game for most of her life. At first the punters were suspicious of the young interloper with her pale eyes and her flat expressionless face whom they vaguely recognised as an occasional waitress at the club. But within a couple of days she was the darling of the £1 game. The reasons were simple really; if you played with Cilla you won money, if you played against her you lost. Also, she was never rude to her partner. No matter what atrocity a partner committed at the table she kept her cool and moved on to the next hand. What this meant in practice was that she squeezed the best game out of the rabbits with whom she played. So not only did they come out on top when they played with Cilla, they felt good about themselves as well.

At the end of the week she was moved up to the £3 game. Two days after that Artur asked her to make up a table at the £5 game. Now she was beginning to play bridge.

There were basically three types of players at the £5 game. There were the poor players. They tended to be slightly more accomplished than the players at the £1 table, but more importantly they were richer and could afford their losses easily. This group was an assortment of wealthy widows, ladies who lunched, gentlemen of means, and a few others who could afford £150 for an afternoon's worth of bridge. The game was not simply a mental challenge for these people, TGR's was their second home; a place where they could find entertainment, company and solace.

Then there were the decent players, the tournament play-ers, who came along occasionally to try their luck at the rubber game where bridge was played for money. They were often quite upset when they lost. What did they expect, they were still rabbits after all.

Finally there were the foxes, the small group of players who consistently won money from everybody else. The foxes aimed to inhabit the £10 or £15 games; that was where the pickings were richest. But sometimes they had to make do with a £5 table instead. The foxes were usually young male professional players who sought to earn their living from bridge. Sometimes they played for the club which meant that

TGR's covered their losses and took a percentage of their winnings. Sometimes they played for themselves, which meant that they were always in danger of being cleaned out entirely by a prolonged losing streak.

Cilla had seen lots of these young foxes come and go during her association with TGR's. The route they took was often the same. They started at the lower tables playing in the £3 and £5 games. As they became more confident and experienced they progressed to the £10 and £15 tables. Finally, they felt they could cut it in the £50 game. At this point a significant number of them lost all their profit and often everything else they had. They went home with their tails between their legs and were never seen at TGR's again. Perhaps these ones weren't foxes after all.

The £50 table was the most interesting game of all; it was generally known as the Big Game. This was where Vlad sat down most afternoons. He was a fairly capable player. What he lacked in skill he made up for with intuition. He wasn't a fox; he was a larger carnivore than that. Foxes were his prey. Apart from Vlad and the young would-be professional players, the £50 table was populated by the ultra-rich and the true experts; the world-class performers who came from all over the globe to play bridge at TGR's and were revered by everybody else.

There was Zia Mahmood, the great Pakistani player, ever popular with the ladies, who wore cream linen suits and split his time between London and New York; Michael Courtney, the crazy Australian, whose capacity to imbibe alcohol had no impact whatsoever on his perfect card play. Then there was the English contingent: Robert Sheehan, tight-lipped and taciturn, sometimes playing an entire session in silence; David Price, bearded and baritone; and his regular tournament partner Colin Simpson, who was ex-Special Branch and had once shot dead a terrorist. Occasionally even Bob Hamman, the mighty American, ranked number one in the bridge world would turn up at TGR's to play. His motto was simple: "Winning is not the most important thing. It is the only thing."

Vladimir Haugr did not win at the big game, but he didn't lose heavily either. He seemed to regard his losses as the price he paid to keep such illustrious company. He truly loved rubber bridge and viewed it as some sort of gladiatorial sport for the mind. In any case his losses could usually be written off or put to some other good use.

Cilla observed the cast at TGR's with interest but she had no aspirations beyond the £5 game. That would have been foolish. She might be a fox in other arenas but at the bridge table she knew perfectly well that she still had long ears and a fluffy white tail. When she broke even at the end of her second week she felt happy. In any case, although the bridge was interesting, it was purely a means to an end. It provided her with a plausible reason to spend her afternoons and evenings at TGR's.

For some reason Vlad took it upon himself to act as some sort of personal bridge mentor to Cilla. Sometimes he took her out for an early dinner in the space between the afternoon and the evening game. Often Zia or Michael or some of the others accompanied them. They would eat Lebanese food, drink, smoke and argue vigorously about who should have played what card on the opening lead. On one occasion, Daniel, Vlad's son, came out with them as part of a larger group. He sat as far away from Cilla as possible and avoided meeting her eye. Perhaps he had some inkling of what it was that she did for his father after all.

If he was still around at the end of the evening, Vlad liked to have a nightcap with Cilla at the bar after all the punters and the staff had gone home. He wanted to review the evening's hands and hear about the bids she had made, the hands she had played, the problems she had encountered. He rarely talked shop and only once asked her if she had any news about Smithy and the Mint.

Vlad's concern for Cilla's development as a player was almost touching. Viewed through the prism of bridge he was an affable, larger-than-life character with an insatiable appetite for cards. He wasn't an expert by any means. Experts avoid mistakes. Vlad played more for the honour and the glory of the game. He had a habit of taking spectacular gambles which paid off more often than they should have done. In this sense, although he was inferior to the elite with whom he played, he was still a dangerous and unpredictable opponent.

Which was something that Cilla had to remind herself of: he was a dangerous and unpredictable opponent. In his capacity as bridge mentor it was all too easy to like him, this gargantuan man with his booming voice and his hearty opinions. If she told him about something clever or brave she had done at the bridge table he would clap her on the back and call her a "dirty dog". When she admitted her blunders he would reassure her saying, "mistakes are good. You cannot learn to play by your successes, only by your mistakes." Then with a smile: "So long as you don't keep making the same ones."

Sometimes, feeling mellow after two midnight brandies, Cilla seriously considered whether it would be possible to throw herself on Vladimir Haugr's mercy and simply ask to go free. Her debt to him was paid, it was time to let her go. Then she could kill Paul Levine quietly, take the seventy-five thousand, add it to the rest and leave with something like four hundred thousand after expenses; not four hundred thousand cash, which would be next to useless, but a fully laundered four hundred thousand pounds deposited in a clean, legitimate bank account for which she was the named account holder. If she did that she could give up the elaborate ruse that she was trying to pull off and just walk away.

Walk away.

But in her heart of hearts she knew that he would never let her go. She was too valuable an asset. She wasn't a fox at all. She wasn't even a rabbit. She was just a little trained bird tethered inside a gilded cage. The cage door was open and the length of the chain allowed her to fly a short distance but in the end it held fast and there was nowhere to go except back to the cage.

In any case, the idea of throwing herself on the mercy of Vladimir Haugr was a contradiction in terms. He did not have the capacity for mercy, any more than she did. There was nothing to do but to continue with the deception and hope that the cloak of bridge would mask her ulterior motives.

Whenever Cilla found herself in danger of liking Vlad too much she tried recalling some of the people she had murdered for him.

Maurice Malinowski, the backgammon swindler, who had sweated his way to a heart attack on the floor of WHSmiths at Heathrow Terminal 2; Vita and Eric von Breda, a pair of notorious bridge cheats who had succeeded in winning the TGR's auction pairs by using illegal hand signals to relay information. Those two deaths had gone down in history as a double suicide.

Then there were the employees: Maria, a delivery mule who repeatedly overcharged clients and kept the change; another one, Cilla couldn't remember his name, only that he was a small ferrety-looking man who had snorted more product than he sold and had badmouthed Vlad to boot;

and finally Jacob, who had been cutting the coke and had to be made an example of. She had poisoned the first two and botched up the third.

But this didn't help. It was difficult to blame Vlad for ordering the expiration of such silly and dishonest people. In his position she might well have done the same. But there were others as well.

Three customers could be included on this list, all of whom had unpaid gambling debts. Two suppliers also had to go because Vlad wanted to take over their territory.

Finally there was his ex-girlfriend Katrina. Cilla did not like thinking about this death because she suspected that it was not one life that had ended, but two. Vlad enjoyed women, but only in the plural. He considered himself to be something of a connoisseur. Like many men that Cilla had observed, he seemed to have a particular type. Dark-haired, olive-skinned, buxom girls in their early twenties were like catnip for him. But none of the relationships ever lasted very long. Vlad was more interested in the thrill of the chase than in the subsequent domesticity. He didn't like to be tied down. So women came and went; Katrina had lasted longer than most. But when he tried to move on she wouldn't have it. There were tears and scenes. She kept turning up, unannounced, to the bridge club and embarrassing him. It was unwise to embarrass a man like Vladimir Haugr; he did not respond well to it. When Katrina, in a state of hysteria, threatened to tell the police about some of his less-than-legitimate activities, he opted to engage Cilla's services. She remembered that she had used insulin as the catalyst. Whilst Katrina lay in a coma dying Cilla had followed this up with a large dose of glucose. This wasn't done as an attempt to save her, merely to confuse the pathologist in the event of an autopsy. It was when she was administering the second injection that she noticed the pelvic swelling, but by that time it was too late to do anything about it.

"You failed to mention that she was pregnant," Cilla had said to Vlad afterwards.

He sniffed disdainfully. "Probably not mine," had been his only response.

It was good to remember Katrina and how she had died. It helped Cilla to maintain focus.

Over the course of the month that Cilla spent at TGR's she didn't always play bridge. Sometimes she just watched the others play. This was known as "kibitzing". She would sit down behind Vlad or Michael Courtney or one of the others and observe the decisions they made with their cards. There was always something new to learn. Kibitzing other players did not strike anyone as odd; it was standard behaviour for a novice bridge player wanting to improve. In the main the experts enjoyed having an audience; they liked to perform for the crowd. Zia always had several people peering quietly over his shoulder and on the occasions when Bob Hamman turned up, word would quickly get around and there might be twenty people vying with each other to sit behind him.

On the days that Cilla was watching rather than playing she would often give a hand to the kitchen staff at the same time. When the club was full of players and kibitzers the dirty dishes and coffee cups would pile up on the side tables; the ashtrays would overflow. The staff often found it difficult to keep up with the orders and the clearing up. So sometimes Cilla would vacate her chair, collect a tray and do a sweep of the room. She would deliver the debris to the kitchen and load the dishwasher. When she came back she would bring fresh ashtrays and the outstanding orders of coffee with her. Once again, this did not strike anyone, even Vlad, as strange. Cilla was an accepted feature at TGR's; as a player, as a waitress; she wasn't invisible as such, she was just part of the general scenery.

In fact the only person who questioned her presence there was Nancy.

"What are you doing here?" she said when she first saw Cilla sitting at the £1 table.

Since Cilla held nine cards in her hand and was in the middle of declaring a delicate contract of three spades, this question seemed rather redundant.

"Playing," she responded shortly.

"Since when do you play bridge?" Nancy persisted.

The two crones who were defending the contract scowled in Nancy's direction. "Shh," they both said simultaneously.

Nancy raised her eyes skyward and retreated to the kitchen.

"But really, why are you here?" she said to Cilla later that afternoon outside the cloakroom.

"I'm learning to play bridge," Cilla repeated.

"With those rude old biddies?" Nancy said incredulously. "I can't think of anything worse."

"Is that what you say to Nick Sandqvist?" Cilla asked. She was referring to a young handsome Swedish player on whom Nancy had an obvious crush.

"He plays in the big game," Nancy replied loftily. "It's different."

"Until he loses all his money and has to sleep on a park bench," Cilla reminded her. "Then he goes back to the £1 game."

"Well he's not sleeping on a park bench at the moment," Nancy said pertly. She looked rather pleased with herself.

"Well, well, lucky you," Cilla commented as she walked away.

Nancy exhibited a similar reaction when she discovered

that Cilla was clearing up crockery from the playing area and loading the dishwasher.

"What are you doing?" she said. "This isn't your job."

"Just lending a helping hand," Cilla replied evenly.

But Nancy remained unconvinced.

"Are you for real? Since when did you ever help anyone?" she demanded. "In any case, you'll help me out of a job if you carry on like this. If you do it for free, why should they pay me?" She looked at Cilla shrewdly. "I know you're up to something," she said. "I don't know what it is but I know you are."

But Cilla merely gave Nancy one of her blank impassive smiles. Without warning Nancy reached out and took one of Cilla's hands in both of her own.

"Be careful," Nancy said. "Whatever it is, be careful."

"I'm always careful," Cilla replied and she gently withdrew her hand.

After that conversation Cilla was more circumspect about clearing up the playing area. Even so, at the end of the month she had compiled what she needed:

A glass

A coffee cup

Three cigarette butts

A plate.

It wasn't much of a haul but it was sufficient. The most difficult aspect of the process had been making sure that the items that she had collected were uncontaminated. They needed to have Vladimir Haugr's fingerprints and DNA on them and no-one else's.

If Nancy made him a coffee and brought it out to the playing area then the cup and saucer were useless. They would have Nancy's fingerprints all over them. If Cilla went into the kitchen, looked at the order list and saw that Vlad wanted a

coffee, she could make it herself. But once delivered and consumed she could not prevent another member of staff from
collecting the empty cup. Now the specimen was lost. On a
couple of occasions she had managed to collect the cup only
to be intercepted in the kitchen by Artur or Nancy or one of
the others before she had had the opportunity to bag the item.

Arguably, it might have been easier just to poison Vlad and
be done with it; but Cilla doubted that she would get away
with this course of action. No matter how absorbed he was in
the bridge game, when she brought him his coffee he always
looked her up and down, scrutinising, scanning, checking for
shifts and anomalies. She wasn't even sure that he was aware
he did this; it was just a form of instinct. In any case, to lace
Vlad's coffee would have been a cowardly and dishonourable
act. Cilla didn't want to poison him, she wanted to outwit
him. He was the very last in a line of individuals who had
tried to use and control her. She didn't want to kill him. She
wanted to rub his face in the dirt and force him to accept
defeat. Most importantly she wanted him to know who it was
that had defeated him.

Collecting Vlad's cigarette butts was equally difficult. Cilla
had to follow the journey of the cigarette from Vlad's mouth
to the ashtray without getting it mixed up with the multitude
of other butts in there. Even if she could discern which one
was his, if it touched another butt this rendered it useless. She
was satisfied to have obtained and bagged up three.

The most prized item of all was the plate. That was simply
a lucky catch. Late one evening when the two of them sat
drinking at the bar Vlad had decided that he wanted a sandwich. They took their glasses into the kitchen and he opened
the fridge. Once he had assembled his ingredients he looked
for a plate. It had been a busy evening and the cupboards
were bare so he opened the steaming dishwasher, which

had just finished its cycle. He took out one of the mid-sized salad plates and began to examine it thoroughly. Vlad was a fastidious man and he liked his crockery to be scrupulously clean. The first one he selected failed to meet his exacting standards so he left it on the sideboard and took another. He made a chicken-and-avocado sandwich and wolfed it down talking all the while about suit combinations.

"Do you understand, Cilla?" he was saying. "If you have nine cards in a suit headed by the Ace, King, Jack you should generally play off Ace and King. You hope that the suit breaks 2:2 and you drop the Queen. But when you have eight cards the odds change. Now you must take the finesse."

But for once Cilla was barely listening.

"Yes," she said absently. "I know that rule."

All she could think about was the plate that Vlad had rejected; the beautiful, unadulterated plate sitting on the sideboard. The clean, warm, slightly damp plate smothered in his fingerprints; fingerprints which could be harvested.

17

Feelings

Another office; another meeting; a new file; the same old drill.

Colonel Nikonov slid one of two identical folders across his desk for Cilla to look at.

"Codename: Ace of Spades," he announced.

Cilla nodded and opened the file.

"The photographs are of Vladimir Haugr," Colonel Nikonov continued. "Half-Romanian, half-Norwegian; based in London; controls two casinos; has an interest in a third. He also owns a bridge club. But his real revenue comes from cocaine distribution."

"Is he the target?" Cilla asked. "Colonel Comrade Colonel," she added as an afterthought.

"Yes, but not directly," Colonel Nikonov replied. "We have been supporting Mr Haugr's operation for some time. The dissemination of cocaine as a force for decadence and corruption to assist in the dissolution of the capitalist system is one of a number of covert tactics used to undermine Western so-called democracies. We provide Mr Haugr with some storage capacity and safe passage for his product via Cuba in return for a percentage of his profits."

There were five photographs in total. They had been taken in quick succession and showed a man standing outside Marble Arch tube station smoking a cigarette and gesticulating. The most notable feature of the man was his size. He was quite simply bigger than all the commuters around him; not just taller but formed on an altogether larger scale. The other thing which struck Cilla was that although the station appeared to be busy there was a consistent space around the man as if he were exuding some sort of forcefield which others could not penetrate. She kept these observations to herself. As Cilla examined the pictures she realised that he was in fact speaking to another man who was in shot for three of the five photos.

"Lately, Mr Haugr has become less cooperative," Colonel Nikonov explained. "Relations with Cuba are not what they were and this has caused transport delays. Mr Haugr has responded by withholding funds. We think he may be planning to source his product elsewhere. We are also concerned about his level of notoriety. We have repeatedly requested that he keeps a low profile and does not attract attention to himself. He gives us every assurance and then ignores us. It is all very well to eliminate enemies but one must do so in a prudent and inconspicuous manner. You, of all people, understand this." The Colonel nodded at Cilla as if in deference to her skillset.

"And how does Mr Haugr eliminate his enemies, Colonel Comrade Colonel?" Cilla enquired.

"He impales them on railings." The Colonel adjusted his steel-rimmed glasses and wrinkled his nose slightly as if he found the activity distasteful. "The British authorities are becoming increasingly aware of his activities. There is intelligence that MI2 have compiled a dossier. We wish to reassert control and to remind Mr Haugr of where lobsters spend the winter."

Colonel Nikonov favoured old idioms. What he meant was it was time that Vladimir Haugr was taught a lesson.

"Who is the other man in the photographs?" Cilla asked.

"Well observed," Colonel Nikonov commented. "This individual is Frankie Osborne. He is Haugr's right-hand man. This is your target."

Cilla scrutinised the last photograph. It was the only one which showed Frankie Osborne facing forward. In the other two photos where he was visible she could only see his profile. He was a stocky fellow, nearly half a metre shorter than his companion, with greying curly hair. By comparison to Vladimir Haugr he looked like a gnome. The other difference between the two men was the expressions on their faces. Vladimir Haugr looked irate. He was waving his hands around and his mouth was open as if he were shouting. By comparison Frankie Osborne looked far more relaxed, mischievous even, with a hint of a smile playing on his rather thick lips. There was something about his expression that reminded Cilla of a painting she had once seen of the Ancient Greek god Pan.

"Wet or Dry?" she asked.

"Dry."

Cilla looked up from the photograph. "If Frankie Osborne dies of natural causes how does this bring Mr Haugr back in line?"

Colonel Nikonov pursed his lips. "This is an informal conversation, Cilla, so I am prepared to overlook the impertinent manner in which you are addressing me but you would do well to remember not to question your orders."

"Yes, Colonel Comrade Colonel," Cilla responded; she felt immensely tired.

"Once you have dispatched the target you will inform Mr Haugr of his death. You will explain to him if he fails to comply with our directives he will meet with a similar fate."

This was new. Cilla was a sniper; she had never been asked to relay messages before. She looked back at one of the photographs of Vladimir Haugr. He really was a very large man. If Frankie Osborne was his partner he might be less than thrilled to receive news of his demise.

"What should I do if he refuses, Colonel Comrade Colonel?"

"Refuses?"

"Refuses to comply with our directives."

"I see, yes. Once you have spoken with Mr Haugr you will report back. Then we will decide how to proceed."

Eliminating Frankie Osborne looked like a textbook case. Fat middle-aged men were always easy to kill. Heart attack, cardiac arrest, embolism, stroke, you could just take your pick. The file also told her that he was a heavy smoker which made it even more straightforward.

She chose an embolism. Cilla had been working on a brand-new toxin with the help of Olga Guseva. They had developed the compound together and it had been extremely successful in trials on both pigs and humans. The catalyst was an organophosphate clotting agent which caused a central venous thrombus. This had the effect of backing up the vital blood supply to the brain. It was the biological equivalent of a car accident blocking traffic. The end result was a catastrophic brain haemorrhage. The only issue with the drug was that it had to be administered intravenously which made the process somewhat cumbersome and time-consuming. But Cilla was dying to try it out in the field, and since smokers are far more likely to experience a deep-vein clot than non-smokers, Frankie Osborne was the ideal candidate.

He was forty-eight years old and an accountant by trade. Married but separated. As far as his association with Vladimir Haugr was concerned, Frankie Osborne didn't really get his hands dirty. He just dealt with the money. He maximised the losses, minimised the gains and then funnelled any remaining profit through a complex network of companies based in the Cayman Islands. When he wasn't laundering funds he played bridge. Sometimes he played at Vladimir Haugr's club in Bayswater: The Great Rose, generally known as TGR's. Sometimes he played in tournaments.

Bridge tournaments took place all over the UK. As far as Cilla could discern, the bridge players descended like locusts on some random hotel, played their funny card game for several days and then left again. Frankie Osborne attended all of the major events. Further research informed her that the next tournament was something called the "Spring Meeting" and took place in Brighton over the May bank holiday weekend. This was good. It would provide her with the ideal opportunity.

Cilla had never been to Brighton before. She liked going to new places. This one was a spa resort located on the coast in the south-east of England. The architecture of the town was largely Regency and Victorian: tall white buildings with ornate balconies and balustrades. At the very centre was a bizarre mosque-like construction known as the Royal Pavilion. But in contrast to its formal buildings the town had a relaxed bohemian atmosphere which reminded her of West Berlin. It was full of little lanes with vegetarian restaurants and vintage clothing stalls. There were street performers and buskers on every corner. Cilla walked past a man painted bronze sitting on nothing in the pose of the Thinker. She stopped and watched him for a full ten minutes but he never flinched, so she put a pound coin into his tin, at which point he stood up and gave her a gracious bow.

The bridge tournament took place at the Metropole Hotel on the sea front. Cilla had checked into a room the day before the event started. This gave her time to explore the venue and to watch as the preparations for the bridge tournament were made. It was a large-scale event; what looked like hundreds of card tables were put up in three separate conference rooms over two floors. The organisers hung a players' starting list in the lobby and Cilla found Frankie Osborne's name about three-quarters of the way down. She also took one of the leaflets laid out to provide players with the session times.

On the afternoon that the tournament began she sat in reception and watched the players arrive. Frankie Osborne turned up at about 4 p.m. and she was relieved to see him queue at the front desk to check in. She had rather banked on the fact that he would be staying at the playing venue. Cilla maintained a discreet distance, followed him to his room and took note of the room number.

Having a copy of the playing schedule made life very easy. She knew exactly when his room would be empty and since she had already lifted one of the skeleton cards from a clean-er's cart there was nothing to prevent her from gaining access. At about 9.30 p.m., when the evening bridge session was in full swing, Cilla quietly let herself into Frankie Osborne's hotel room.

Her purpose in being there was twofold. Firstly it was a reconnaissance exercise. She wanted to check the contents of the room; to examine the man's possessions in detail. What sort of medication was he taking? Had he brought any weapons with him? Was there evidence to suggest that this would be anything other than a routine Dry Job?

A thorough search yielded nothing of consequence. His overnight case contained a change of clothes, two bridge books and a packet of condoms. His toiletries bag held the usual items and the only medication he was taking was statins. This indicated that he must have high cholesterol which, if anything, was an advantage.

Secondly Cilla wanted to do a dummy run-through of the job itself. It was always good practice to do this if it were possible, which wasn't very often. The room was effectively L-shaped. It opened into a short hall with a bathroom door to the right and a cupboard door to the left. At the end of the hall the space expanded into a square, most of which was taken up by a double bed.

Her plan was to occupy the cupboard from 10.30 p.m. the following evening. The bridge finished at around 11 and presumably Frankie Osborne would return to his room at some point and go to bed. When Cilla was sure that he was asleep she would emerge from her hiding place. She would further sedate him using a large dose of zopiclone and then, once half an hour had passed, she would set up the intravenous line and administer the clotting agent.

Cilla checked the cupboard thoroughly. It opened and closed with a sliding mechanism. There was a good space on one side where she could position herself behind two spare pillows. Even if, for some reason, he opened the door he would be unable to see her. She practised sliding the door open from the inside several times. It was awkward but feasible.

When she had finished Cilla vacated the room and walked down the corridor to the main lift. Up or down? She knew that she should try and get a good night's rest in preparation for the long day tomorrow, but she couldn't face going to bed yet. It was always the same before a job; there was always a sense of effervescence in her head and a deep knot of tension in her chest, not anxiety or fear exactly, since these were not feelings that she was accustomed to, more a sense of pressure building from within, pressure which demanded release.

Instead of going back to her room Cilla took the lift down to the Metropole bar and ordered a beer. The evening bridge session had not yet finished and the bar was half-empty. The loudest occupants were a party of twelve or so young women in fancy dress. All of them wore the same pink sash positioned diagonally across their outfits, emblazoned with the phrase "Nicole's Nasty".

"Why are they dressed like that?" Cilla said to the bar-tender as she paid for her drink.

"Hen night," he replied succinctly, taking her money. But this answer left her none the wiser. For all her immersion into British culture, Cilla had never come across the term before. She sat drinking her beer and watching them out of the corner of her eye. One of the women wore a pink diamante tiara and was engaged in filling shot glasses with tequila and shouting down the table to her friends.

The room began to fill steadily and Cilla realised that the bridge must have finished. Players poured into the bar waving their money and trying to catch the attention of the bartender. They were an odd crowd. Some were posh and smartly dressed, others were scruffy. Several looked as though they might be on day release from a local institution. She spotted Frankie Osborne amongst them. He bought two bottles of red wine and commandeered the table next to hers with five or six others. By listening carefully she could catch scraps of their conversation amongst the general din.

"He bid four spades and I doubled him. The contract was

cold but he butchered it and managed to go two off so we got five hundred."

"Did you bid six hearts on Board 19?"

"No, I made a slam try but partner never showed me his shortage so I gave up."

"That's because I only had an eleven count."

"Eleven working points and a fit. You have to show me your singleton. If you don't get that then, in a nutshell, you know nothing about bridge."

On it went. The snippets made no more sense than the hen party. The only thing that Cilla understood was the term "in a nutshell". It was over two thousand years old and originated from Pliny the Elder's book *Natural History*, one of the largest single works to have survived from the Roman Empire. In it, Pliny mentioned that a copy of Homer's epic poem *The Iliad* had been written in a font so small that the entire tome could be enclosed within a single nutshell. But this hardly seemed relevant here and, disheartened, she finished her beer and retreated to her hotel room.

In any case, she had completed her study of the Romans and the Greeks some time ago and had moved on to medieval philosophy and mathematics. Cilla spent the rest of the night reading a book about Fibonacci and how he had introduced the Hindu–Arabic numeral system into Europe in the thirteenth century after travelling around the Mediterranean coast, meeting with many merchants and learning about their system of arithmetic and bookkeeping. This she found easy to understand.

The cupboard was warm and close, more so than Cilla had anticipated. From the noises that she could hear under her feet it sounded as if the hot-water pipes ran beneath the floor.

After sitting in a semi-foetal position for an hour she decided to remove her gloves and her balaclava. She could put them back on before she slid open the door. Another fifteen minutes passed and she took off her top. Her torso was slick with sweat and her mouth was dry. Still Frankie Osborne did not return to his room. After a further hour of crouching in that black confined space the unthinkable happened: Cilla fell asleep.

She awoke to the sound of a crash followed by giggling. Then a male voice said: "Be careful." And another voice, female, replied, "If I was being careful I wouldn't be here." There was more giggling, followed by some whispering and fumbling noises. Cilla cursed herself. Why hadn't she just done the job the night before? There was nothing to do now but remain where she was, waiting, sweating and trying not to think about her raging thirst.

Presently she heard the heavy squeak of bed springs, sporadic at first but then gathering pace and rhythm. Frankie Osborne began to make some grunting noises, his companion let out a series of soft moans. Although, for all Cilla knew, it could have been the other way around. Maybe she was grunting and he was moaning, who could tell? Eventually the noises died away and Cilla heard the sound of a match being lit. There was more whispering and then the padding of feet around the room and the sound of a toilet being flushed. Cilla was aware of the main door being opened, clicked shut again and then finally, thankfully, silence.

She checked the digital display on her watch. It was 4.32. The sun would begin to rise soon. She waited for a further twenty minutes, dressed herself, put on a fresh pair of gloves and slowly slid open the cupboard door. Then she paused again. Nothing. Slowly and painfully Cilla emerged from her hiding place. Six hours of squatting seemed to have left her body in a state of rigor mortis. She extended her limbs out quietly like a cat stretching and looked around the room. After the inky blackness of the cupboard's interior Cilla could see quite clearly. The place stank of alcohol, cigarettes and another slightly sickly smell that she couldn't identify. There was an empty bottle of brandy on one of the bedside tables with one glass. Another glass was lying on the floor. Frankie Osborne was alone, passed out on the bed, half-covered by bedclothes. He still had one sock on. Four pillows lay scattered around him. Cilla locked the hotel room door internally and crept towards the unconscious man. The combination of sex and alcohol appeared to have left him comatose. He was lying on his side in a state of abandon like some sleeping satyr, his barrel chest rising and falling with his breath. Frankie Osborne was not a handsome man, and he was old, but there was something coarse and visceral about him which was not altogether unappealing. And clearly someone, the woman, whoever she was, had found him attractive enough to engage in sexual intercourse with him. Much as she wanted to consider the matter further Cilla was aware of a more pressing and immediate problem. There was no longer sufficient time to perform the embolism induction procedure; it took five hours, sometimes longer. She would need to think of something else.

In the event of the failure of Plan A, Plan B would have been to intercept Frankie Osborne on a London street, on his way either to or from TGR's. The retractable guiding pin was loaded with ricin and ready to go. Unfortunately it was in London along with some of Cilla's other luggage, left at the bed and breakfast in Acton where she had been holed up for a couple of days before making her way to Brighton.

What to do? Cilla felt loath to retreat when she had Frankie Osborne right there in front of her, unconscious and accessible, lying on the bed like a ripe plum ready to be picked.

She looked at Frankie; she looked at the pillow beside him. It was just too tempting not to try.

When she got back to her own room the first thing that Cilla did was to drink three glasses of water. Then she filled up the basin and dipped her whole face into the bowl. The shock of the cold helped clear her thoughts. The job wasn't finished yet, there was still work to do. She dried off, put her blonde wig back on, donned yet another pair of gloves and returned to Frankie Osborne's room with the two spare pillows from her own cupboard, a pack of baby wipes and a spray bottle filled with diluted bleach. Cilla spent half an hour wiping down the cupboard inside and out. When she was finished she gave the carpet a light misting of bleach and positioned the fresh pillows where the old ones had been. She was confident that all of the DNA from her sweat had been either collected or corrupted, it didn't really matter which.

Before departing she took a final look at the body on the bed. It was now 6 a.m. and Frankie Osborne had been dead for nearly an hour. The contrast between a live person and a corpse was always revealing. Within minutes of dying the body exposed itself for what it was: a shell, now empty. The pallor changed, the muscles relaxed: the corpse entered a state of primary flaccidity. He didn't look appealing now.

But then a thought occurred to Cilla. She had been very careful when she smothered Frankie Osborne with the pillow. There would be a post-mortem, that was inevitable. Dead bodies in beds had to be investigated. The finding would be that he had died as a result of either sleep apnoea or accidental asphyxiation with excessive alcohol consumption as a contributing factor. It would be registered as a death by natural causes.

So why would Vladimir Haugr believe that Cilla had killed him?

223

When she tried to tell him there was every possibility that he wouldn't take her seriously. He would look at her, a small, slim, rather ordinary-looking young woman, and assume that she was some sort of fantasist. Cilla needed to have evidence, some sort of trophy, something that would not be missed, but would be sufficiently meaningful to Vladimir Haugr so that he would know, beyond doubt, that Cilla was telling the truth. It needed to be something personal. In the end she took the signet ring from the little finger of Frankie Osborne's left hand and one of the bridge books in his overnight bag. She chose *Play These Hands with Me* by Terence Reece because it looked as if it had been a present according to the inscription on the flyleaf:

To Frankie, who taught me much of what I know. Robbo

And she hoped that these items would be enough.

Normally, in the immediate aftermath of a successfully completed assassination Cilla experienced a familiar sequence of emotions, one after the other. The first was euphoria, wave upon wave of it, sweeping across her like the sea. As the swell settled this gave way to an overwhelming feeling of relief, warm water entombing her body in its gentle hold. Then a deep sense of calm and well-being would pass over her; a perception of being at one with the universe. And at the end of it all was sleep: blissful, dreamless sleep, sometimes for as long as fifteen hours.

It hadn't always been like this. She hadn't felt this way the first time, all those years ago, when she'd shot that wretch from Bunker 6 with her crossbow. All that she'd felt then was a sort of sickened awe. But once that line had been crossed and she became used to her role in the world Cilla began to find satisfaction in her work. The aversion subsided but the sense of awe never left her, instead it blossomed.

224

Most of the time Cilla did not really experience emotions in the way that she had observed other people experiencing them, or in the way that she had read about them in books: happiness, sadness, joy, misery, excitement, fear, she knew what the words meant but they did not mean very much to her. The only emotion she was really aware of was a sort of dull rage which settled on her from time to time like fog. So she looked forward to the blissful range of sensations which would take over after a good kill: euphoria, relief, calm. She hankered for them like a baby hungers for milk.

But this time they would not come. There was nothing. The deep knot inside her chest remained embedded and taut. Apart from a nap in the cupboard she had not slept properly for over forty-eight hours but as she lay on her hotel bed staring at the ceiling her eyes seemed to be held open with barbed wire.

And she knew exactly why this was. She still had to speak to Vladimir Haugr.

"Mr Haugr, Mr Haugr, may I have a word with you?"

It was four hours later. Cilla had been standing on the Bayswater Road for an hour and a half waiting for Vladimir Haugr to arrive at his bridge club. When she realised that there would be no release, no relief and no sleep until the second part of the mission was complete she got up, showered, packed her bag and made her way back to London. There was no reason to delay talking to the man. In fact there might be an advantage in talking to him before Frankie Osborne's demise became public knowledge. He might not believe her at first, but he would certainly believe her once his partner's death was confirmed.

Now Vladimir Haugr was striding down the Bayswater

Road with a long, confident gait so that Cilla had to trot to keep up with him.

"Mr Haugr," she repeated.

He slowed his pace and looked down at her.

"You want to talk to me darling?" he said.

"Yes."

"Is it about a job?" he enquired benignly. They had reached the TGR's premises and Vladimir Haugr was standing at the top of the stone steps with every intention of walking down them to the basement and the bridge club entrance. "You have to speak to Artur about it. He's the manager." He descended several steps whilst looking her up and down nonchalantly. "You seem like a nice girl, I can put in a word for you."

"I don't want a job," Cilla said. "I have a message from the Committee for State Security."

Vladimir Haugr stopped and turned around properly. He looked at her again, this time with a degree of interest.

"You are KGB?" he asked quietly. His tone was no longer friendly.

"No, not exactly, but I am authorised to pass on a message to you."

"So the KGB employ little English girls now, is that it?" He still didn't really look as though he was taking her seriously.

"Make a notch on your nose," Cilla said in Russian. It was another of Colonel Nikonov's favourite expressions. Roughly translated it meant: take notice of what I'm saying and commit it to your memory.

Now she had his attention.

"My employers insist that you honour your business arrangement with them," Cilla said, switching back to English.

"What business arrangement?" he replied. He was standing on the third step down and their eyes were nearly level.

226

"Storage and safe passage comes at an agreed cost," Cilla reminded him. "You owe a percentage."

"You're five years out of date, girlie," Vladimir Haugr replied scathingly.

"What do you mean?"

"I mean I haven't done business with your shitty government for five years. What is this percentage I owe them? I owe nothing to those scumbags."

Cilla's mind began to race. She felt as though the firm ground on which she thought she had been standing had turned to quicksand. Meanwhile Vladimir Haugr stood in front of her, his fists clenched, his expression increasingly enraged. As his fury grew she had the impression that any moment now he would reach out with those massive hands of his, take hold of her small skull and crush it. Cilla took several careful steps backwards.

"Excuse me Mr Haugr," she said evenly. "Forgive my intrusion. It would appear that I have been misinformed." And with that Cilla did what she had been trained to do in such situations: she slipped away.

The more she thought about it, the less sense it made.

Her instructions had been as follows: go to England. Kill Frankie Osborne. Inform Vladimir Haugr of Frankie Osborne's death. Pass on the message to him from the KGB. Report back to Colonel Nikonov.

But when she had passed on the message to Vladimir Haugr he had disclaimed all knowledge of any current association with the Soviet State. He wasn't lying, quite the opposite. He had been filled with righteous indignation that could have easily spilled over into violence. In retrospect it was fortunate that she hadn't told him about the murder of

Frankie Osborne. He would have killed her if she had, of that Cilla was certain.

And then it came to her: she hadn't told Vladimir Haugr about the death of Frankie Osborne. She had changed the order of instructions, not purposefully, or with intent, but simply because it made sense to pass on the message first and then use the death of Frankie Osborne as leverage.

But this was not what she had been instructed to do by Colonel Nikonov. She had been told to inform Vladimir Haugr about the death of Frankie Osborne first and then to pass on the message afterwards. If she done that then he would have killed her.

Which could mean only one thing: Colonel Nikonov wanted her dead.

Why?

Did he think she was a traitor, a double agent cooperating with the West? Two of her intended targets had survived attempts to assassinate them. Did he somehow know that she had chosen to spare the life of Stefan Kuhn? Was it retribution for making him look foolish in front of the Stasi? Or did he simply dislike her? Was it just Colonel Nikonov who wanted her dead or was she now an enemy of the State? Was there any difference? If Colonel Nikonov had branded her as "undesirable" then her removal simply constituted a cleansing of the ranks. Cilla had seen this done before. She recalled Professor Kuznetsova, one day the privileged and respected Director of Operations at an elite military boarding school, the next sent who knows where. Maybe the Professor had been subject to an administrative resettlement order, maybe she had been shot. This was the way in which Soviet society operated. One moment you were in favour, the next you were not. A false move, a mistake, a foolish remark, some small thing which invoked the ire of a superior; any action taken by an individual could be deemed to threaten the State and as such constitute a counter-revolutionary activity punishable by death. So it didn't really matter what Cilla had done. It didn't matter at all. The fact was that she had done it and now they wanted rid of her.

It was a lot to process. The knot inside her chest seemed to twist and tighten its hold.

The only advantage that Cilla possessed was time. As a lone operator once she was out in the field she managed her agenda without interference. She had informed Colonel Nikonov of the approximate date that the assassination of Frankie Osborne would take place but she had leeway with regard to making contact with Vladimir Haugr. The Colonel did not know that she had already spoken to him. It was quite reasonable that she might wait several days before doing this.

So there was no rush, no need to take a hasty decision. The bed and breakfast in Acton was booked until Wednesday, which gave her three days to think, to consider her options, to work out how she was going to secure some sort of future for herself.

Cilla vacated her room only to eat and to go to the cash-point. She took out £150 each day on the debit card that she had been given, the maximum she was entitled to. She would use the same card to pay for her room when she checked out and then she would dispose of it.

This would mean that, come Wednesday, Cilla would be left with £600 and the contents of her luggage. It did not amount to very much. There were her precious things: her locket and her bolt, which she took with her everywhere, her talismans. She had four changes of clothes, a jacket and two pairs of shoes. She had her blonde wig. She had brought some equipment with her: syringes, a catheter, the guiding pin, hidden away in a concealed compartment in her suitcase.

Finally she had her stores: compounds, toxins, poisons, in both liquid and powder form, disguised amongst her toiletries. She didn't like to rely on Plan A and B anymore, these days she preferred to bring the whole alphabet. That was it, that was the lot, these items represented everything that Cilla possessed in the world.

As far as she could see she had four options.

Option 1: Report back to Colonel Nikonov and return behind the Iron Curtain as if nothing was wrong. Maybe she was mistaken, maybe she was paranoid, maybe there was no plot to kill her. Perhaps it was simply that an error had been made. Errors were made all the time. Think of all those missions, planned then aborted because something changed, or somewhere someone got something wrong. Even if a decision had been made to have her purged she suspected that this decision had been taken solely by the Colonel. Otherwise she would have just been arrested at the Turgenev Institute and carted off in the usual way. Maybe when she got back she could seek an audience with General Barkov and denounce Colonel Nikonov to him. Maybe the General would listen to Cilla. After all he had commended her twice and put her forward to receive a Hero of the Soviet Union award. That had to mean something didn't it? Didn't it? Or was the sad truth of the matter that it meant nothing at all?

Option 2: Go it alone. She would have £600. Her passport was valid for a month. Whatever the mission, her passport was always valid for a month. She could eke out the money for a few weeks, retreat to some bumfuck little town somewhere, get a crappy job which paid in cash, grow old and die. If anything, this option was actually less appealing than the previous one.

Option 3: Defect. This alternative at least had some

superficial advantages. She would be safe. She could make a deal. The British government would rub their hands with glee if she turned herself over to them; all the juicy secrets she could tell. But what of the murders she had committed, especially the last of them, a British national killed on British soil; a British national, moreover, with no links whatsoever to the Soviet Union; an innocent. Would they really let her get away with that? Or would they make their promises, extract every last piece of information she had to give them and then lock her up and throw away the key? That might be the worst outcome of all.

And there was something shameful and dishonourable about defecting to the British authorities in such circumstances, not because she would be betraying the Motherland or any of that Socialist nonsense; it was more that she would demean herself by committing such an act. She was a soldier after all, and as a soldier she should fall on her sword as Brutus had done in ancient Rome; which brought her neatly to Option 4.

Option 4: Kill herself. Cilla had considered this alternative a number of times since the first time; the time she had considered throwing herself over a precipice after Luna's death. She could not decide whether suicide represented an act of heroism or one of cowardice. All the philosophy and history that she had read never seemed to answer this question definitively. There were always arguments for both sides.

And all the while a fifth option kept turning itself over in the back of her mind. What she needed was a new ally, a protector, someone powerful who could make use of her services in return for a safe house and a retainer, someone who would allow her to remain off grid. In any case, she had an apology to make. And if he killed her, well, that would just mean that she had taken Option 4 after all. It was a brave choice, a noble choice. She would put her head inside the lion's jaws and let him decide.

❦

This time she did not waylay him on the Bayswater Road. Cilla waited until she had seen Vladimir Haugr enter the bridge club premises and then a few minutes later she descended the stone steps and knocked on the door. A sallow-looking man answered it.

"Yes?" he said.

"I want to see Mr Haugr," Cilla replied.

"He's not here," the man replied dismissively.

"Please tell him that the little English girl needs to see him," Cilla requested.

"I said he's not here," the man repeated irritably.

"I'll wait," Cilla said, and she sat down on the stone steps. The man slammed the door. It was a sunny morning and although the small basement patio spent most of the day in shade there was a short window of time when the sun was directly overhead and its rays poured down into the court-yard. Cilla closed her eyes and tilted her head up towards the light. The warmth of the rays bathed her face and she found this comforting.

About half an hour later the door opened again. It was the same man.

"Mr Haugr will see you now," he said and ushered Cilla inside. He led her down a corridor, through a large empty room laid out with card tables and a bar, down a second cor-ridor past the kitchen to a final door on the right where they stopped. The man gave a couple of tentative knocks.

"Come," came the low response. They went inside.

Vladimir Haugr was seated on a black leather swivel chair in front of rather than behind his desk. If anything he looked even larger seated than he had done standing up. Next to him was a small wooden chair which was positioned at a right angle to the desk so that it faced his chair. He looked at Cilla, smiled and patted the wooden seat. The sallow man hung at the doorway waiting to see what would happen next.

"Thank you Artur. That will be all." The sallow man retreated and closed the door. Cilla sat down on the wooden chair. Vladimir Haugr turned to her still smiling.

"Back again," he said. "Do you have another message for me, little English girl?"

"No," Cilla replied. She had tried to rehearse this conversation several times in her head. It never went well. "I was sent on an operation here. I now believe that it was a puppet play."

"Puppet play?" Vladimir Haugr repeated uncomprehendingly. "What is puppet play?"

"It's a term they use sometimes. It means to outmanoeuvre your opponent so that they unwittingly do something that leads to their own death."

Vladimir Haugr said nothing but at least he was listening.

"I believe that I was sent to give you a message so that you would kill me," Cilla continued cautiously. She looked at the floor as she spoke; she did not wish to provoke him.

"But I didn't kill you," Vladimir Haugr retorted. "If I had wanted to kill you I would have killed you."

"I didn't give you the whole message," Cilla admitted.

"So now you are going to give me the whole message and then I will kill you?" he said affably.

"That's one possible outcome."

"A possible outcome? So there is more than one?" Vladimir Haugr grinned. He was clearly enjoying himself.

"Another outcome is that you will employ me instead."

"Employ you? One minute I'm going to kill you and the

233

next I'm going to offer you a job. You want to be a waitress, is that it?"

"No," Cilla said. "I have a very specialised set of skills. I believe that these might be of use to you."

"What you have is a death wish," Vladimir Haugr declared. "But go on, you tell me about your special skills. And in return I promise not to kill you as long as you keep me amused."

"I dispose of people."

Now he laughed out loud.

"Ha," he said. "You dispose of people? Does this mean you stick them in a dustbin or do you actually kill them?"

"I kill them."

"But I thought we'd established that I was the one who killed people. So why would I need someone else to do this for me?"

Cilla was silent for a moment; she was aware that she needed to choose her words very carefully. She didn't want to insult or aggravate the man but at the same time she needed to take the opportunity to assert herself.

"I've read your file," she said slowly. "When you kill some-one you do so brutishly and blatantly. Whilst I'm sure that this inspires fear and awe, it also attracts attention." Finally she lifted her head and met Vladimir Haugr's gaze with her own. Her irises glittered as if they were made of diamonds. "When I dispose of someone I do so covertly and discreetly, so much so that the event is never classified as murder. It is recorded as a suicide, or an accident, or as a death by natural causes."

Even though she wanted to look away from him Cilla found herself unable to do so. Vladimir Haugr narrowed his eyes slightly and tilted his head. It was as if he were looking at her properly for the very first time, peering right inside to examine her little black heart and everything else she was made of. It was useless to resist so she relaxed and gave herself up to the moment.

"What was the rest of the message?" he said softly and she had no choice but to answer.

"I killed Frankie Osborne," Cilla replied. There it was, it was out and could not be taken back.

"How did you kill him?"

"I suffocated him."

"No, not possible. If you do this the police can tell. The eyes will be bloodshot."

"Not if you use the right technique." Cilla reached towards her bag. "May I show you something?" she said. Vladimir Haugr nodded curtly. She took out the bridge book and the signet ring and handed them to him. He scrutinised the ring for a moment and placed it on the desk. Then he opened the book to its flyleaf and read the inscription.

"I cannot undo what's been done," Cilla said. "The best I can offer is two lives in return for the one that was taken. Give me two names, two identities and I will dispose of them for you. If you are satisfied with my work perhaps you would consider offering me a position in your organisation."

"Tell me how he died," Vladimir Haugr instructed her.

So Cilla told him. She left nothing out. When she got to the part where she could hear moaning and grunting from her hiding place inside the cupboard he roared with laughter.

"That man," he said. "He had such a way with women. They could never resist."

She continued with the story until its very end. Finally Cilla fell silent waiting for his judgement, his final decision. Vladimir Haugr leant back in his chair still holding the bridge book, turning it over in his huge hands.

"You have some fucking nerve coming here," he said.

"I'll give you that. I should get rid of you, I really should."
It almost seemed as if he were talking to himself. "But then again." He leant forward. "Suppose I give you a job, what is it you want in return?"

"Security. Safety. Somewhere to live. Money."

"What about your government? What will they do?"

"I haven't been in contact with my handler since I arrived. When he doesn't hear from me he will assume that you killed me and got rid of the body; which is what he wanted anyway."

"Why does he want you dead?"

"I'm not sure; maybe because I kept forgetting to address him as my commanding officer."

Vladimir Haugr sniffed and looked thoughtful for a moment. "Well I don't give a fuck how you address me," he said. "But there is one thing that we need to establish." He leant in closer towards Cilla so that when he spoke she could feel his breath on her cheek. "You know how I kill people, don't you, what my modus operandi is?" The Latin term rolled off his tongue with a flourish.

Cilla nodded.

"Well I have one in the cellar here. It's not a railing as such, it's actually a piece of old scaffolding pipe that I had modified. I keep it for special cases, for people who have really pissed me off. Would you like to see it?"

Cilla shook her head.

"Wise decision. But let me tell you this, little English girl. If you ever try to dispose of me, if you try to fuck me over, if you ever seek to betray me, I will know. Then I will take you down to that cellar. Do you understand?"

Cilla nodded.

And so, her association with Vladimir Haugr began.

He provided her with an apartment, a reasonable retainer

and expenses in return for five jobs a year and later on, when he knew her better and trusted her, as much as Vladimir Haugr ever trusted anyone, some babysitting.

Cilla loved her little flat on the Hammersmith Road, located halfway between Brook Green and Shepherds Bush. She had slept alone in hotel rooms of course, but she had never really had a bedroom of her own before, let alone an entire apartment at her disposal. The best thing about it was the garden which stretched all the way down to the railway line. Vlad even bought her a little greenhouse and a potting shed so that she could continue with her research.

Still the knot of tension in Cilla's chest did not really dissipate. She wasn't frightened, she didn't do frightened, but she still felt the need to look over her shoulder all the time, just in case one of the other remaining operatives had been sent to locate her.

But then in the November of that year a momentous event occurred, something which changed her perspective of everything: the Berlin Wall fell. Cilla saw it on television whilst eating a Chinese takeaway on the sofa. She watched in disbelief as the Ossis swarmed through the checkpoints where they were met by the Wessis with flowers and champagne. Soon afterwards a bunch of West Berliners actually climbed the wall and were joined there by some East Berlin youngsters. There was wild rejoicing and some of them even started to hack pieces off. She looked for Stefan Kuhn amongst the sea of happy faces, and even though she never saw him, she knew he must be there.

After that Cilla began to sleep in her bed, rather than under it, as she had been doing for the past few months. And more importantly than that she realised something that she had never quite understood before: nothing is eternal; it is all just a holding pattern, before the next paradigm shift occurs. Even the Motherland, that vast Socialist juggernaut which had dominated and overshadowed the first twenty years of her life, was itself beginning to look like a temporary structure. Cilla was pleased that she had worked this out for herself rather than reading about it in a book. It was time to look forwards rather than backwards over her shoulder. It was time to embrace a new era.

18

Endings

Everything was in place. One night Cilla went out into her garden at 3 a.m. and dug up £350,000. Each of the seven sites where £50,000 was buried had been marked by a hybrid tea rose so the money wasn't very difficult to find. The oldest of the bundles had been buried for more than two years but when she unwrapped it all the notes were dry and serviceable; and it still smelt like money rather than soil.

To this, she added Paul Levine's deposit of £25,000 and the £50,000 she had got for the old lady in Tunbridge Wells. All of it was handed over to Smithy. His cut was fifty, twenty-five for the documentation and twenty-five for his silence. He passed on the remaining £375,000 to a third party so that a legitimate bank account could be set up in Cilla's new name. For cleaning the money their cut was ten percent. Cilla was now the proud owner of a cheque book and a debit card. At least once a day she liked to insert the card into a cash-point machine and look at her balance: the digital display of

£337,500 never failed to please and placate her. To this she would add the money from Amy Levine, not all at once, but over a period of months. Even if she deducted a few thousand pounds for living expenses in the immediate future, this still left Cilla with a clear £400,000.

She had collected £75,000 from Amy Levine a couple of days earlier. Amy had been instructed to take the children and Matilde to her parents for the coming weekend. There was no issue in getting Matilde to accompany them since the au pair refused to stay in the house alone with Paul anyway. The stockbroker's wife understood what was expected of her. She knew that, in all likelihood, she would receive a phone call or a visit from the police informing her that her husband had died. The manner of his death would come as a shock; which was expedient since it would mean that she wouldn't need to act when she heard the news, it would just all come naturally. The best lies are always the ones which are interwoven with the truth. Amy knew to tell the police that Paul had begged her for money, that she had withdrawn all her savings and pawned her precious engagement ring in order to provide him with seventy-five thousand in cash. That was all that Amy Levine needed to know. As long as she played the part of grieving widow with a sufficient degree of gusto she would have fulfilled her part of the bargain.

Four hundred thousand pounds: it was a tidy sum. Not a fortune, not as much as Amy Levine would receive. During their last meeting she had confided to Cilla that Paul had insisted on setting up joint life insurance policies for them both six months earlier. No wonder he wanted her dead. Now she would be the one to benefit instead. There would be enough to pay off the mortgage, raise the children, finance her tennis lessons and the personal trainer. She wouldn't fall foul of the "forfeiture rule" because there would be nothing to link her to her husband's death. The insurance company could investigate as much as they pleased. Paul Levine would have been murdered, true, but the perpetrator would be known, and it wouldn't be Amy Levine.

Cilla didn't begrudge the stockbroker's wife her pay-out. All Cilla wanted was her £400,000. It would be enough; enough to start a new life, enough for a house, furniture, a car, driving lessons and a little plastic surgery to complete the transformation. Cilla could get a job, pay taxes, go on holiday. All for £400,000, blood money built on a pile of corpses, but money has no memory. And nor would Cilla. She would do what she needed to do. She would commit this one final heinous act and then she would shed her skin and move on.

It was 9.30 p.m. on Saturday evening when Cilla let herself into the Levines' house for the last time. She had seen Paul go out half an hour earlier and it seemed unlikely that he would be back for a while. Cilla used the time to set up. Everything she needed was in a large holdall: the champagne, the drugs, the catheter, masking tape, a baseball bat, a pair of pliers, scissors, her cleaning equipment; also the special items, the glass (plus five others like it), the cigarette butts and the fingerprints, six in total, one taken from the coffee cup and five lifted from the base of the plate, all of them stored on cellophane.

She started off in the basement. She found the thermostat and put the heating on at full blast. She put the champagne in the fridge and placed the five dummy glasses in a kitchen cupboard to join the Levines' other tumblers and glassware in there. It was important that the sixth glass, the one she had taken from TGR's, would not stand out in any way. It

241

needed to be one of a set so that there could be no indication it had been planted.

Then Cilla made her way up to the top of the house with her holdall. There were two bedrooms up there and a bathroom. One bedroom was used by Matilde and the other was spare. The action would need to take place in Matilde's room since this was at the front of the house. But neither of the chairs on the top floor were suitable since both lacked arms. In the end Cilla took the high-backed Windsor out of Amy's room and dragged it upstairs. It had a nicely carved section running down the middle. Cilla wiped the chair clean and then transferred two prints onto the back of the carved section, at the top, where they would be likely to be found when it was dusted by police. She put two more on the handle of the bedroom door.

The holdall with the rest of its contents went under the bed, out of sight but accessible.

The next thing to do was to check the windows. They were traditional two-panel sash frames which opened and closed with a cord pulley system. Both were locked with fasteners and egress window stops but Cilla found the key for the stops on one of the upper rails. The left-hand window would not open at all. It had probably been painted shut at some point, but the right one moved up and down smoothly. Once she had the lower sash panel fully opened Cilla threw the three cigarette butts out of it. Then she leant over the sill to gauge the trajectory that would be required later that night. She had left the kitchen light on so that she could see below.

The iron railings which separated the house from the street were 1.3 metres away from the building. Cilla knew this because she had already measured the distance. If Paul Levine was simply hauled out of the window there was every possibility that he would miss the railings altogether and plummet to the basement. The fall would kill him, certainly, but it wouldn't be good enough. He needed to end up on those railings. It was the trademark, the signature, nothing less would do.

Cilla had seen this happen only once. In the early days when she first knew Vlad, he had invited her to attend one of his special sessions. The subject was a high-roller with large unpaid gambling debts and the man had just been declared bankrupt so there was no hope of repayment. Vlad and two of his henchmen barged into the man's flat late at night wearing hazmat suits and masks. They strapped the poor bastard to a chair, taped up his mouth and went to work on him. Cilla did not participate in the activities, she was merely there to observe. Perhaps she was supposed to be impressed, or afraid, or simply reminded of the lengths that Vlad would go to in order to impose his will. After a while, when everyone was tired and bored, Vlad ordered one of his men to untie the bloody lump that sat with its head drooping to one side. The man was still alive but barely. As he was unstrapped and his body began to slide towards the floor Vlad stepped forward and caught him. He lifted the man up gently, cradling him in his arms as if he were no heavier than a child, and walked towards the open window.

"How far?" he enquired. The other henchman leant out and peered down into the darkness.

"Three metres, give or take," he replied.

"OK," Vlad said. He planted himself in front of the window, made a quarter turn away from it, stepped back with his left foot and lowered his body slightly, bending at the hips and knees. He lifted up the load so that the man's body was level with his jaw line. Vlad pivoted gently on the spot a couple of times in preparation, inhaling and exhaling through his mouth. Then he exploded into motion. The man's body sailed out of the window. Vlad arched his back, flexed his shoulders, turned towards Cilla and smiled.

"Impressive," she remarked since it was clearly expected of her.

"It's a through and through on two spikes," one of the others said excitedly. "Nice work boss."

"But brazen," Cilla continued. "If you keep this up eventually they'll come for you."

"Sometimes it is necessary," Vlad responded. "It lets the other cunts know what's in store for them if they don't pay what is owed." He took off his mask and began to remove the hazmat suit, peeling off the wet upper half and rolling the material carefully down his legs. "Anyway, I have you," he said contentedly. Vlad stepped out of the suit entirely and kicked it away. "So I don't need to do anymore dirty work if I don't want to. That's your job now."

The problem was that Cilla could not launch Paul Levine out of the third-floor window as if he were a shot put. It wasn't physically possible. She sat down on the bed to consider the matter. Then she moved the high-backed Windsor chair so that it sat in front of the open window and practised tilting it backwards so that the crest rail sat on the sill. If she levered the whole chair onto the sill then Paul Levine would slide out of the window at an angle. Of course, this was easy to do with an empty chair. It might be a different matter with a body seated in it.

Finally Cilla placed the sixth glass in the middle of the dressing table to the left of the chair. She practised the action of standing in front of the chair, drinking from the glass, or perhaps offering it to the person seated on the chair and setting it down on the table. Incorporating the necessary adjustments for height and arm length Cilla then moved it eight centimetres.

244

She shut the window, leaving it unlocked, and went back downstairs to the ground floor and into the study which also doubled as Paul Levine's bedroom. The web had been woven, the fly would approach. All that was left to do was to wait.

🐛

It was 2.34 a.m. when Cilla heard the sound of a key turning in the front door. She waited until she heard the door close before standing up and going out into the hall. Paul Levine was standing there pale and unsteady, taking off his jacket. He looked drunk, or stoned, or both.

"Mr Levine," she said.

He was predictably startled and peered down the passage at her with bloodshot eyes. At first he didn't appear to recognise who she was but eventually he said:

"You. What are you doing here?"

"I've come to tell you that the job is complete."

"What?"

"Your wife is dead."

"But I just spoke to her earlier today."

"And now she is dead, as we agreed."

Paul Levine did not react to this statement. He simply stood, transfixed, mouth open, one hand extended still holding his jacket. Perhaps he was in shock.

"Your wife is dead," Cilla repeated helpfully.

"She's dead," he acknowledged eventually and the act of saying this seemed to release him from his fugue state. He reached forward and hung his jacket on the coat stand.

"I don't have the money," he blurted out. "Not on me."

"I'm not expecting to be paid now," Cilla reassured him, "but I always like to let clients know personally when a job has been concluded, so that we may toast the successful completion of the project and our partnership."

245

"What?"

"I have taken the liberty of chilling a bottle of champagne in your fridge downstairs." It sounded clumsy when she said it out loud, but Paul Levine didn't seem to notice.

"Amy's dead, oh God she's really dead. She's fucking dead," he muttered, half to himself. He turned to Cilla. "Are you sure that it looked like an accident?"

"Not an accident, better than that, natural causes," Cilla said soothingly. "Let's go down to the kitchen and I'll tell you all about it."

"Why is it so hot in here?" he said as she guided him along the hall, down the stairs, and sat him on a chair at the kitchen table. The cork came out of the bottle easily and Cilla filled two champagne flutes nearly to the brim. Flunitrazepam tended to froth when it came into contact with liquid and the champagne bubbles served to disguise this. She handed one of the flutes to Paul and sat down opposite him.

"To a job well done," she said, raising her glass towards his. Still dazed, he picked his glass up and clinked it with hers almost from force of habit, then raised it to his lips. Beads of sweat had begun to appear on his forehead and his upper lip looked damp. That was one objective complete.

There were four tasks ahead of Cilla now:

Ensure that Paul Levine drank his glass of champagne.

Keep him talking for twenty minutes until the Flunitrazepam took effect.

Get him to accompany her to the top of the house.

Make him cry.

The first two were fairly straightforward. She would tell him how she killed his wife and he would drink his champagne. The third was a matter of timing. She needed to get him upstairs once he became suggestible and before he became incompetent. But the fourth, how to make him cry, that was the one that concerned her.

Some people cry with almost no provocation whatsoever; show them a sick puppy or a starving kitten and that's it, they're off, bawling their eyes out like a baby. Others barely cry at all. Who knew where Paul Levine lay on this spectrum. Perhaps the disinhibiting effect of the Flunitrazepam would be helpful. But helpful or not, Cilla needed those tears, those tiny drops of saline, as many of them as she could squeeze out of those bewildered bloodshot eyes.

She told him all about his wife's death. Of course it was not actually his wife's death she was describing since his wife was alive and well in Saxbys Mead with her parents. What Cilla actually told him about was the death of Maria the mule a couple of years earlier, poisoned in her sleep with the last of the Batrachotoxin. She added a few choice details about Amy's peaceful childlike demeanour and how beautiful she had looked as she lay unconscious. This did not have the intended effect.

"Bitch," was his only comment as he took a large gulp of champagne and Cilla recalled the torture request he had made during their second meeting. There was clearly no point trying to paint Amy as a dying Madonna when she had already been reclassified as a whore.

"Why bitch?" she said instead.

"Nothing I ever did was good enough. It was just nag nag nag. Mow the lawn. Nag. Empty the dishwasher. Nag. And even when I did there was never any fucking sex, not once the kids came along. She just kept telling me she was too tired, but I knew what was going on. It was that fucking trainer of hers. He was giving her one, I know he was." Paul Levine was getting angry rather than upset which was not the aim of this line of enquiry and yet Cilla could not help but ask:

"So why not just separate? Get divorced. Isn't that what people do?"

"No!" he shouted. "No, no, no. She promised to love me and to honour me until death us do part. She was a fucking liar."

How did people end up like this? They started out in love, got married, made children, created a family and ended up each wanting to destroy the other. Sometimes Cilla envied other people their emotions, the way in which they got caught up and swept away by them, and sometimes, like now, she felt grateful to be unencumbered.

Paul Levine tipped the stem of his glass upwards, swallowed its contents and deposited the empty vessel rather heavily on the table. His eyes were beginning to look unfocused and the pupils were dilating.

"There's one other thing I'm curious about, Paul. Do you mind if I call you Paul?" Cilla said.

"Call me what you like," Paul replied. He tapped his glass. "More please," he requested in a sing-song voice.

Another glass wouldn't really do any harm and it would keep him occupied so Cilla refilled it.

"I'm curious about the coke," she said.

Paul looked furtive like a small boy with something to hide. "What coke?" he said.

"The coke that you sell," Cilla replied casually.

"I don't sell any coke," Paul Levine insisted.

Cilla looked thoughtful for a moment. "No, you don't," she agreed. "But I don't think you're giving it away either. What do you get in return?"

"It's a secret," he replied.

"You can tell me," she said coaxingly. "I'm good at keeping secrets."

Paul Levine smiled slyly and leant across the table towards

her. "Information," he whispered loudly. "I got into a bit of a rut, wasn't making any money. In fact I lost a load of money; my money, clients' money, the company's money. Ssh." He put his finger to his lips. "Nobody knows. Now I've got this new system I'm going to make it all back. I give them coke, they tell me stuff, then I know when to go long and when to go short."

The candour of these admissions appeared to indicate that the Flunitrazepam was taking effect. It was important to get him moving before he was incapable of doing so. The crying would have to wait.

"Why don't we go upstairs now?" Cilla suggested brightly. "We could go and look at Matilde's room."

"I'd like that," Paul responded, rising rather shakily from his chair. "She's so beautiful isn't she? And she has a lovely voice. She calls me Mr Paul, isn't that sweet?"

The only real difference between men and women, or the only one that counted, in Cilla's opinion, was the difference in physical strength. If Vlad was here now he could have simply picked Paul Levine up, slung him over one shoulder and carried him to the top floor of the house. Even an average-sized man could have waited until the Flunitrazepam rendered Paul unconscious and dragged him up to Matilde's room. Cilla did not have either of these options. Instead she had to cajole and wheedle the stockbroker up three floors whilst he was still vaguely compos mentis. Twice he sat down on a step saying that he was tired and it took all Cilla's powers of persuasion to convince him to climb the final flight of stairs.

The only source of illumination in Matilde's bedroom came from a small lamp on the dressing table. Its range extended about two metres from the bulb.

"What's that doing there?" Paul demanded pointing at

the high-backed Windsor chair parked in front of the right window. "That doesn't belong in here."

"I put it there so that you would have somewhere to sit," Cilla replied.

"But I want to lie down. I like lying down in here, it smells of her." Paul Levine made to move towards Matilde's bed; Cilla blocked his path.

"Sit in the chair," she said firmly. "I need to tell you something; something about Matilde."

"What about her?" he said.

"Sit down and I'll tell you," Cilla insisted.

Paul Levine staggered several steps and slumped down into the high-backed Windsor chair, eyeing Cilla reproachfully as he did so.

"Tell me now," he demanded.

"Matilde doesn't love you," Cilla said slowly and clearly.

"What?"

"She doesn't love you. She thinks you're a pervert."

"No," Paul Levine howled. "That's not true."

"Yes it is. You stole her underwear didn't you?" Cilla pressed on.

"She gave it to me," he wailed.

"No she didn't. You stole it. She thinks you're nothing but a dirty old man. She wouldn't touch you with a barge pole. But you already know that don't you?"

There was a moment of hesitation, an effort to maintain control, but then Paul's face collapsed. His eyes brimmed over and two large globules began to roll down his face, one after another; fat salty pearls which coursed their way over his cheekbones towards his chin. He began to sob in earnest making small choking sounds as he wept. There were more than enough tears now. He put his hands on the arms of the chair and tried to stand up but his legs refused to bear any weight. Cilla stood there regarding him in his increasingly helpless state and sighed.

"It's OK Paul, you can stop crying now," she said quietly. "Matilde does love you really."

"What? But you said she didn't," he stuttered.

"I was just teasing you. I'm sorry."

"That's a mean thing to do," he moaned. "You're just like my wife. Why are women such bitches?"

It was an interesting question that the stockbroker had raised and in different circumstances Cilla would have enjoyed debating the matter further with him. Her own view was that it all came back to the disparity in physical strength between the sexes. Most women could not impose their will forcibly, as men were able to do, so they had to find more subversive methods. But now was hardly the time for such a discussion and instead she said, "I'm sorry Paul, you're right, it was mean of me. Why don't you shut your eyes now?"

He barely had a choice in the matter. The effects of the Flunitrazepam meant that his eyes were closing of their own accord.

"Imagine that you and Matilde are on a beach together. You're lying on warm sand and the sun is shining down." As she spoke Cilla crept towards the bed and retrieved the holdall from beneath it. She took out the masking tape, the scissors and the baseball bat. "The only sound is the soft lap of water as waves break onto the shore." She stood in front of the chair and began to secure the stockbroker to it with the masking tape, wrapping it around his torso three times. He didn't resist. She taped his wrists to the arms of the chair. "Matilde takes hold of your hand and she tells you how much she loves you." His fingers seemed to reach out with this statement so she held them gently for a moment with her own. The tears were drying now. Although his face

251

was still streaked the expression on it had grown peaceful and contented. Whether this was because he was listening to her or because he had fallen asleep, Cilla was unsure. It really didn't matter. "You feel very happy and contented," she continued, taking hold of the baseball bat as she spoke. "You love Matilde and she loves you. Everything is good with the world." Cilla lined up her knuckles and swung the bat back over her shoulder. She brought it down with full force onto Paul Levine's left temple. The purpose of this was to cause his brain to swing violently against the lining of his skull. It wouldn't kill him, it would just knock him out completely. It wasn't meant to kill him; not yet. She wanted him unconscious but alive.

Cilla went down to the kitchen and turned the heating thermostat back to its original level. She washed the two champagne glasses and put them back into the cupboard with the others. She poured the rest of the bottle down the sink, rinsed the bowl with water and checked the kitchen for any other evidence of her presence. When she was satisfied she switched off the light and made her way back upstairs, flicking off any other switches as she ascended.

The only light in the house still on was the lamp on the dressing table in Matilde's bedroom. It cast a dim glow on the man slumped in the chair. There wasn't really enough light for Cilla to work with but, in truth, she had no particular desire to see what she was doing too clearly. The procedure would be distasteful enough even in this half-light. She put the empty champagne bottle into her holdall, took out the catheter and the pliers, put on a second pair of gloves and taped up Paul Levine's mouth. There was little or no possibility of his regaining consciousness but this added an authentic touch to proceedings.

The thing about torture is that it always involves effluence:

blood, sweat, tears, urine, diarrhoea and vomit. The first three of these are a given, but at least one of the others is always present. Given a choice between urine, diarrhoea and vomit, urine is the least offensive and the easiest to extract. Cilla kept reminding herself of this as she unzipped Paul Levine's flies, found his penis and inserted the catheter. His bladder must have been fairly full because once she had the tube in place a vigorous flow of warm yellow fluid doused his right trouser leg.

Next came the body and the face. Cilla used the baseball bat on the knees, the chest and the shoulders. Then she broke his nose and crushed one cheekbone and an eye socket. With the pliers she chopped off two fingers from his left hand. Onto one of these she transferred the last of Vlad's prints before throwing both of the fingers to the floor. She checked Paul Levine's pulse; he was still alive. From her perspective it would have been easier to commit these atrocities on a dead body rather than a living one, but that would have defeated the object of the exercise. One of the first physiological changes that occurs in death is that blood stops flowing around the body. This enables an autopsy to reveal whether injuries have been committed pre- or post-mortem. Sadists don't tend to torture the dead, after all where is the sport in that, which meant that Paul Levine's heart needed to keep beating, to keep pumping blood around his body, right until the bitter end.

Cilla paused and stepped back to survey her work. The stockbroker was unrecognisable as himself, and he strongly resembled the other bloody lump on a chair that Cilla had seen two years earlier. She put all her equipment back into the holdall except for the scissors. She cut through the tape that bound Paul Levine's wrists to the chair and ripped off the piece over his mouth. Finally she opened the window to its widest setting and turned off the lamp on the dressing table.

It was time.

Tipping the chair backwards so that the crest rail met the window sill took some effort but Cilla was able to tilt it sufficiently so that the chair balanced precariously on its back legs and the sill. The next part of the procedure was more taxing. She squatted on the floor in front of the chair and put the scissors in her mouth. Then she placed her shoulders underneath the seat and gripped both front legs with her hands. Her face was positioned neatly into Paul Levine's wet sour crotch. Bearing the weight of the chair on her shoulders Cilla tried to stand up. Nothing happened. She stopped, drew breath, tensed again and attempted to deadlift the chair to a standing position. It didn't move.

If she couldn't lift the chair onto the sill and propel Paul Levine out of the window and onto those railings below then the whole of tonight's endeavour would have been pointless. She would have to revert to Plan B, which wasn't so much of a plan as a form of capitulation. She would kill Paul, wipe the prints off the chair, the door handle and the finger, put the glass from the dressing table back into her holdall along with the rest of her stuff and retreat. She would go back to the bridge club as though nothing had happened and it would be business as usual. Her coup would have failed. Then one day, probably sooner rather than later, she would be doing some job and she would make another mistake and this time she would pay for it with her life. Or maybe Vlad would simply tire of her and take her down to the cellar for a bit of fun. Or perhaps she would simply decide that enough was enough and take the hero's way out, or the coward's way out, depending on how you looked at it.

And all because she couldn't lift a fucking chair.

Cilla took the scissors out of her mouth and started tapping one of the chair legs with the blades. The steady beat was like a metronome and it helped her think. Colonel Dubrovsky, her old headmaster, would have said it wasn't that she couldn't lift the chair, but that she didn't want to lift the chair enough. He had personally supervised a number of the Impulse and Behaviour Regulation sessions at Academy 43 and he had some interesting ideas about pushing past limits and breaking boundaries. On the other hand he was probably dead now or relocated to the Northern mines, which presumably was not what he had wanted. But still. Maybe there was some truth to it. Maybe, when she thought about it, there was some ambivalence, some part of her that didn't want to let go. This way of life was all that Cilla had ever really known and she was very good at what she did.

Twice, in the past, she had had the opportunity to give it all up, to take another path, and twice she had elected to carry on. What was different this time? There was the money that she had saved up, that helped. There was her epiphany; the realisation, fused with blood and tessellating fish, that she had reached an ultimate dead end, or soon would, a gaping black hole which would consume her. But more than that she was aware that her life did not belong to her; she was someone else's creature and always had been. The only things that really belonged to her were a few scars, a locket, a piece of charred paper and the bolt from a crossbow that she had decided not to fire; these were the things that represented the choices that she had made for herself rather than those that had been made for her. In the end that was what it all came down to: she wanted the right to choose.

Cilla put the scissors back in her mouth. This time she did not tense. Instead she took one long deep breath into her diaphragm, her stomach and her spine. She imagined the oxygen filling her whole body. She exhaled slowly, relaxing her shoulders as she did so, and she stood up, pushing the chair forward simultaneously so that the weight of it slid onto the windowsill. Cilla edged the load forwards. She wanted to extend the chair out of the window as far as she could without losing control so that chair and body toppled out together. When she had gone as far as she dared she leant forward, took the scissors out of her mouth with her right hand and began to cut the masking tape that still bound Paul Levine to the chair. It was slow going, there were three layers of tape to get through. Even when she had severed it entirely the tape still clung to his clothes and he remained seated, his head and arms flung backwards hanging out of the window, his legs still within. Maintaining a firm grip of the chair with her left hand, Cilla clutched hold of a handful of tape with her right and ripped it free. The stockbroker's body slithered backwards and in an instant it had gone. Cilla hauled the chair back inside, closed and locked the window.

Within forty-five seconds she was leaving the house, descending the steps from the Levines' front door, opening the gate and closing it behind her, pausing for a moment to survey the scene. Now was the moment of truth. Would Paul Levine's body have fallen to the basement or would it be visible to all, impaled on the railings?

There was nothing to see; her heart sank; it had all been in vain. Then Cilla caught sight of the arm in the street. At first sight it looked as if the arm had become detached from its body and was simply lying there on its own, pale and lifeless. But as her gaze travelled up the arm she saw that it was still attached to its shoulder and through that shoulder protruded the long black bloody spike of an iron railing.

Cilla was already walking briskly away, going over the image in her mind, trying to make sense of it. The horizontal top rail should have prevented the shoulder from sliding all the way down the railing. Perhaps it was missing at that point or weak and had been broken by the weight of the falling body. No matter. The result wasn't perfect, it wasn't a through and through on two spikes, but it would do. Even the most obtuse detective would be able to add up the evidence left behind at the scene and come up with Vladimir Haugr's name. There was no hazmat suit to protect him this time.

The night air was cool and fresh on her face. Cilla took off her wig and stuffed it into her pocket. She wouldn't need it anymore. The last thing left to do was to go home and pack two bags. One would contain her essentials, the few things that she would take with her on her new journey. The other would contain all the links to her past, her plants, her stores, her equipment, the True-to-Life baby doll and its wardrobe of little clothes. Then first thing tomorrow she would make a trip to various dumps and recycling centres around the capital, disposing of a few items at each. Finally, she would go to Smithy's place in Amersham to collect the last of her documents: an honours degree in Philosophy from Leeds University.

She wondered why she didn't feel better as she strode towards Shepherds Bush: more relieved, more elated, more excited at the prospect of the future. But in her heart, or rather the dark core which functioned as a heart, Cilla knew why. It was the final heinous act; it still needed to be completed and she would have no peace until it was done.

19

Choices II

Loose ends must always be tied.

Colonel Dubrovsky taught her that. He drummed it into the children at Academy 43 over and over again after they began using live targets on the archery range, rather than aiming at a dartboard, after it became clear what the training programmes at the school were actually training pupils to do.

The tying of loose ends was essential if a covert mission were to remain covert. Any link that allowed an operation to be traced back to its origins had to be severed, no matter the cost.

A loose end could be anything: a murder weapon left behind at the scene or abandoned thoughtlessly, revealing CCTV footage, a witness. Most loose ends occurred due to carelessness on the part of the operative, but some were unavoidable.

Occasionally the Colonel would invent a theoretical

mission and create a scenario within that mission which involved a loose end. Then he would ask the class for proposals as to how the loose end should be tied. Whenever that loose end involved a witness, there was only one sensible course of action that could be followed. The witness must be eliminated.

Smithy was a loose end.

It was impossible to know how long it would take the police to examine the crime scene, process the evidence and draw the inevitable conclusion that Vladimir Haugr had tortured and killed Paul Levine. Or how long after that it would take for them to arrest him. It might be a few days, it might be weeks, or months. Cilla did not want to wait around to find out. She wanted to pick up the last of her documents and go.

There was no choice in this matter. She could not risk encountering Vladimir Haugr again. If she saw him, even once, his sensitive antennae would immediately detect that something was amiss. He would start asking questions, he wouldn't believe the answers, he would lose faith and the cellar would beckon. Cilla would find herself processed into a bloody lump of meat and there would be no Flunitrazepam or sharp blow to the head to ease the transition. In fact it was more likely that every effort would be made to keep her alive and conscious, so that she could still experience the exquisite sensation of the scaffolding pipe at the end of it all. Vlad once boasted to her that he had kept someone alive for five whole days in that cellar. He probably ate his dinner down there as well. There was no doubt about it, she had to leave, and she had to leave immediately.

But it would not take more than a couple of days before her absence was noted. When she didn't show up at the bridge club Vladimir Haugr would start to wonder. Then he would look for her. When he couldn't locate her he would probably start by talking to Nancy. Since Nancy knew nothing she was in no danger. After that it wouldn't take him very long to go and find Smithy. Even if Smithy ran away, Vlad would find him, Vlad would hunt him down.

Smithy would not betray her, not on purpose anyway. But once Vlad went to work on him he would be unable to resist. It would probably only take a couple of teeth and a fingernail or two before Smithy gave up all the information he had: her new name, her passport details, her bank account. And then they'd kill him anyway, in some vile and unnecessary manner.

Better surely that Cilla tied up the loose end herself. She could make it quick and painless, he would never see it coming. And then they would both be safe. And she could move on and begin her life again.

It was no big thing, not really; just one more death, one more corpse to be thrown on the pile, a pile so large that Smithy's body would simply converge with the others, indistinguishable from the mass. Once it was done Cilla would walk away. Inside her head she would take a can of petrol and she would pour it on that pile. She would take a match and she would set the pile alight. And she would never think of it again.

It was 7.30 a.m. on Sunday morning when Cilla found herself standing outside the detached Amersham bungalow where Smithy lived. All the curtains were drawn which was not unusual given the time of day. Nevertheless she could not remember having seen them closed before. Cilla stood in the road for several minutes, fingering the green locket around her neck, before she approached the front door. Something felt off. Or was it simply her own resistance to the task that she had set herself? But as she finally pressed her finger to the doorbell and heard its shrill retort she knew for certain that something was wrong. The heavy footsteps approaching the door were not Smithy's. It took quite a few seconds between the initial sound of those footsteps and the opening of the front door. Longer than the length of time that a child was given as a head start when they had chosen Flee and their opponent had chosen Chase all those years ago at Academy 43; more than long enough for Cilla. She could have high-tailed it down the street at breakneck speed if she had opted to do so. She was a good runner and it was unlikely that anyone would have caught her. But Cilla didn't do that. She just stood on the step with her hands in her jacket pockets waiting for the front door to open. In spite of all her training, all her knowledge and experience, everything that it had taken to survive for all these years, she couldn't help but choose Fight. Or perhaps it wasn't really a choice at all: it was just her nature.

"Cilla," Vlad said, as he opened the door. "What a pleasant surprise. I wasn't expecting to see you here. Or maybe I was, I'm not quite sure. Come in, come in."

There was nothing left to do but to enter the lion's den.

"So what are you doing here so early in the morning?" Vlad continued affably as she slipped past him into the long empty hall. The kitchen door was to her left and the lounge entrance was to her right. Further back were three more doors. One housed the bathroom and the other two led to the bungalow's bedrooms. All the doors were shut and there was no sign of Smithy.

"I just came to check on the Mint," Cilla replied evenly. She stood very still and alert, her head cocked slightly to one side, her hands firmly in her pockets. She could feel Vlad's eyes fixed on the back of her head as he closed the front door behind her. There were a series of clicks as he inserted the key into the deadlock and turned it. Then she heard him slide the heavy-duty bolt into place. In her left-hand pocket Cilla's fingers curled around Plan A: a hypodermic syringe filled with fentanyl, a synthetic opioid which was up to a hundred times stronger than heroin. It was meant to have been for Smithy. She had wanted to provide him with a quick easy exit wrapped up in one last incredible high. In her right pocket was Plan B: her blowpipe loaded with the same dose of curare that it had not been necessary to use on Amy Levine, just in case Smithy turned out to be difficult about the fentanyl. Both of these plans seemed rather redundant now.

"Where is Smithy anyway? Is he still asleep?" she enquired, turning smoothly back towards Vlad as she spoke, careful not to let any inflection seep into her voice, to maintain an expression of calm composure.

"You want to see the pretty boy," Vlad said. "Of course you do." He jerked his head towards the right. Cilla turned and took a step towards the lounge door. She could feel her pulse slowing down. Everything seemed to be decelerating around her as if it was all taking place underwater. It was always that way when base Cilla began to rise to the surface.

"He's not looking so pretty right now," Vlad commented with a low chuckle as she turned the handle.

The lounge was a fog of cigarette smoke. Everything was in disarray, broken and strewn about the room. Cilla had a grim sense of déjà vu at the sight which met her eyes. The only piece of furniture which was still upright was a regency mahogany dining chair on which Smithy was seated, his hands taped to the cross rail at the back. Two of Vlad's henchman loitered uneasily on either side of him with dull witless expressions on their faces. How was it that she had just dealt with a man strapped to a chair and now here she was faced with another? Smithy still vaguely resembled Smithy so Vlad and his boys couldn't have been there for all that long, but his nose had been broken so viciously that it sat in a swollen slant towards one cheekbone on a face which was streaked with red and purple, angular and distorted like a Picasso painting. What was even more shocking than the destruction of Smithy's beautiful nose was the reaction that seeing this elicited in Cilla herself. She felt the pain of its wreckage. She felt the panic in Smithy's dark eyes as though it were her own; his terror seemed to pass through her like a jolt of ice-cold electricity. Her heart, normally located firmly in her chest, seemed to rise of its own accord upwards through her oesophagus until it sat tentatively at the top of her throat, just below her mouth. And where her heart should have been was a space, a black bottomless pit of longing and yearning for something that she could not name. Cilla thought about the syringe of fentanyl in her left-hand pocket and what she had planned to do with it. And she realised that she had intended to kill Smithy not because he was a loose end but because she knew that he would never want her in the way that she wanted him and that this knowledge was intolerable.

Strange how these epiphanies only seemed to occur in situations of stress.

"So what's he done now?" she said casually to Vlad.

"You know, I'm not actually sure yet," Vlad replied pushing past her into the lounge and dropping down onto one knee so that he could inspect the damage to Smithy's face. "All I know is that I woke up at 3.30 a.m. this morning with a sense of—" He stopped mid-sentence and deliberated for a moment. "A sense of foreboding," he concluded. "I tossed and turned for a couple of hours but it just would not go away." Vlad stood up again to his full massive height. "Do

263

you remember that contract of seven hearts I told you about, Cilla, the one where I went down because the trumps were five nil. It is the same exact feeling; I still have it now here in my gut." Vlad patted his belly with a fist. "So I got up and I came here."

He fell silent, glowering down at Cilla, watching and waiting to see how she would react.

"And?" was all she said.

"And nothing," Vlad admitted grudgingly. "We searched the place and the only things we found were the Mint, a bunch of fucking postage stamps and this." He reached into his back pocket and brought out a folded piece of paper which he tossed towards Cilla.

She could feel the quality of the paper as she unfolded it; Smithy had used aged parchment. The black lettering was written in raised ink. He had awarded her a First Class Honours Degree in the Field of Philosophy. At the bottom left-hand corner was a large embossed hallmark bearing the words "The Seal of the University of Leeds" in elevated capital letters around its circumference. Cilla held the document in her right hand and let her left one fall to her side so that it could edge its way back to the door handle as she spoke.

"What is this?" she said indifferently.

"I don't really know. Maybe nothing, maybe something," Vlad replied. "I asked the pretty boy about it and he lied to me. So I sat him down and I asked him again. But every time I touch him he keeps fainting like a little girl. And then you turn up," he concluded thoughtfully.

"Maybe it's just a freelance job, some fake documentation that somebody ordered," Cilla suggested.

A faint smile began to flicker at one corner of Vlad's mouth.

"Do you know, that's just what he said." Vlad leant down

to the floor and picked up another of the regency dining chairs setting it upright next to Smithy's.

"I think I want to ask you some questions now Cilla. Would you care to sit down?"

Cilla shook her head. "Ask away," she replied. "But I think I'll stay where I am."

Maintaining her position in the doorway with a light grip on the door handle seemed to be the best and safest alternative for the moment. If Vlad's two goons tried to rush her she should have time to slam the door in their faces. This might buy her a couple of seconds and when they broke through she could use the fentanyl on one of them, or maybe even both of them if she could time it right. There was easily enough there to deal with two grown men. Cilla didn't think any further than this. She just planned for the next five minutes, always the next five minutes. If she was still alive at the end of that then she could consider her options again.

"Who does that belong to?" Vlad enquired pointing at the certificate in her hand.

"It's mine," Cilla replied. There was no point in lying to him now.

"And why do you have it?" he continued.

"Because I wish to leave your employ," she explained.

"You wish to leave my employ," Vlad repeated slowly and ominously. "And why is that? Has someone made you a better offer?"

"No," she replied. "I just don't want to kill people anymore."

This made no sense to Vlad at all. It was as if she had said that she wanted to give up breathing or eating food. "Why not?" he asked.

"Because!" Cilla shouted. "Because I'm twenty-two years old. At least I think I'm twenty-two years old. You know I might be out a year. It's possible that I'm actually twenty-one or maybe I'm twenty-three, I'm not really sure. But the point is that I am young, and there's a life out there for me, which I won't get to live if I carry on working for you." The words poured out of her like water breaking through a dam.

"But I thought you were happy," Vlad remonstrated. "You were the one who came and asked me for a job, have you forgotten that? Have you forgotten the chance that I gave you and the debt that you owe?"

"No," she said miserably.

"And what about your bridge?" he persevered. "You were coming along so nicely."

But Cilla said nothing and just stood in the doorway watching Vlad as he clenched and unclenched his fists repeatedly.

"Cilla, you give up this nonsense now," he growled at last. "We'll go out and get some breakfast. We can talk things over, sort them out. Maybe come up with a new arrangement, one that will give you more freedom, more opportunity."

If circumstances had been different this would have been a very tempting offer. It was the lure of the familiar. But there was the small matter of Paul Levine, dead and impaled on a railing, to be considered. The crime would likely have been discovered by now, the police called in. Maybe a forensics team was already on site, dusting down the premises, bagging up evidence, scratching their heads and trying to fit all the pieces of the puzzle into place. Still, Cilla had been up all night and she was beginning to feel hungry. At least breakfast with Vlad would defuse the current situation she was in.

"What about him?" she nodded at the mute mauled figure taped to a chair in the middle of the room. Vlad shrugged his shoulders.

"I have what I came for. The Mint is fully operational now; I got him to test it for me, several times. We'll take it with

266

us." He smiled, almost benignly, revealing the gold canine on one side that Cilla rarely got to see. "I have no further use for him. Let's you and me go now, my boys will take care of things here."

Choices, choices, difficult choices. Cilla had come to kill Smithy and yet now she felt torn between choosing to save her own skin which would mean leaving him to his sad inevitable fate, or opting, against all the odds, to try and save them both.

"No," she repeated, more firmly this time, and the word was a surprise even to herself.

The upward curve of Vlad's mouth inverted itself.

"I warned you Cilla, I warned you what would happen if you tried to fuck me over. I've given you every chance and all you do is to throw them in my face." He looked so angry, so irate, and yet even so there was something almost sorrowful in Vlad's expression. Then his face closed down, he gave a brief low whistle and the two henchmen sprang towards the door.

They were nothing more than guard dogs really, Dobermans that were trained to attack on command. Of course if they had actually been dogs, rather than human beings, their reactions might have been quicker. But it wouldn't have made any difference, not really, because base Cilla was there now, breaking through the surface, ready to take command.

In the same moment that the men charged, Cilla retreated and slammed the door. She hung on to the doorknob with her left hand, extending her arm and leaning backwards so that all her weight was concentrated into the handle. She scrunched up the paper in her right hand and reached diagonally across her body. The ball of paper went into her jacket pocket. The syringe of fentanyl came out. She manoeuvred her right foot backwards so that she could maintain her balance and simultaneously released the doorknob. As Cilla let go she rotated one hundred and eighty degrees on her front foot so that she was repositioned to the side of the door primed and loaded for whatever came through it.

Dealing with the first one was relatively straightforward. As the man burst into the hall she snapped forward and stuck him in the upper arm, making certain not to push the plunger all the way down and withdrawing it swiftly as he yelped in surprise and collapsed.

The problem was that this served as a warning to the second thug who came crashing through after him. He veered out of her reach and located himself at a safe distance, heaving from leg to leg, his arms and hands semi-outstretched in a wrestler's starting position, watching for the opportunity to close in and take her down.

Now Cilla was at a disadvantage. He had a clear view of the hypodermic and he knew to avoid it. He was advancing forwards, backing her up against the front door. At any moment now he would make his move and his brute strength would overwhelm her. There was only one chance. Cilla darted towards him, her right arm raised as if she intended to puncture him in the shoulder and as she did so she offered him her head. He took the bait, seizing hold of the attacking arm with one hand and sinking his fingers into her hair with the other. Once he had a good firm hold he yanked her head back violently and as he did so the wig came off in his hand. For a moment he stood there, staring at the large clump of hair with astonishment and in that same instant Cilla dropped the syringe, caught it with her other hand and injected her assailant in the thigh. There was less fentanyl in this dose so it took him longer to fall. But the pressure on her arm eased immediately allowing Cilla to wriggle out of his grasp and to run down the hall.

By the time he hit the floor she was already inside Smithy's bedroom and had closed the door behind her.

Vladimir Haugr watched the latter part of this scene unfold from the doorway to the lounge. He observed the struggle by the front door. As Cilla came sprinting past him it was even possible that he might have reached out and seized her. But he didn't feel like doing that. He preferred to take his time. Now that Cilla was in the bedroom she was trapped. There was nowhere for her to run. Vlad stepped over the first body and padded towards the front door. The second man lay there, his breathing ragged and shallow, the needle still poking out of his trouser leg. Vlad kicked the syringe away. Who knew what unpleasant concoction it had contained. Poison; a typical woman's weapon; underhand and deceitful. But the syringe was empty now.

Vlad knew all of Cilla's little tricks. He was aware of her armoury of small weapons, crossbows, blowpipes and the rest. She probably still had something up her sleeve, some nasty fatal dose. But in order to administer it she would have to take him by surprise and he already knew what lay behind that bedroom door. He and his boys had ransacked the room earlier in their search for the source of Vlad's sense of unease. The mattress was half off the bed so there was no chance that Cilla could be concealed beneath it. The window was glued shut, ruling that out as a means of escape. In fact the more he thought about it the more certain Vlad became that the bedroom offered little or no opportunity to hide. But for all his size, his strength and his bravado Vladimir Haugr was a careful man. He had not risen to the position of feudal warlord by taking unnecessary risks. He returned to the doorway of the lounge and glanced around the room, ignoring Smithy, searching amongst the detritus for something that he could use. His eyes alighted on an overmantel mirror which lay broken on the floor. The glass was smashed but the wooden framework was still intact and it had a length of chain hanging at the back which would suit his purpose exactly. He picked up the mirror, shook off the broken glass and wrapped the chain securely around his left arm. With his new shield in place Vlad moved down the hall towards the bedroom door.

He turned the handle carefully and then kicked open the door, smashing it into the wall on the right-hand side and holding up his shield to the left. But there was no sign of Cilla. Vlad made a panoramic scan of the room. Almost everything was as he had left it: the mattress aslant and scored down the middle, the duvet ripped apart into strips, the crumpled sheet and pillows on the floor. The drawers still hung out of the chest, spewing their contents around them. Only one thing was different. The doors to the armoire were shut. Vlad had left them open. He advanced towards the wardrobe stealthily keeping his shield raised. He had no intention of opening those cupboard doors. That would be what Cilla wanted him to do. She would be lying in wait, ready to perform some final act of treachery. Instead he unwrapped the chain from his arm and rewrapped it tightly around the two handles in front of him. Now the armoire could not be opened at all and this would serve as his protection. With slow steady precision, like the repeated fall of an axe, Vlad began to kick the doors of the wardrobe.

If curare is administered into a large vein or an artery it will take effect within the space of a minute. But if the dose lands in muscle tissue it can take up to half an hour before the recipient is paralysed. The difference between these two lengths of time was the difference between life and death. Cilla might be able to survive for a minute after she had discharged her load, but she wouldn't last any longer.

As she rose up from the floor, a small silent spectre, emerging from the bedsheet like a newly formed moth, Cilla was also aware that none of Vlad's arteries were readily available to her. They were all protected by his clothing, his constant movement and fluctuation, as he kicked the cupboard over and over again. The only bare piece of flesh that was visible to her was the back of his neck, those few centimetres between hairline and collar. There were vertebral and internal carotid arteries located there but these were obscured by the bones of his neck at the top of his spine. Which led her to think about Vlad's spinal cord, snaking its way downwards and, more importantly, about the space between the dura mater and the vertebral wall. Cilla wondered how long the curare would take to activate if it were administered directly into the cerebrospinal fluid within that epidural space. There was no easy answer to this question and only one way to find out. But she couldn't use the blowpipe. Her breath would never exert sufficient pressure to allow the arrow to perforate the layers of clothing, skin and ligament. It would need to be done manually. So she took the blowpipe out of her jacket pocket, released the dart into her left palm, and gripped it, dagger-like, with her right hand. She waited for a few moments, swaying backwards and forwards, adjusting herself to the rhythm of his movement, then she took three steps and stabbed Vlad in the back.

He roared; a long guttural sound which seemed to emanate from deep within his chest. His hands were on her in an instant, hoisting her small frame high into the air and shaking her until she could feel her eyeballs and her teeth rattling within her skull. All Cilla could do was to remind herself to relax, to let her limbs flow freely and not to tense up. Nothing much mattered anymore. One way or the other, it was all over now.

If he'd had access to railings Vlad would have skewered Cilla upon them. But there were no railings in Smithy's bedroom so he had to content himself with hurling her at the wall.

❧

"I don't want to do it," Cilla whispered to Amelia who was standing in front of her in the queue.

"What?" Amelia responded, slightly startled, unsure if she had heard her friend correctly.

"I don't want to do it," Cilla repeated urgently.

The two of them were standing outside, in line, at the bottom of the scaffold. There were two children directly in front of them and two more had already begun to climb the ladder.

"You have to do it," Amelia retorted, stating the obvious, which was really no help at all.

So far ten children had made the ascent to the top of the two-storey structure. Of these, nine had walked across the platform and jumped. One refused and had to descend the way he had come. He was marched away by Comrade Guseva and since this was the second time that this particular boy had failed a test, Cilla knew that they wouldn't be seeing him again. Of the nine jumpers eight had landed successfully, stood up and walked or limped away. But the ninth jumper, a girl, hadn't got up. She had just lain there on the hard mat, listless and unmoving, her head sitting at an odd angle to her neck, until she was stretchered off. Soon it would be Cilla's turn to jump.

"I don't want to," she insisted now, hissing her words through gritted teeth.

"Why not?" Amelia wanted to know. "Are you afraid?" But Cilla didn't answer. Amelia knew better than to draw attention to

272

the two of them so even now she didn't turn around. She just reached out a hand discreetly until she encountered one of Cilla's small wrists. "Don't worry," Amelia said, squeezing it briefly. "I'll be there with you. I'll show you how."

The scaffold and its platform had appeared quite suddenly in the grounds of Academy 43 the day before, erected in a matter of hours by the labourers from Bunker 6. The purpose of the structure was to conclude a seminar that pupils had attended on jumping and falling as part of their Tactics for Retreat and Evasion course.

The seminar itself had been largely theoretical. Pupils were taught about the science of terminal velocity and the threshold for sustaining critical damage from a vertical descent. They were shown a video of a man jumping from a helicopter and free falling onto a large pile of cardboard boxes seemingly without injury. This video was played several times, twice in slow motion, to demonstrate how the man relaxed his body, spread his limbs, then tucked in his chin, bent his knees slightly and landed at an angle so that the energy of the impact could be transferred into a rolling motion. Each time he landed on the boxes the man leapt up, grinned and gave a big thumbs up to the camera. Cilla did not feel comforted by his enthusiasm. Afterwards there were a series of slides and diagrams which explained the man's falling technique in detail. Finally pupils were invited to the gymnasium to practise falling for themselves. Now they were expected to put what they had learnt into practice from the top of the two-storey scaffold.

"Come on," Amelia instructed her. "It's our turn."

Pupils went up the ladder in twos. Cilla kept her eyes firmly on Amelia's feet as she made her ascent and avoided looking down at all costs. She hauled herself up onto the platform and stood up, shivering slightly in the breeze. Amelia was waiting for her.

"I don't think I can do it," Cilla said shakily.

"Yes you can," Amelia reassured her. "You'll be fine. You won't hurt yourself."

273

"How do you know?"

"Because I know. Just watch me do it. When I get up from the mat, then it's your turn."

But Cilla just stood there, stubborn, wretched, and Amelia could sense the inertia setting in like cement.

"Let's swap places," Amelia suggested. "You go first, then I'll follow."

"They'll notice."

"It doesn't matter. They won't care. I'll just say that you pushed in front of me like you always do. Come on Cilla, you can do this. I know you can. Just put one foot in front of the other. That's right; one foot in front of the other. Keep moving; keep going; come on, you're nearly there, nearly there. There you are. Now relax. Relax. That's good. You're ready. You're ready now Cilla."

The bungalow was very quiet as Cilla slowly came to. It took her a while to recall where she was and she had no idea how long she'd been out for. She'd had the strangest dream, so real that it didn't feel like a dream at all, but more like a fragment of memory. But it couldn't have been a memory because the events of the dream were inaccurate. Children hadn't gone up the scaffold in pairs; they'd gone up one at a time. And she hadn't hesitated at the top. She'd just jumped.

Cilla kept her eyes closed for a few moments longer, not yet willing to commit to consciousness, and she used the time to take stock of her body. Her head was groggy and she could feel something oozing past her ear. One leg felt bruised and battered; her right collarbone was very tender which almost certainly meant that it was broken. Again. But apart from these injuries the rest of her felt relatively unscathed and intact.

A scraping noise nearby caused her eyes to flick open

involuntarily. Vlad lay on the floor opposite her in an almost symmetrical position. The noise had been his shoe twitching against the wooden floor. She could sense the effort and exertion that he expended internally as he tried to move his body. But Vlad's will was no match for Cilla's curare. It would hold him in its vice-like grip for hours. If his spinal cord had been perforated by the dart the paralysis could well be permanent. He might even die. But for the time being he remained conscious and his eyes blazed at her furiously.

Cilla reached into her pocket and brought out the scrunched-up ball of paper. She smoothed it out carefully trying to eradicate as many of the creases as she could with her numb tired fingers. She wanted to look at her name again written in black raised ink: Alexandria Fleming. It had a nice ring to it. Fleming, for Amelia, from all those years ago. Alexandria, for herself; her original name. Could she still use it, this name, now that Vlad had seen the document? She glanced over at his immobile body; sensed it thrashing inwardly and without effect. Yes, it would be OK. Even if he remembered the name, which he probably wouldn't, he was broken now. She had nothing left to fear from him. And in any case, no-one would actually call her Alexandria. They never had, it was too much of a mouthful. She would be Sasha, or Sashenka, as she had been in the beginning, before the sleek black car came and took her away.

The past seemed to stretch backwards like a long black tunnel lined with the bodies of the dead. Most of them had names. A few of them didn't. But here was an end to the slaughter. Now it was done, and Cilla vowed to herself, as she lay on the floor of Smithy's bedroom, that she would try, very hard, not to kill anyone else.

It was an easy promise to make; one that might be hard to keep. Murder was a deeply ingrained habit and, after all,

275

it was the only thing that Cilla had ever been good at. She would miss the rush, there was no doubt about that, nothing else would ever come close. She would live as a fox amongst rabbits and chickens, a predator in disguise, teeth hidden, claws retracted. It was the only way.

Her mind turned away from the people that she had killed towards the ones that she hadn't, those rare individuals who had encountered her and survived.

There was Amy Levine, the stockbroker's wife, free to bring up her children and play tennis.

Stefan Kuhn, hero, saxophonist, residing in a united Germany.

Finally there was her brother Tomas. She hadn't thought about Tomas, not really, for a very long time. She recalled the way he had followed her everywhere when he was tiny. "Asha, Asha, Asha," he would call out in his silly baby voice because he couldn't pronounce her name properly; she remembered the tears he would shed when he fell over, the tears he shed when he realised that she was going away. She recalled the essay that she had written when she had first arrived at Academy 43, the one entitled "Who is your favourite family member and why?" If she had written about Tomas he would be dead now; but she hadn't and he was alive. Did that count for something? Tomas would be eighteen years old now. What sort of man had he become? What was he doing? What were his plans? The Soviet Union was often in the news these days. It was crumbling. All the satellite states seemed to be breaking off, rejecting the rhetoric, declaring independence and organising free democratic elections. Maybe this would create new opportunities for Tomas, opportunities that extended beyond joining the farm collective or working in a factory.

Cilla forced herself back to the present and realised her degree certificate had slipped out of her hands and onto the floor so she reached out painfully and retrieved it again. She was feeling immensely tired but she knew that she couldn't let her mind wander anymore; she had to make a plan.

The henchmen in the hall would be dead by now so they were of no concern. It would probably be best to leave Vlad well alone. If she killed him then the police might start looking for someone else to hold responsible for the carnage. If she left him alive, as the last man standing, then he would take the blame. If he ever regained the power of speech he would probably still take the blame because that would be preferable to admitting the alternative; that he and his men had been annihilated by a little girl. But just to make sure she would retrieve the syringe, wipe off her prints and place it carefully into Vladimir Haugr's hand. Then she would dislodge the dart from his spinal column, clean it, add one of the henchmen's fingerprints and put it carefully back into place. Now the whole fiasco would resemble some sort of gangland coup gone wrong. Finally Cilla would open the curtains in the lounge, not much, just a chink, just enough for someone to peep inside, observe the vandalised room and glimpse the body of a dead man lying in the doorway. Once she was safely away Cilla would make a short call to the police, posing as a concerned neighbour, who preferred not to give her name, worried about all the noise and the goings-on at number 33 that morning.

This left only Smithy to consider. He was still a loose end, but Cilla didn't want to kill him anymore; she didn't want to break her promise. If he was still alive, sitting in the lounge, taped to that chair, then she would release him and she would take him with her. They could hole up somewhere for a bit. She would look after him, tend to his wounds, nurse him back to health. His broken nose would heal in time and he could have surgery, if necessary, to return it to its proper position on his face. Although, on reflection, it might be just as well to leave the nose a little bit wonky. Perhaps if Smithy were slightly less beautiful then he might regard Cilla as slightly more so; especially once her hair started to grow properly. In any case he would have to be grateful to her, for saving his life, for looking after him, and gratitude was something she could work with.

It was a good plan and Cilla was satisfied with it. But when she tried to stand up a great weariness came over her and she had to lie down again. Vlad was still glaring in her direction, which made her feel uncomfortable, so she closed her eyes to avoid him. It was quite pleasant to lie there with her eyes shut. There was no real hurry. Perhaps she could allow herself a cat nap, just a short one, before she tried to get up again. As she curled into a crescent and drifted towards unconsciousness Cilla was aware of a new sensation: something that was settling over her like a warm blanket. At first she wasn't sure about it, she had never experienced anything like it before. But then she realised what the feeling was: she felt happy.

Nothing stirred in the bungalow. Vlad's blazing eyes made no sound.

Acknowledgements

With thanks:

To Robbie Burns who read each chapter as it was written and encouraged me to write the next one.

To the early readers of my first draft: Sigmund and Paula Gjesdal, Margaret Nygren, and Susanna Gross; who gave me the confidence to hope that this book could reach a wider audience.

To my agent Laura Macdougall and her assistant Olivia Davies for their unwavering support.

To my publishers at Muswell Press: Kate and Sarah Beal for taking a chance on me and for their wisdom and patience.

To Ellis Moore at Bolinda for securing the audio rights and for being "obsessed" with this dark little novel.

To my daughters: Claudia and Eve without whom I would be a lot more like Cilla than I am.

MURDER BY
NATURAL CAUSES